ED GA

GABRIEL MILLER
Serial Killer

THE DERNFORD PRESS

The copyright of this book has been asserted by Ed Garron/ G. P. Denny / The Dernford Press © 2025. No part of this book may be copied or reproduced electronically or in print without the written permission of the author. This is a work of fiction, all characters, institutions and situations depicted are purely the work of imagination. Any resemblance to persons living or deceased is therefore purely coincidental.

GABRIEL MILLER
SERIAL KILLER

Ladies and gentlemen of the jury! Before coming to your decision as to the defendant's innocence or guilt, I now ask you to take your time and read these diary extracts which you may or may not think relevant to the very serious case of murder now before you...

Contents:

Chapter One: Ridealong With A Killer

Chapter Two: A Few Surprises In Orford

Chapter Three: A Visit To The Scene Of A Crime

Chapter Four: Inside The Lair Of The Beast

Chapter Five: Old Man Tranmer Had A Farm

Chapter Six: Another Visit To The Scene Of A Murder

Chapter Seven: Gerald Hadiscoe

Chapter Eight: The Making Of A Thief

Chapter Nine: Fleur

Chapter Ten: Gabriel Miller, Deer Killer

Chapter Eleven: The Reverend Alan Clitheroe

Chapter Twelve: The Catastrophe

Chapter Thirteen: The Long Arm Of The Law

Chapter Fourteen: A Killer On The Loose

Chapter Fifteen: Bed Bugs And Broken Legs

Chapter Sixteen: Caught In The Act

Chapter Seventeen: A Hard Task Master

Chapter Eighteen: Partners In Crime

Chapter Nineteen: The Stuff Of Nightmares

Chapter Twenty: Unexpected Visitors

Chapter Twenty-one: Pure Evil

Chapter Twenty-two: The Tarot Cards Again

Chapter Twenty-three: The Rat Hunt

Chapter Twenty-four: Anot

Waveney
Kessingland
Homersfield
St. Cross
Sth. Elmham
Benacre
Mendham
All Saints
Sth. Elmham
Covehithe
Metfield
Westhall
Fressingfield
Blyford
Halesworth
Blyth
Southwold
Wenhaston
Stradbroke
Bramfield
Blythburgh
Walberswick
Laxfield
Heveningham
Dunwich
Peasenhall
Westleton
Middleton
NORTH
SEA
Dennington
Badingham
Yoxford
Fordley
Kenton
Saxtead
Green
Theberton
Minsmere
Saxmundham
Framlingham
Leiston
Sizewell
Earl
Soham
A12
Thorpeness
Framsden
Snape
Letheringham
Aldeburgh
Helmingham
Wickham
Market
Iken
Tunstall
Bredfield
Ufford
Sudbourne
Alde
Butley
Orford
Woodbridge
Sutton Hoo Tumuli
Orford
Ness
IPSWICH
Sutton
Shottisham
Ore
Waldringfield
SUFFOLK
Bawdsey
Nacton
Orwell
Levington
Deben
Chelmondiston
Erwarton
Shotley

CHAPTER ONE:
RIDEALONG... WITH A KILLER

Thursday July 10th

I am sitting alongside Gabriel Miller in his brand new silver Scudo van on our way to yet another killing. Gabriel doesn't know it yet, but I am the man who is going to bring him to justice. The police may have eliminated him from their enquiries, but I am absolutely sure they made a big mistake by letting him go after only a few hours of questioning him. The tricky bit is avoiding becoming one of his victims before I present the police with the evidence. The funny thing is that I don't feel the least bit scared. In fact, I feel instinctively that Gabriel is *not* going to murder me. You see, he runs a pest control company and took me on as his busy summertime assistant. Luckily, he seems to like me and in any case I don't fit the profile of one of his victims. They were nearly all married women, aged around forty, five of them so far, and each one killed with a single blow to the head, the death-blow given with a sharp instrument such as a hatchet or small wood-axe.

I know for a fact that Gabriel sometimes carries just such a tool – or weapon – right there in the big left-hand pocket on the side of his cargo pants. At other times the hatchet is kept in a tool box in his van, alongside a machete, a sheath-knife, a claw hammer and several wrenches and crow-bars. Any one of these objects could be used to carry out a murder, but it's the small hatchet that fits the bill as a possible murder weapon. It's the ultra-sharp, small-bladed type used and endorsed by TV explorer Ray Mears, and is hand-crafted, the razor-sharp blade guarded by a hand-stitched leather cover when it's not in use. How could the police have overlooked the fact that Gabriel Miller walks around equipped to slaughter? I mean, who needs or carries a small axe in his pocket? And the fact that the fourth victim was found three months ago on the allotment next to the one tended by Gabriel and his family surely points to the fact that my boss is guilty, guilty, guilty as hell!

The odd thing though, was that despite him being interrogated and investigated by the police, not a shred of evidence could be found to link him to the murder. In my opinion this is because he thoroughly cleaned and sanitised his hatchet, or maybe he throws the 'used' ones away and buys another for each new job. Alternatively, he could keep the actual murder weapon hidden or buried ready for each new crime.

After five brutal murders you'd think the police would have checked this out, but I don't think they're doing their job properly, not after they arrested a man called Gerald Hadiscoe who walked into Suffolk police headquarters at Martlesham Heath and boldly claimed to be the serial killer. This man is a nutter from Framlingham who claims he heard voices that told him to take the lives of those women. The newspapers were, for a while, full of stories celebrating the end of Hadiscoe's reign of terror. But there are several details about this man's confession that just don't add up, and not one piece of conclusive forensic evidence to link him to a single murder. Some of the officers on the case want to open up the investigations again, but Chief Constable Richard Garnham has forbidden this because he believes Hadiscoe is guilty. I know all this, because my mum is secretary to the Chief Constable and constantly updates me with all kinds of police gossip she's not supposed to talk about.

I have also acquired the awful habit of snooping through her work stuff on the computer in her home office after I guessed her ridiculously weak passwords. I know this is a terrible thing to do, but I think the end justifies the means. After all, we are talking about a serial killer here, and I am convinced he will strike again. I am painfully aware, too, that my mother is a woman of the same age range, hair colour and level of attractiveness of the victims so far. She, however, like most people working within Suffolk Constabulary, firmly believes the East Coast Killer has already been caught. I too had this mistaken belief, until something happened that changed my mind for good.

Two weeks ago I answered Gabriel Miller's ad in the local rag and applied to him for a summer job to help pay for my future course at Anglia Ruskin University. She casually revealed that back in April he'd been questioned about the murder at Fordley, which is Gabriel's home village, and released the same day. Mum said that a few days after Gabriel had been questioned the forensics team received their results from the lab, and found that there was nothing to link him to the case.

My mother told me all this the day before I was to meet him for a job interview. I remember that I thought all this information about Gabriel Miller was fascinating stuff, but had, like my mother, not the least suspicion he was anything other than a simple, hard-working pest controller with absolutely nothing to hide.

How wrong I was! As soon as I met him in person, I took one look at him and knew he was the murderer. It was written all over his face, his body language, and even the clothes he wore. Have you ever had that feeling deep in your gut, without actually having any proof, that you were right about something and had to act on it? Well, that's what happened to me. And while we were chatting at the interview, I suddenly remembered the Eastern Daily Post had put up a reward of fifty thousand pounds for information leading to the conviction of the 'East Coast Killer' as they'd dubbed the murderer.

The thing was, I had absolutely no proof, but I hatched the plan of working as his assistant and watching, waiting for him to give me a clue or shred of evidence enough for me to go to the police and get him arrested. Now, this was a pretty dangerous thing to do, to go working for a killer and put myself in harm's way. But I calculated that he wouldn't be interested in killing me. After all, the victims were all women aged between thirty-five and forty-five, and in any case a murderer who'd so far concealed himself so well was not going to give himself away by doing away with his own employee... or so I hoped.

Now, after being utterly convinced he was the serial killer, what I found astounding was that the police forensics team hadn't nailed him yet with their supposedly brilliant scientific methods. When you consider the weapon used was a small axe, you'd think the killer blow, or blows, would splatter blood all over the attacker. But no blood was found, no tell-tale DNA or clothes fibres from the victim killed near Gabriel Miller's house, nor from any of the others, for that matter, were discovered having transferred onto Gabriel's clothing or possessions. Nor were any of his DNA, fibres and so on, found on any victim. So much for modern forensic techniques!

As regards the murder at Fordley, the crime took place at an allotments site adjoining the Millers' back garden. Apparently, the ground was too hard for footprints to be identified, which is a shame, because I think they would have led straight to Hawthorn Cottage, the Millers' home. Having thought about it a lot, I think Gabriel Miller simply slipped out of his house just before nine that morning and killed the poor woman with a single blow delivered at arm's length, then slunk back home without his family noticing he'd gone out. Then, when the body was discovered by a neighbour entering the allotment's main gate at nine-thirty a.m. and the first police were on their way to the village, Gabriel Miller had only to emerge from his house and feign shock and surprise. Of course, he was closely questioned, and his van, clothes and belongings submitted to the forensics unit's scrutiny, which, far from proving his guilt, actually got him eliminated from their enquiries.

Well, despite the police losing interest in Gabriel Miller, I *know* he's guilty. I feel it in my bones. He's a man who knows how to keep secrets all right, I've discovered that in the time I've been working for him. Every day, I see his dark arts, see more and more evidence of a cunning and deceptive killer. But I just need that one piece of concrete evidence that will see him convicted, and get me that reward money.

Talk about hiding in plain sight! A self-employed pest controller for over twenty years, Gabriel Miller is exactly the type of person you would *expect* to be a mass murderer. After all, *he kills for a living.* And just look at the way the man dresses: cargo pants with a hatchet handle sticking out of a side pocket, black army boots with neatly tied laces, and over his skinny chest an olive green army-style pullover with leather-suede elbow and shoulder patches. As for the clean-shaven slightly tanned face, his features may be regular enough, but his small mouth twists in odd contortions as he speaks his local-accented nonsense. The striking thing about him is the wide jackdaw-like grey-blue eyes. They're usually very expressive, almost hypnotic, yet at the same time actually give nothing away of the inner man away, if you know what I mean.

Sometimes those eyes are darting and clever like a comedian about to tell you a very funny joke. Other times he is capable of fixing you with a long and searching look as he tries to work out what you're thinking. I'll tell you another thing too, that though he often smiles, especially after telling you one of his funny yarns, that strange little smile is made without real humour. The mouth smiles, but the eyes, though expressive, are cold and cruel. That's how I see him. Look, I'm only eighteen, you may think I'm not very experienced as a judge of character, and you may be right. But I know what I feel and what I've seen. So, by the time I've finished this little account of 'what I did in my summer holidays', I've a funny feeling I'm going to be proven right, and I, Ivan Salter, will be the one who, against all the odds, brings Britain's most dangerous serial killer to justice.

Each day I watch him, see his 'gift of the gab' kind of charm used to chat up his customers. I think his way of killing is to lure gullible women into a false sense of security and get them into a suitable isolated place before hacking them down.

Oh yes, he certainly knows how to talk to people, does Gabriel Miller. Women in particular seem taken in by his small talk. This often takes the form of subtle flattery, praising the smartness of a garden, the good behaviour of a dog, the prettiness of a child.

His talk is corny, but oddly effective.

'New dress?' he asked one pretty young woman

'I got this in a charity shop,' she said.

'Well it looks like new', he said.

'I've had it six months,' she countered.

'Well, it looks new on you, anyhow', he insisted.

The woman's cheeks were pink now, and she gave him a funny look, *and it wasn't one of disgust!*

Hearing and seeing all this, I was cringing, but the woman was laughing. She knew it was all flattery, but she just lapped it up, at least till she saw the size of the bill he gave her.

I saw two pregnant women from different households get the standard three questions: *'When's it due?'* Then: *'Do you want a boy or girl?'* And finally: *'Hospital or home birth?'* He rounded off the conversations with the same quip: *'I remember when my wife had our first baby, a little boy, best day of our lives!'*

If he really fancies a woman he says *'Have you been working out?'* and when she says 'no', as is usually the case, he'll say *'Could've fooled me, with legs like that!'*

Compliments sometimes resulted in a bigger tip, I observed, though Gabriel's fees were huge enough already. New customers in particular were likely to tip him, perhaps thinking he worked for a company, rather than being self-employed, not knowing that every working day Gabriel was pulling in a cartload of cash.

Once, at the end of a job he went through the flattery routine to a woman in Saxmundham, making her laugh, but her husband came out from behind a garden gate, slapped some money in his hand, and told him to move on in no uncertain terms.

When dealing with men he was more business-like and deadpan, except for elderly gentlemen, who he seemed to assume were all suffering from dementia and patronised accordingly.

This morning we are driving to a killing - not a murder victim, of course, but a rat running around in a hotel kitchen that will very shortly end up dead. Sitting between me and Gabriel perched on the little third seat that Scudo vans have in the centre of the cab is a Jack Russell terrier called Nancy. This dog is a deadly 'ratter', who I predict will make short work of the rat if it's still hiding in the kitchen of the Six Bells Hotel in Southwold. Every job involves some unfortunate creature or creatures ending up dead. This morning we've killed off a few thousand wasps with permethrin dusting powder, annihilated ants' nests in a lawn with liquid cypermethrin insecticide, and shot five feral pigeons in a grain store. I get to clean up the mess and dead bodies, and I'm probably already reaching the maximum permitted daily dose of dangerous pesticides. At the wasp nest job I got a cloud of permethrin dust in my face, and the ant-killer liquid gave off terrible fumes that made me feel sick.

It's a miracle Gabriel is still alive at forty-two, as he uses a variety of deadly chemicals to massacre mice, rats, ants, cockroaches, bed-bugs, fleas, flies and so on. He's a regular a one-man army of pest destruction. Some of his 'target species' as he calls them, are protected by the law, like the bumble bees in a garden he destroyed two days ago, and I suppose that is why he made me sign a non-disclosure agreement. I can't imagine his silly home-written document was designed to stop me turning him in for murder! On the other hand, maybe, when he thinks I'm completely under his spell, he'll casually tell me of those five murders he carried out, you never know. Perhaps he intends to get me fully trained and primed, then hand me the hatchet and say: 'There you go, Ivan, I've shown you how to do it, now it's your turn...'

But I think that laughable non-disclosure agreement was probably aimed more at preventing me from shopping him for breaking a load of wildlife laws and regulations in his everyday work. So far I've watched Gabriel kill off three nests of bumble bees for nervous householders, and shift some badgers from a newly-established sett in a garden by rolling fir cones soaked in diesel oil into their tunnels. Then there were the rabbits he blew up with his 'Rodenator', a device that emits oxygen and propane gas into burrows which are subsequently ignited to give the poor bunnies a nasty and untimely end. I know for a fact that operators in the UK are only supposed to collapse empty animal tunnels with this device, but Gabriel told me bluntly that 'everyone in pest control uses the Rodenator this way.' You should have seen him smile as a dead rabbit was blown right out of a hole, all singed and mutilated.

On the subject of breaking the law, only last Thursday I witnessed the most shocking thing I've ever seen in my life. And, if I'd had any doubt of Gabriel's savagery and guilt before that day, what I saw at Doves' Farm convinced me that my instincts were correct.

Edna Dove is a widow who farms five hundred acres with the help of her teenage son Charlie. Edna has two fingers and a thumb on one hand, having had, Gabriel tells me, a little accident involving a cattle-beet pulping machine in her girlhood. She was about forty, small and plump, and dressed in dirty jeans and a blue cotton top with holes all over it. Her hair was greyish-white, tied back with an elastic band, and she wore wellington boots even though the temperature was about thirty degrees centigrade. I had already gathered on the way that she had a special job for Gabriel. But, when I asked him exactly what it was we had to do at Doves' Farm he had only smiled wryly, and told me *'Wait and see'*. So I guessed it was something a bit unusual, and so it turned out.

'Be sure to make it quick,' said Edna.

'Oh yes,' said Gabriel, 'It'll be quick all right.'

Gabriel Miller walked up to Mrs Dove's thirty-year-old Jersey cow and patted it on the flank. Its thick hide quivered as if fending off a pesky fly. Then, taking out his special Ray Mears survival hatchet with his lethal left hand, Gabriel, quick as a flash brought back his arm and fetched the beast a mighty blow to the flat area right between its eyes. The poor animal dropped onto its knees with never a moan, just a strange snorting noise as its final exhalation was expelled through its mouth and nostrils. The blood poured out of the wound – a lot of blood – and, as the cow's tongue lolled, Gabriel gently pushed it over onto its side where it lay in the dust with its feet twitching oddly for a second or two.

'Ah well, that's that then,' said Edna Dove, her face strangely blank.

'Yes, that's that,' said Gabriel, pursing his lips as he contemplated his work.

'I'll get Charlie to take her down the meadow with the JCB and bury her. Didn't seem right to have her taken to the slaughterhouse and cut up for dog meat, not after she'd given me so many years of good milk. She was a bit of a pet, you see. Much better this way.'

'Yes, much better this way,' said Gabriel, still looking at the cow.

'Now, what do I owe you?'

'Oh, whatever you think,' said Gabriel.

'Here,' said Edna Dove, and thrust a fifty pound note into his right palm, the one that wasn't gripping a bloody hatchet

Gabriel glanced momentarily at the money, nodded in thanks to Edna, then stuffed his violently gotten gains into a trouser pocket.

'Got to get going,' he said. 'We've got a hornets' nest in a garage roof to see to, over Aldeburgh way.'

He cleaned his Ray Mears special edition survival hatchet under a tap in the yard. A minute later he was drying it with tissue paper off the roll he always kept in the back of the van. I wondered at the time if he'd been spattered with microscopic particles of cow blood. Television police dramas try to tell us there's always a trail of forensic evidence to betray the story of violent skulduggery, but I already had my doubts.

On the way to Aldeburgh I glanced at Gabriel. He was still looking thoughtful, and for once he wasn't talkative as he drove. Finally he said:

'That was a horrible job, Ivan, but somebody had to do it. Sorry you had to see that. Still, it was necessary - that cow was almost unable to stand, and her time had come. Edna wanted it done the old-fashioned way. She knew it would be instant and humane if I did it. Technically she wasn't supposed to bury it on her land, so don't breathe a word of it to anybody.'

'All right,' I said.

'Good boy. Now, let's get these hornets done, I need to get home early tonight, Naomi and I are going to see a show in Ipswich and the A12 is a bugger for road-works at the moment.'

On the way to the next job I asked him:

'Have you killed cows before?'

'Once or twice,' he said, 'It's not something I would ordinarily do, but Edna is an old friend. We go back a few years, you see.'

Our next task that day was to eliminate a hornets' nest, and even that job (strictly legal for a change) revealed something more of the inner demon that inhabits Gabriel Miller. I was told we might both have to get 'suited-up' as Gabriel put it, in protective beekeepers jackets, but as it turned out, we both did the dastardly and dangerous deed in our shirtsleeves with Gabriel's usual contempt for health and safety.

We parked on the driveway of a big bungalow in Aldeburgh. After Gabriel had spoken to the householder, an elderly widower as it turned out, we gingerly looked into the wooden garage that housed the offending nest. With one side of the double doors open there was enough light to see in, and there in a corner was our target. Six or so big, brownish insects were buzzing ominously around a rugby ball sized paper nest, hanging from the roof. It was just above head height, right at the back of the building and easy enough to get to.

Gabriel went close up to have a good look at it, pursing his lips and scratching his chin, as he spent a minute watching the insects. I knew he was weighing up his mode of attack. Then he walked back to the van and slid open the side door to select the appropriate chemical weaponry. Meanwhile, the householder, after some initial curiosity, had beaten a hasty retreat into his kitchen.

Much to my surprise, though we had two beekeepers' suits in the van, Gabriel, without a shred of protection over his cotton shirt and cargo pants, walked calmly back into the open garage and squirted insecticidal foam from a can straight into the hole at the bottom. Only one hornet went for him, but he saw it coming for his head, and nonchalantly batted it away with the flat of his hand. To my surprise, it turned tail and flew out of the garage, passing right by my head, but luckily ignoring me. The other hornets kept circling Gabriel in a rather threatening manner, but didn't actually attack. As he stepped backwards, the big brown insects in the nest began dropping out of the hole in the bottom of the structure and falling on the ground. They made a low, moaning sort of buzz as they expired.

'Get an empty cardboard box from the van, Ivan, and put it under the nest,' Gabriel ordered. I collected an empty box marked *RAT BAIT STATIONS*, opened the leaves wide at the top to act like a funnel, and nervously approached the nest.

Seeing my hesitation, Gabriel took a second aerosol

can of insecticide from out of one of his voluminous side pockets and walked up close to the nest again. Deftly, he sprayed the circling hornets one by one and they dropped to the ground.

'It's OK, Ivan,' he said, 'You won't get stung, this is a quiet colony, you can see by their behaviour. Every nest is different, this is a gentle one, no need to put on a bee suit, so long as we don't break it open till they're all dead.'

Taking his word for it, I quickly put the box in place and backed off. Hornets, white with foam, duly dropped into the box, and moaned away for a few minutes. There were several hundred in the nest, and it took about ten minutes for all the insects to drop down. Then Gabriel approached again and ran a pen knife between the top of the paper nest and the beam it was attached to. The whole nest dropped neatly into the box. Gabriel turned to me and winked.

'Get a broom and sweep up all those other dead ones and bits of debris, please,' he said, and off he went to knock on the house door to get his sixty-five pounds.

I had a long, hard look at the squirming mass of dying hornets in the box. Their nest had split open, and the circular stacks of cells housing the grubs were visible, a whole city of innocent wildlife destroyed in a few minutes. Some of the cells had emerging hornets halfway out of their cells, killed when the foam had touched them.

Gabriel came back with the cash in his hand.

'That was an easy one,' he said.

One solitary hornet carrying a caterpillar had just returned to the area where the nest had been. Gabriel raised his aerosol can and took careful aim. The hornet came down with the first puff, landing on the concrete garage floor and Gabriel put his foot on it. He picked it up by one wing, and dropped it in the box.

'Another one bites the dust,' he laughed, and turned on his heel and went off to the van to put his cans of aerosol away, leaving me to clear up while he rolled himself one of the thin Golden Virginia cigarettes he smoked every so often in the day.

It was obvious from all I'd seen up to then, that when it came to danger, Gabriel Miller felt not the tiniest, weakest pulse of fear in his body. Only the day before this I'd watched him run up a ladder to the second storey of an old folk's home in Leiston and climb up onto the pitched roof, and, with no safety equipment or protective clothes, deposit permethrin dust down a chimney. As he explained back down on the ground, he had to polish off the colony of wild honey bees because some of the worker bees were falling down the flue and emerging in a living room to terrify the elderly residents.

'Ah well,' he'd said, 'That's another sixty-five quid in the kitty.'

I remember he had a honey bee, its tiny legs still covered in yellow pollen, stuck by its stinging rump to the front of his shirt. He pulled it out with his finger tips, pinched it tightly and cast it aside.

I wondered then, if he'd killed and cast aside those five women as easily and casually as he dealt with these wild creatures. As easily as he'd axed that cow, and pushed it over onto the ground. Where were the usual human emotions of sympathy and empathy? Perhaps, I thought, his parents, when he was a baby, had somehow washed those two imposters out of his system and thrown them away with the proverbial bathwater...

And so, today, we arrive at the Six Bells Hotel in Southwold, just off the seafront. Our destination is the yard at the back of the kitchen. A rat has been spotted going into a food storage cupboard and the staff are nervous of going in to get the things they need for this afternoon's high tea.

'It was *huge,*' says a man in a chef's hat.

'It ran right past me,' says a pretty girl in an apron worn over the front of a flowery summer dress.

'Don't worry,' says Gabriel, 'We'll have it sorted in a jiffy.'

He has Nancy tucked under his arm. Usually the terrier looked sleepy and bored, but at this moment she's alert and animated, a wicked glint in her eye. Her head is cocked on one side ready to home in on a scurrying rat.

'Anybody squeamish, leave the room now,' says Gabriel. The chef and the girl look at each other, but both stay put.

'Ivan, close all the doors, please,' says Gabriel.

For the first time, I notice he's wearing thick leather gauntlets, and he's tucked his trousers into his socks. Taking the hint, I bend over and tuck my own trouser legs into my socks in the same way.

'Why did you do that?' asks the chef.

Gabriel answers for me:

'To stop them going up into his trousers, of course. I'd advise you to do the same.'

The chef gives a nervous laugh and does as he's told. The girl merely shrugs, and holds her ground over by the sink and dishwasher area. She's bare-legged and wearing sandals, but evidently intent on watching the rat-hunt.

I duly close the door to the yard, and the one leading through to the dining area, leaving only the one to the storage cupboard open. Gabriel sets Nancy down on the ground, and she runs around the main kitchen, sniffing under work-benches and behind various obstacles.

Then she comes to the cupboard and stops. She cocks her head on one side, takes a couple of steps forward and points with her nose to a stack of cardboard boxes.

'Oh-oh,' says Gabriel very softly, 'Mr. Ratty is behind those boxes.'

From inside the cupboard, he lifts one off the top of the stack and uses it to partially block the doorway. One by one he shifts more boxes until he's blocked off the doorway to a height of about three feet.

I peer over the boxes, see Nancy stock-still and pointing with her nose at the last two boxes which are not quite against the wall. Evidently, the rat is in that narrow gap.

'Here we go,' says Gabriel, lifting the first box. Nothing stirs, and he passes it to me through the doorway. I put it down and wait.

Then, just as Gabriel reaches down to move the last box, the rat bolts, jumping clean over the boxes in the doorway, followed by Nancy. As the chef steps out of the way, the kitchen girl gives out a short shriek of surprise, and Nancy and the rat do a couple of circuits around the kitchen floor. To my horror, I see the rat heading straight for me and jump! But it doesn't land on me, but leaps straight back into the store cupboard. Quick as lightning Gabriel stoops down and there is a high-pitched squeal.

Nancy jumps back over the boxes into the cupboard, but she's too late: Gabriel holds the rat aloft in one hand like a wicket-keeper who has just taken a particularly fine catch. *And the rat is still alive!*

'Oh my God!' says the girl, 'What are you going to do with it now? Are you going to let it go outside?'

This makes me smile. Obviously, she doesn't know much about the subtle arts of pest control.

'Oh, I don't think I'll be letting it go,' says Gabriel, carefully examining the rat face to face. It is quite a big one, but he has it firmly round the body so that it can't crane its neck to get a bite at the gauntlet.

Meanwhile, the dog is watching the rat, fixated and tense as a coiled spring.

'Are you ready, Nancy?' asks Gabriel, lowering his arm so that the rat comes closer to Nancy's muzzle. 'One, two, three, GO!'

He drops the rat right into Nancy's mouth. There is a snap, a squeal, and a sudden toss of the dog's head as she throws the rodent into the air and catches it before it hits the ground. You can actually hear the crunching of bones as her jaw crushes it for a few seconds. Then she drops the lifeless body on the kitchen floor, nuzzles it once, then looks up at her master, her tail now wagging slowly.

Gabriel turns to the man in the chef's hat.

'Well,' he says, smiling, 'That's that. Now, can I possibly interest you in an all-inclusive pest control contract? I happen to have a draft copy right here in my pocket – and I can offer you a very reasonable price.'

CHAPTER TWO:
A FEW SURPRISES IN ORFORD

Friday 11th July

It's 8.30 in the morning and we are on our way to Orford, famous for its medieval castle, its two gastro-pubs and the most expensive bakery in the country from which I cannot afford to buy a cake, never mind the vegan sausage rolls at five pounds each. The fishermen's cottages have all become holiday homes, and the larger houses, also unoccupied for much of the year, are the haunts of billionaire Londoners who complain they can't get a gardener or cleaner for love or money. The truth is, people on an income of less than a hundred thousand pounds simply can't afford a house anywhere near Orford. A systematic 'ethnic cleansing by cash' has made the quaint little fishermen, the cleaners, the gardeners, farm workers and other impoverished rude and rustic mechanicals, in effect, an extinct species.

On the upside, enterprising men like Gabriel Miller (forced to live a good few miles away) can fleece them for a few quid now and again, a sort of 'Robin Hood' revenge tactic that takes the form of expensive cleaning, gardening or pest control companies or individuals saddling stupid householders with huge bills. Typically, this takes the form of doing a relatively simple job and spinning it out for as long as possible, making it as complicated as possible, and dressing it up in as much jargon as possible, so that the householder feels compelled to cough up the extra cost firmly presented to them.

'We've got fleas,' says the fat old lady from Crabbe House, Quay Street, Orford, 'and we don't even have a dog or cat.'

'I see,' says Gabriel, with a funny little smile, his eyes darting around the house to weigh up the situation. 'And has anyone with dogs or cats ever visited or stayed here in the past few months?'

'Why... yes, we let my daughter and her husband stay in the place in June. They brought their two Schnauzers and since then we've occasionally found the odd flea, until this week, when the ground floor suddenly became absolutely infested with hundreds of them. Look, they're on my ankles right now.'

'So I see,' says Gabriel, taking a step back.

'Oh dear,' says the lady, 'Where can they all be coming from?'

'Most likely the warm weather has caused a lot of flea eggs to hatch all at once,' smiles Gabriel. 'Well, like I said on the phone, you'll need to vacate the house for the morning, as the chemicals take a while to disperse after the treatment.'

'Are these chemicals dangerous at all?' asks the woman, 'I mean to humans?'

'Not at all,' says Gabriel, 'The chemicals we use are specially selected and *act only on the cholinesterase of invertebrate species.*'

Gabriel often came up with these well-rehearsed pieces of jargon for bamboozling his gullible clientele.

'And how much is all this going to cost me?' asks the woman.

'Not much,' says Gabriel. 'It's a standard treatment that comes in at one hundred and ninety-five. The big companies charge much more, of course.'

'Oh well, it's got to be done. My husband and I are off to an antiques fair at Snape Maltings, then we're going to do our shopping at Waitrose in Saxmundham, so we'll be back at about twelve. Can you be finished by then?'

'I'll make sure it's all ready for you by then,' replies Gabriel. 'If you could meet me back at twelve noon that would work out well for both of us...'

'Very well,' says the lady, going back into the house. 'Lionel, Lionel, we have to go out right now, the men are coming to fumigate.'

'I'm all ready, my poppet,' says Lionel, walking into the hallway in his splendid salmon-coloured trousers and blue and white striped sleeveless shirt.

'Give those pesky fleas an extra squirt for me, will you gentlemen?' he says with a wink, as he selects a straw fedora from off the hat-stand.

Ten minutes later and the householders are long gone. Gabriel and I each have a ten litre pressure spray hanging by a strap on our shoulders, loaded with the latest, most effective anti-flea chemical on the market. According to the label, *Anti-Flea Formula No.1* contains micro-encapsulated cypermethrin with an IGR (Insect Growth Regulator). We also have canisters of 'fogging spray' to kill the fleas trying to escape up the walls and curtains, or in hard to reach cracks and recesses. All in all, it is a bad day to be a flea at Crabbe House, Quay Street, Orford.

For once, Gabriel issues us with overalls and proper gas masks. They have little labels which tell me they have *'double charcoal P3R particulate filters'*, which sounds reassuring. As it isn't my first time spraying for insects, Gabriel decides to let me loose on the stairs, landing and four big bedrooms, my orders being to lightly spray all carpets, rugs, soft furnishings and curtains. Beds and anything draping off them were strictly off-limit, as are any hard floors, painted or papered walls, towels, toothbrushes or toilet seats. These are my orders, and I decide to stick to them to reduce the chance of killing a customer.

Meanwhile, Gabriel sets about spraying the ground floor carpets, sofas, chairs, cushions, curtains and so on. I have seen him doing this before, and he is usually very thorough. 'Do it right first time, and you don't get called back,' he'd explained. 'Also, move the furniture and leave it a few inches from its usual position so the householder knows you've done a thorough job.'

Fleas are tricky to eliminate because of their habit of depositing their eggs in huge numbers in every crack, crevice and gap in the furniture and structure of a room. Deep-pile carpets and spaces between floorboards are favourite sites for eggs, along with gaps on the underside of chairs and sofas. It is very common for fleas to re-infest a property after the most thorough treatments because the eggs are very difficult to neutralise. That is where the Insect Growth Regulator chemical kicks in. It prevents the newly-hatched fleas from morphing into adults. God knows what it might do to humans, but the label at least deems it *safe when used as directed.*

One hour exactly into the treatment and Gabriel and I have finished stage one of our task. Next comes the fogging. This involves setting off self-emptying cans in every room or area, but to save money Gabriel goes from room to room, starting upstairs, letting off about a quarter can in each room and running to the next one. Once the nozzle is activated the canister can't be switched off, so it's important to move about fairly swiftly. In this way Gabriel can do the bedrooms, landing, stairs, kitchen, living room, study, utility room, dining room, hall, three bathrooms and various cupboards using only four cans instead of the recommended amount, which I think is about eight for a house of this size.

Gabriel meets me on the front porch, and is careful to make sure he has the key on the outside to avoid us being locked out. He removes his mask, the sweat pouring down his face.

'Too bloody hot in these overalls,' he says, taking a seat on the garden wall. 'Still, that's a job well done, there won't be a flea, fly or spider left in there now.'

He sets his shoulder bag down on the ground and unzips his overalls and pulls them down over his waist. He reaches inside his trouser pocket for his tobacco pouch and lighter. Soon he is puffing happily at one of his thin cigarettes.

'What do we do now?' I ask; 'It's only quarter past ten

and the owners won't be back till twelve.'

'Oh, I've got a friend I have to see for a while,' he says. At that moment a woman got out of a car on the other side of the street. She was blonde, about thirty-five and quite pretty.

'Oh Gabriel,' she says, 'I'm over here, I've been waiting for you.'

She comes across the street beaming at Gabriel, who has miraculously shed his overalls like an insect metamorphosing into its next growth stage. Evidently the IGR hasn't taken effect on him.

He kisses the woman on the cheek, and goes across the street to get in her car.

'Let Nancy out and give her water,' says Gabriel. 'At half past eleven go back in the house with your mask on and open a window in every room. You got that?'

'I got it,' I reply, trying to disguise the surprise I feel at seeing this latest turn of events.

Gabriel climbs on board and the blonde woman drives him away, leaving me to take care of the dog, and finish off the job. A cushy morning, after all, and one that had come with a big surprise.

I consider, for a moment or two, on seeing Gabriel disappear with the woman, that perhaps he will lure her into the woods and chop her down with his hatchet; but, upon reflection, I reckon this unlikely, as Gabriel, of course, knows I'd witnessed their departure together.

Gabriel returns at ten to twelve, the pretty blonde

dropping him off and even blowing him a kiss as she departs. He seems a little pink in the face, and the first thing he does is roll a cigarette.

'Did you open the windows like I said?' he asks.

'Yes, the house should be thoroughly aired by now.'

'Good,' he says, fumbling in his pocket for his lighter.

About three minutes later Lionel and the fat old Lady pull into the driveway.

'That's good timing,' says Gabriel. He goes over to the van and comes back with a cardboard box containing about a dozen empty fogging canisters.

'All finished, old sport?' asks Lionel.

'Just airing the rooms ready for you,' says Gabriel; 'Some of the windows are still open.'

'It's all right, we'll close them,' says the lady. 'Now, how much do I owe you?'

Gabriel hands her the invoice and she gives a little theatrical start, and her cheeks grow visibly pale.

'But this says three hundred and twenty pounds and forty pence.'

'Yes, that's right, madam, we had to use a lot more chemical than I'd estimated – the fleas had got everywhere, right under all the beds, in all the cupboards, even under the kitchen sink. We used six extra cans, and they cost twelve pounds each at cost price. Then there's VAT, so it comes to three-twenty and forty pence. It's all itemised there for you.'

'Well,' says the lady, 'I've only got two hundred in cash.'

The husband, who is watching on bemusedly, now

chips in and says, taking out his wallet, 'It's all right poppet, give him the two hundred, I've got enough to pay the rest.'

There follows an uncomfortable few moments as she extracts her money, and Lionel adds another hundred and thirty, saying to Gabriel with a broad grin:

'Never mind the change, there's a tip there for the boy, old sport!'

'Thank you very much,' I say awkwardly, getting into the van, even though I know I am never going to get my extra nine pounds and sixty pence.

Gabriel stuffs all the money into his cargo pants pocket, picks up his cardboard box of twelve canisters and puts them in the side door.

Just as he's getting on board, Lionel appears in the crack of the front door and calls out, laughing:

'Three hundred and twenty quid for a flea treatment – gets more like London here every day, old sport!'

And he quietly closed the door.

Our route home takes us through Tunstall Forest, a man-made stretch of woodland covering several thousand acres. Along a footpath that runs in the middle of a forest fire-break, on Wednesday 19th February, murder victim number two was savagely hacked down. Melanie Kitson, according to the newspaper reports and police statements on national television, had been walking her dog when she was attacked with 'a small bladed weapon' as the police had phrased it. This was the first time they suggested that there may be a murderer on the loose who will strike again. Melanie, like everybody in the area, had hoped the Walberswick murder back in January had been a one-off, but alas, we were all to learn otherwise...

We drive within a half-mile of the killing, which took place about noon, close to the village of Sudbourne, the victim hit and killed almost instantly with a hatchet or similar implement. Her dog, a yellow Labrador, remained faithfully by the body until another dog walker discovered the body at about three p.m.

I remember watching the evening news with my mother when the murder was announced. We listened spellbound as the grim details were read out, ending with an appeal for information from anyone who was in the area who might have seen something suspicious.

'Oh God,' my mother had said, as the details were aired. 'I've been to that forest scores of times with our dog. I won't ever be going again.'

'And that woman,' I said, 'She came from Theberton, which is just up the road. Not only that, she was aged forty-three with white-blonde hair, and drove a Ford Mondeo. She was single and fond of walking her dog in the countryside.'

We were silent for several long moments, conscious of the fact that this description also fitted my mother almost exactly, except that my mum was two years older and drove a Ford Fiesta, rather than a Mondeo.

'Promise me you won't go out alone, Mum,' I said, reaching out my arms for a hug.

'You don't need to ask me,' she said, almost crushing me in her embrace. 'I'll take the dog for walks along our village street, in front of the houses. And you must take care too, until this maniac is caught.'

'I promise,' I said.'

Well, that was back in February, now we are in July. The police have had Gerald Joseph Hadiscoe in custody since June 10th when he walked into police HQ at Martlesham Heath near Ipswich and 'admitted' that he was the East Coast Killer. Two days later he was charged with five counts of murder, and straight away the Criminal Investigation Department team switched their activity from hunting for a killer to corroborating Hadiscoe's confessions.

My mother told me the Chief Constable himself is convinced of Gerald Hadiscoe's guilt, and has given the Suffolk CID team working on the case strict orders to keep him informed by providing him with daily updates. My mother has signed the Official Secrets Act, but she is still nevertheless in the habit of letting slip this kind of information, usually when we are chatting at mealtimes.

On Thursdays she works from home while the Chief Constable is off 'doing his rounds' as he calls it, visiting regional police stations, making public appearances and generally seeing to things outside Martlesham HQ. So, every Thursday, my mother is busy in her home office typing up reports, sending and receiving emails and generally getting the Chief Constable's diary organised for the days ahead. She goes to bed at 10.00 p.m. regularly as clockwork, and takes an anti-depressant each evening that first makes her sleepy and then more or less knocks her out till early the next morning.

Now, I ashamed to be confessing this, but I am an inquisitive, not to say rather crafty sort of person. I happen to have guessed (with very few attempts) my mother's work password of IVAN, and her police work PIN code of 30 03 07, which just happens to be the birthday of her only child. This gets me into Suffolk Constabulary's PDCS, which stands for Police Data and Communications System. My mother would never in a hundred years dream her beloved son would be so devious as to hack into her personal and work affairs. I am not proud of what I do, but if I am to get the reward money I need just a little help to point me in the right direction. Then, when I get the evidence I need to convict Gabriel Miller, I will make out that I discovered his guilt by own genius, hard work and clever calculations, meaning neither I nor my mother will get into trouble. Well, that at least, is the plan.

Only last night I had a look through her work emails and the files she had prepared for her boss the Chief Constable. The most interesting thing I discovered was in a file that was marked *'Summary for CC/Latest developments/East coast murders'*.

It stated that the officers working on the case had found the same size twelve boot or shoe imprints at the second and third scenes of crime. The footwear was apparently smooth-soled, with some damage to the left heel. There was some jubilation in the CID team that Hadiscoe took a size twelve shoe, though the actual footwear with the damaged heel had not yet been found in his house or car.

Of course not – because he's not the East Coast Killer! Now, I happen to know that Gabriel Miller takes a size nine shoe but I am not at all put off by the size twelve information, in fact I think eliminating suspects because of shoe size isn't such a great idea. A serial killer might easily be clever enough to throw off suspicion by changing their shoe size and wear something bigger, perhaps making it fit by putting on two pairs of thick woollen socks. Also, having a pair of boots or shoes hidden in some secret place – perhaps along with the murder weapon – obviously isn't out of the question.

My mother, because she knows all the latest developments in the East Coast Killer case, has swallowed the idea of a murderer in size twelve boots hook, line and sinker. According to one email, only a couple of renegade CID officers think Hadiscoe may not be the killer, and the senior officers have ordered them to toe the line and work on the assumption that Hadiscoe is guilty. By all accounts, Hadiscoe knew all the minute details of the murder sites, but I think he gained this knowledge by visiting each scene of crime long after the event. He also claims he heard voices that told him to kill the women. Well, if he's not guilty, the man must be well and truly insane to go claiming he committed the five murders and try to heap all the blame, scorn and notoriety on himself.

Talking of insanity, my snoops through my mother's files turned up another very interesting document, composed by no less than three criminal psychologists. I printed out a copy of it for my own secret folder, though I'm not sure it's actually very helpful. Most of it is laughably obvious and if this is the best Suffolk Constabulary can come up with, it's no wonder they take so long to solve their murder cases.

It was dated May 20th, so it precedes the confession and subsequent charging of Gerald J. Hadiscoe.

```
           PSYCHOLOGICAL PROFILE:
             EAST COAST MURDERS
1. The perpetrator is most likely a male aged
between 15 and 75.
2.  The  primary  motive  for  killing  is  a
sexual thrill obtained by violent murder.
3.  The violent psychology of the perpetrator
is  most  likely  hidden  and  invisible  to
friends and family, work colleagues and so
on.
4.  The  strong  likelihood  is  that  the
perpetrator is a local man who does not like
to travel far from his home range.
6. It is likely the perpetrator prefers an
unobtrusive vehicle of unremarkable or common
type, as no distinctive or memorable vehicle
has been seen in the area of the killings to
date.
7. The perpetrator is likely to have a deep
resentment  of  women  he  finds  sexually
attractive, most likely a fixation on blonde
or light haired females between the age of 35
and 45.
```

8. The wounds inflicted in each act of murder makes it likely that the perpetrator has a liking for killing very swiftly with a single blow.

9. The rearrangement of the victims' garments such as the raising of skirts and partially removing underclothes, but without sexual assault taking place, is a significant feature found at all the scenes of crimes. The lack of deposited DNA and clothes fibres suggests the perpetrator wore gloves or carried out the rearrangements with an object such as a stick so as to avoid leaving any forensic trace.

10. The location of each murder has been carefully selected in an isolated place out of sight of CCTV cameras or witnesses. If the murders are opportunistic, an inordinate degree of luck has so far aided the perpetrator. However, the strong likelihood is that very careful planning and extreme cunning are the reasons the murderer has so far evaded detection.

All very interesting, but there's nothing whatsoever here that would actually help *catch* a killer. But what the information might do is assist in the wrongful conviction of Gerald Hadiscoe, if all three psychologists were to put their heads together and swear that these ten statements are applicable to him.

I have to say again, how appalled and disappointed my mother would be if she knew I'd been snooping through her papers and hacking into her computer to get confidential information like this. It is only by sheer good fortune that the Chief Constable has taken such a personal interest in the case, and demands his summaries of the case. Normally, I understand, the top dog doesn't get so involved in individual cases, leaving the day to day running of his departments entirely to his subordinate officers.

I wonder what Chief Constable Richard Garnham would say if you knew that his personal and confidential emails and files were being hacked into by his personal assistant's son. And he wouldn't be too happy either if he knew my mum was breaching the Official Secrets Act by telling her teenage son various snippets of information from the updates he received.

I know that my probing for information is a very bad and risky thing to do. But how else am I to get the inside information I need to carry out my plan? That reward money would pay my way through college. And just imagine the book I could write when I finally bring Gabriel Miller before a court of justice...

First, however, there is the tricky business of proving he's guilty. The other evening I casually tried to get my mother to reveal whether Gabriel had been a person of interest in the East Coast Killer case. She gave me a furtive look, and then I knew she was about to tell me something she shouldn't.

'Now, don't you go talking about this to anybody else,' she said, 'but there was a lot of interest in him before Gerald Hadiscoe came forward. As I told you before, Gabriel Miller was investigated at the time of the Fordley murder. Two weeks later, some case detectives had considered bringing him in for a second interview, this time at HQ at Martlesham.'

Then she actually *laughed* as she told me:

'Can you imagine, your boss Gabriel Miller being an actual serial killer? That would be a turnout for the books!'

'Do you not think,' I said cagily, 'That he sort of fits the bill?'

Again, she laughed.

'Oh,' she said, 'Gabriel is a funny old sort, but I don't think he's a killer – at least not of human beings.'

'How can you be so sure?'

'I told you before, I met him when he came on a Thursday to kill off the rats round the neighbour's chicken coop. I talked to him over the fence, and I found him pleasant enough. He does come across as a bit of a ladies' man, but he definitely doesn't seem the type to carry out a murder.'

'Maybe,' I said, 'But aren't killers often just ordinary family men, hiding in plain sight of everybody?'

'That's often the case – but there are reasons why Gabriel Miller was eliminated from police enquiries.'

'Oh, really?' I asked; 'Like what?'

She looked at me with a secretive smile on her lips, and I could see she was trying to decide whether to tell me stuff she shouldn't. Then, not able to help herself she said:

'There was something about his shoe size being too small. Apparently, the killer has a size twelve boot which leaves a distinctive imprint. Some of the crime scenes had this same print. It turns out, your boss's feet are much too small.'

'Really?' I said, feigning surprise.

'Yes, and not a shred of DNA evidence linked him to any one of the crimes. CID officers took his phone, searched his van, his house and outbuildings and took a number of tools and utensils for analysis at police HQ. Within ten days these were all returned to him and not a single item showed any trace of blood or DNA pertaining to the victims.'

'But the police were suspicious enough to do all those tests on him, right? Don't you think that's significant?'

'Not in the least – up until the time Gerald Hadiscoe confessed, a hundred men had been questioned, and the CID team had done dozens of searches of vehicles and buildings, all of which drew a blank.'

'What about DNA left on the victims, surely the police have found something significant by now? I mean to say, there've been five poor women killed.'

'Nothing significant has turned up so far. And I'll tell you one thing, those people at the forensic department are pretty good at what they do. If there'd been any trace of DNA evidence left behind by a murderer, it would have shown up already.'

'But how can there be no evidence at all from this killer? He must have left fibres, or been spattered with blood!'

'*Spattered with blood?* Oh, Ivan, I think you're thinking of all those crime movies and TV series we've watched together – but sometimes real-life cases are not so easy or straightforward. At one of the Chief Constable's briefings they were talking about that very thing and as far as I remember they said the method of killing made it very difficult to catch this murderer. They said he very likely approached the victim using stealth and struck the person with a claw hammer or an axe or whatever it was, without coming into contact with the clothes of the victim. Some of the crimes occurred on a hard surface, so there were no footprints. The other thing was the fact that so far no vehicle had been linked to any of the murder sites and that's really unusual. Even a serial killer has to get from one place to another and there are usually cameras at various points along the roads, for example at petrol stations, traffic lights and on private buildings. But I do know there's work going on at the moment to find out whether Gerald Hadiscoe's car was filmed anywhere near a scene of crime.'

'But they haven't found anything so far?'

'Nothing, so far, and I think the team are having a really hard job trying to pinpoint the movements of a suspicious vehicle in this area. There just aren't enough cameras for them to track a car or van on a journey, say, from Hadiscoe's home in Framlingham to any of the murder sites over here in the east.'

'Do you really think,' I said, 'that this Hadiscoe fellow is the East Coast Killer?'

'Oh, I have no doubt. He's confessed, and virtually the whole department thinks he's guilty.'

'You said "virtually all" – which means at least *some* of the detectives don't agree.'

'There were only two who came forward to voice their doubts, and one of them was a DCI – that's a Detective Chief Inspector – but he's been overruled.'

I was slightly heartened to hear that I wasn't the only one who believed Gerald Hadiscoe wasn't the East Coast Killer. On the other hand, it meant that these two officers would still be on the look-out for the real murderer, making it all the more important I proved Gabriel was the killer before they did.

As it was late, and I'd found out all I'd wanted, I gave my mother a hug, and decided to go to bed. Later, before I drifted off to sleep, I thought of how, when Gabriel Miller was safely locked up behind bars – most probably in a secure wing in Broadmoor Hospital for the criminally insane – I could settle down and write that book about how I, Ivan Salter, ex-pest controller and now author, playwright and screenplay genius, had single-handedly caught one of Britain's most notorious serial killers.

But first, I had to find that one crucial piece of evidence I needed to prove, once and for all, that Gabriel Miller was guilty of those five very ugly murders. I determined to watch him like a hawk, study his behaviour and try to second-guess his cunning method of murder, maybe even find where he keeps his size twelve boots and killing hatchet. It wouldn't be easy, but if anyone at all was in a position to uncover the secrets of Britain's most dangerous man, it was *me*.

CHAPTER THREE:
A VISIT TO THE SCENE OF A CRIME

Monday 14th July

This morning Gabriel and I are off to slaughter some unfortunate grey squirrels that have taken up refuge in the loft space of Walberswick Vicarage and are threatening to burn the place down by chewing through electricity wires. When Gabriel told me of our destination, all I could think of was the murder of Linda Travis-Moore, murder victim number one of the East Coast Killer. She had been struck down as she left St Peter's church on Saturday 18th January. According to the newspapers, the evil deed was done just outside the church porch at about 6.30 p.m.

At that time of day it was, of course dark. The evening was cold and rainy, and Ms. Travis-Moore, a respectable blonde divorcee of forty-four was just on her way home after arranging flowers in the church, an activity she performed every Saturday. She had been alone, and, just after leaving the church, was approached, most probably from behind, and hit with a sharp instrument – such as a small axe – and killed instantly. She was discovered two hours later by the vicar, who had walked over to the church to lock the porch doors for the night.

Half-asleep in my seat in the van, I glance across at Gabriel, who is puffing away on one of his thin little roll-up cigarettes, thankfully with his window open. I am wondering if this man, driving along so matter-of-factly, totally relaxed and seemingly at ease with the world, really is the killer. My instincts say that he is – and yet he has been interviewed, thoroughly investigated and released. This makes me think of the Yorkshire Ripper, Peter Sutcliffe, who was interviewed by the police eleven times before being arrested as he prepared to kill a prostitute in January 1981. He had been murdering women, thirteen in all, for over five years. Some of his work-mates called him 'the killer', and his job of long distance lorry driving gave him obvious and documented opportunities to be in the vicinities of the murders; and yet he was free to carry out his crimes for so long...

Gabriel tosses his cigarette butt out the window. He reaches out his left hand towards me. A slight nervousness washes over me, until his long, tapering fingers settle on Nancy the terrier's neck. She is sitting on the spare seat between us, curled up in a ball, but wakes up and raises her head, sniffing and then licking the hand that caresses her.

On we go, travelling a little too fast as usual, speeding along narrow, winding roads, but I say nothing. I look out the window, and I notice that the countryside along the way is particularly pretty hereabouts, all chocolate box cottages, golden fields of wheat and barley, oak trees, flowery meadows and the occasional farmhouse painted in traditional Suffolk pink. We travel through the village of Westleton, and speed on towards our destination. Ten minutes later, we reach the sign marked 'Walberswick', and see the speed limit sign of twenty miles an hour, which Gabriel ignores.

Until January 18th, Walberswick was famous only as the most trendy holiday home location in England for dozens of TV and film actors, directors, writers, producers and so on, with a smattering of artists, musicians and sculptors thrown in for good measure. The other inhabitants, usually fancying themselves to be of an artistic bent, were of the super-rich London type, with names like Jocasta, Samantha, Tamsin, Giles, Miles, Hugo and Peregrine, you know the type. I expect their conversations post January 18th might have included comments of how much house prices had suffered, and how sluggish the holiday rental market in East Suffolk had lately become. Let's face it, would you like to rent a secluded cottage in a village like Walberswick, Iken, Yoxford, Fordley or Sudbourne with the East Coast Killer on the loose with his nasty little hatchet? And if you are a woman between the ages of thirty-five and forty-five, with blonde or light-coloured hair, there were added reasons to be a little nervous of venturing into the 'heritage coast' area...

But where, you might ask, were the police, those dashing heroes who are generously paid to protect our lives and property? The answer is, back in their police stations, poring over a mountain of paperwork. Serial killing aside, Suffolk is currently undergoing a crime wave of burglaries and farm thefts, the inevitable consequence of cuts in the numbers of rural police officers. Suffolk in the twenty-first century has become the murder capital of the United Kingdom. The five killings of young women in the past six months have put the county on the map for all the wrong reasons. Almost twenty years ago we had the Steven Wright murders, five young women killed over a time span of only two weeks. Since his imprisonment other unsolved murders and attempted abductions pre-dating Wright's arrest have been linked to him, and the press have ruthlessly hammered the local Criminal Investigation Department for incompetence, and they may have a point. Over the last few years there have been other unsolved murders across the county, with Ipswich in particular being a hot-spot. From bodies being found in the woods, to drug dealers stabbing each other on the streets of the county capital, something in Suffolk seems to bring out the worst in people.

'What a beautiful day,' says Gabriel, as we speed along the last narrow country lane to our sunny seaside destination. 'Today we have some squirrels to trap in the Vicarage garden, and I'm going to show you how to set a cage trap and shoot the air rifle. Oh, and I may also show you how to mix up squirrel bait so that the critters simply can't resist it and die at a single feed.'

'Great!' I say, trying to sound enthusiastic, 'Can't wait to find out how to do that.'

I am trying to employ all my acting skills in my attempt to sound keen to learn those horrific things. At first I think I'm coming across rather convincingly. After all, I'm supposed to be studying English and Drama at university this autumn, serial killers permitting.

But Gabriel shoots me such an odd sideways glance at this moment, that in the next few seconds' awkward silence I realise he's somehow seen straight through me and guessed my uneasy train of thought.

'You sure you're up for it?' he asks, frowning; 'Look, I know pest control can be a grim old business sometimes, but look on it this way. If we didn't kill off these rats and mice people would be left in danger of horrible diseases like leptospirosis which is ten times worse than covid. And what about all those stinging insects that are life-threatening to people suffering from allergies?'

'Yes,' I say, 'I agree, we're doing people a great service. And not many people have the guts to face those wasps and hornets.'

'Exactly, Ivan,' he says, breaking into one of his enigmatic smiles again. 'What we're actually doing is taking on difficult and sometimes dangerous jobs that nobody else wants to do. That's why we get paid so much for doing tasks that often take no time at all, you understand?'

'Yes, of course.'

He's still smiling, and periodically glancing across at me, which is giving me the creeps.

'It takes a special kind of person,' he continues, 'to do what we do. There's no room for the squeamish when it comes to pest control...'

His speech trails off as we pull up outside, of all places, Walberswick churchyard. You could knock me down with the proverbial feather – we've stopped not twenty yards from the scene of Linda Travis-Perkins' murder!

I am amazed to see Gabriel get out of the van and walk through the wooden gates towards the porch. He's looking left and right, towards the graves, not at the porch door or the path he's walking on. But then he stops six feet in front of the door, the very spot where the woman was murdered. He bends down, strokes his chin thoughtfully, looks at the ground just to the right side of the path,

Meanwhile, I sit in the van, stroking Nancy, watching to see what he's going to do next. Suddenly he turns towards me, and beckons. I get out and go over to him, a cold chill running down my spine.

'Moles!' he says; 'I have a contract to control the moles here. Can you get me three talpex mole traps out of the van? And the trowel. We'll deal with these little buggers first, then nip down the road to sort out those squirrels.'

Sure enough, there are three large molehills a little way from the path. By the time I come back he's kneeling on the dry grass to that right side of the path. I hand him the traps and trowel and stand patiently on the spot where the woman died,

'I have contracts to control the moles in about two dozen churchyards,' says Gabriel, without looking up. 'As we're visiting the Vicarage, I thought it'd be nice to tell the Reverend Alan Clitheroe we'd made a start on getting the mole problem under control. Now, while I'm doing this bit, have a good look round the churchyard and see if you can see any more hills and runs – you should know what to look for by now.'

By the time I report back to him, he's set all three traps below the ground and marked each spot with a handful of gravel and small stones from the path. Gabriel wipes his dirty hands on the grass, which doesn't do much in the way of cleaning them. That will only be done properly with the detergent and jerry-can of water in the back of the van. There is even a roll of paper towels. Gabriel is very fussy about keeping his hands clean.

As we're sitting in the van ready to move on, Gabriel pauses before turning the ignition key. He lays a hand on my shoulder, and says:

'Now Ivan, you know what happened right next to where we were just setting those traps?'

'Everybody knows,' I say. 'I remember watching the ten o'clock news report – they filmed it right where we were working.'

'Yeah,' says Gabriel, with a wry smile, 'It kind of makes you think, doesn't it?'

'It certainly does,' I say.

'I knew her, you know.'

'Really?' I say, feeling horrified but desperately trying not to look too shocked.

'As a matter of fact, I fumigated her house for fleas last summer. Told the police all about it, in case they were interested. I don't suppose you know they questioned *me* after my neighbour found one of the bodies in the allotments?'

'Really?' I say, trying to look surprised.

'They questioned *everyone* in Fordley,' he says, 'but of course they were more interested in the men. We were all asked to give DNA samples too, which I'm told will be destroyed after the case is closed.'

'At least they caught the crazy coot that did the killing,' I say.

'They didn't *catch* him,' he says, very quietly, reaching toward the ignition key; 'The mad fellow turned himself in.'

'Do you think Gerald Hadiscoe really did the murders?' I hear myself say.

He turns towards me, with one of his strange little smiles.

'Oh, I should think so,' he says. 'I mean, who on earth would ever want to own up to something like that unless he was guilty as hell?'

He turns the key, and the Scudo starts first time. After only a few seconds of travel we pull up outside a set of wooden gates, already opened. There are two weather-beaten signs on a post just over the low, crumbling brick wall. One reads *The Vicarage*. On the other is written *Please use side door*. Beyond the wall, over the close-cropped lawn is a large, Virginia creeper covered house of Georgian red brick

At the side door we meet the Reverend Alan Clitheroe. He is a huge ungainly fellow of about fifty, with a pink face, bald head and brown cow-like eyes, well over six feet tall and weighing, I guess, about eighteen stone, dog-collar and all.

'We have both the fortune and misfortune of having

two large beech trees in the garden,' he explains, 'both of which as you can see, overhang the roof so that the little blighters can bound straight onto the tiles. From there they go into the gutters and chew holes in the soffit. We often hear them bouncing about in the loft and it sometimes sounds as if they're having a game of tag up there.'

'Yes,' says Gabriel gazing up at the trees, 'You've got a drey in the left hand tree, and a big hole in the right hand one ideal for a nest as well. Looks like at least two families have set up shop right next to your house. Could be a drey in the roof space too, if they've been up there a long time.'

At that moment a squirrel emerges from the hole in the right hand tree, and runs along a branch, then stops. It is twitching its tail left and right, as it surveys us on the ground. Gabriel goes swiftly to the back of the van and emerges with his air rifle in its brown leather gun-slip with the gun manufacture's name 'Weihrauch' printed on it in white gothic lettering. In mere seconds he has it unzipped and under his arm. It is quite a big rifle, with an expensive-looking telescopic sight. Gabriel cocks it by pulling down the under-leaver, then takes a lead slug out of a cargo pants pocket and inserts it in the rotating breech.

Propping himself up on his elbows on the bonnet of the van, he eases the rifle butt into his left shoulder and takes aim. The Reverend Alan Clitheroe is looking rather nervous. The air rifle goes off with a *ping!* and the squirrel falls out of the beech tree and lands in the flower bed below. Nancy the terrier leaps out of the open window on the driver's side of the van and dashes over to the dead squirrel. She gives it a couple of bites to make sure it's dead, then trots back to Gabriel and looks up expectantly, her tail slowly wagging.

'Oh, dear, poor thing!' says the vicar, looking at the squirrel. 'Oh well, I suppose it's got to be done – they've ripped up all the insulation in the loft, and the electrician says they've chewed through some wires and it's a miracle they didn't cause a fire. The bishop has ordered me to get it sorted out, and though I hate killing anything, I've taken on board what you said on the phone, that this is the only way to keep them out permanently.'

'That's right.' says Gabriel, rolling a cigarette with one hand, 'Unless you want to cut down both trees, you'll be plagued with squirrels till kingdom come – if you'll pardon the expression.'

'Unfortunately the trees have a preservation order on them,' says Clitheroe, 'so, our hands are tied as regards chopping down the trees. We even have to get approval before the tree surgeon comes to trim them each year.'

'Yes,' says Gabriel, 'and even if the branches that are nearly touching the roof are trimmed, there'll still be some big boughs left which the squirrels can use to jump on and off the roof.'

'Oh dear.'

'It's a clear cut case,' says Gabriel; 'Either the squirrels go, or you'll end up with the wires damaged again. Even if we got the squirrels out of the roof and blocked up every hole they've made in the soffit, within a week they'll make new holes and find their way inside again, causing no end of mischief, and in my experience once they've got the taste for chewing wires and doing damage like that they never stop.'

That's exactly what Dial-a-Kill said,' says the clergyman.

'How much did they quote you?' asks Gabriel.

'Two and a half thousand pounds.'

Gabriel lets out a low whistle of surprise

'Well, I won't be charging the parish quite as much as that,' he smiles.

'You said five hundred on the phone, I think.'

'Yes,' says Gabriel thoughtfully, 'We should be able to do the job within budget. But if it takes a little bit longer than I thought, I might have to charge a *little* more. Squirrels can be persistent, and it's difficult to tell how many there are in the area to re-infest the garden once the initial targets are removed.'

'I see,' said the vicar.

We are all gazing up into the trees. For the moment not a squirrel is in sight.

'They may not show themselves for quite a time,' says Gabriel, 'so now we'll get on with the trapping. Ivan, get the six cage traps from the van and bring them over here. We'll put three by each tree.'

'Just a thought,' says Clitheroe, 'Do we have to kill every single squirrel? After all, it's the ones in the left hand tree which are jumping onto the roof, and, as far as

I know, causing all the trouble.'

'That may be true,' says Gabriel, 'but as soon as the ones on the left hand side are removed, the remaining ones will certainly take over the territory left vacant. Besides, for all we know the damage inside the roof may have been caused by *both* family groups – that's usually the way.'

'Shouldn't you put your traps up in the roof space?' asks the vicar; 'That way you'll catch only the guilty ones that have been trashing the loft.'

'Wouldn't work I'm afraid,' says Gabriel. 'By now *all* the squirrels probably know their way in through those holes in the soffit. At the moment I'm guessing they're only using the loft as a sleeping and playing place, as they have nesting dreys in the trees. But, what with the dryness and the warmth up there in the top of the house, you can bet your boots the squirrels have got that loft marked down as their next place to build a drey. Maybe there's even a nest up there already, I'll have to check, of course. So, you see there's no real way of solving the problem without culling all the little devils.'

'I see,' says the vicar. 'Oh look, there's another one!'

Sure enough, there's a squirrel sitting on a branch on the right hand tree. Gabriel had been in the process of putting his rifle back into the case but now he pulls it out again. He compresses the spring by pulling the under-lever and places another pellet in the rotating breach. In a few seconds he's ready, leaning on the bonnet of his van again, the muzzle of the rifle almost motionless as he lines up his quarry.

The squirrel makes a couple of hops across a bough then stops. We can all see its tail twitching as it looks down on us and contemplates where to go next. The muzzle of the air rifle moves slightly as Gabriel adjusts his aim.

Ping! goes the rifle and the squirrel gives a little jump in the air – but it doesn't fall from the tree. Instead, it slides off the side of the branch and hangs there by one paw.

Quickly Gabriel reloads and takes aim again.

'Oh dear, oh dear!' says the minister, 'The poor thing isn't quite dead.'

'It will be in a moment,' says Gabriel peering through the site.

Ping! goes the rifle and the squirrel drops from the tree, hitting a bird feeding table on its way down, before landing on the lawn. Once again, Nancy runs over to make sure it's dead by giving it a few quick bites.

'That reminds me,' says Gabriel, 'I can see peanuts scattered on the ground by the bird table and feeders. While we're doing the trapping, you'll have to stop feeding the birds. Otherwise the squirrels will be feeding on the peanuts and seeds instead of going for the bait in the cage traps.'

'Yes, of course,' says the vicar, 'I'll tell my husband and son to stop it, they're the ones in charge of the feeders.'

At the words h*usband and son* Gabriel looks up from his gun-sight and gives the vicar a momentary glance, before averting his gaze to the left hand beech tree.

'One other thing,' says Gabriel, 'I hope you don't mind me saying, but when you start feeding the birds again, you need to use the hanging type of feeder with a metal guard around to stop the squirrels getting to the nuts. Putting heaps of peanuts onto a flat platform or even on the ground is only going to attract more squirrels and probably the rats as well. There's a lot of rats in Walberswick, I can tell you that for a fact.'

'I'll tell Nigel straight away,' says the vicar.

Just then, Nigel came out of the house and stood beside the vicar. He was about thirty-five years old, tall and rather handsome, with long sandy hair and a goatee beard. He wore blue skinny jeans, a blue cotton shirt and black boots with pointed toes.

'This is my husband Nigel,' says the vicar. 'He's in the same trade as me, but he hasn't completed his training yet.'

Gabriel looks at him with slightly widened eyes and a funny little smile frozen on his lips.

'Hi,' says Nigel, 'You must be the pest control men.'

'Pleased to meet you,' Gabriel says, glancing from one man to the other.

The vicar now turns to his husband and says:

'Now Nigel, I know you're fond of feeding the birds but, Mr. Miller here says it's been attracting the squirrels so that in future we're going to have to use feeders that are protected by metal guards.'

'That's not a problem,' says Nigel. 'I'll order some from Amazon right away. Oh, is that a dead squirrel on the lawn? I did tell you I didn't want to see any dead creatures, Alan.'

'I'm so sorry,' says the vicar; 'I'll tell you what, you go inside and make us all a cup of tea, and we'll leave Mr. Miller and his assistant to their work.'

Twenty minutes later we have three squirrel cage traps arranged around each of the trunks of the two trees. The traps are each about a metre long and 25 centimetres wide and 25 centimetres tall with an opening at one end. Inside, about halfway along, was a metal plate attached to a wire arm. The arm is linked to a catch that releases the door, which is hinged to the top of the entrance. So, when a squirrel steps on the plate, in an instant the gate slams shut behind the victim. By way of bait there is a pile of last year's chestnuts which Gabriel has kept especially for these occasions. He explains to me that squirrels can't resist going in after the nuts, but non-target species such as birds generally ignored chestnuts. As for the squirrels, even if they hop straight over the metal plate once or twice, eventually they get careless and step on the triggering area.

Nigel brings us both a cup of strong tea on a tray along with a bowl of sugar and a tiny jug of milk. He sets it down on a garden bench.

'We'll be back tomorrow morning to take away the squirrels,' says Gabriel, shovelling about six spoonfuls of sugar into his tea. 'We should have caught a few by then.'

'Are you going to release them somewhere a long way away?' asks Nigel.

Gabriel laughs.

'Absolutely not. It's illegal to release a non-native species back into the wild. So Mr. Weihrauch here will have to deal with them.'

The air rifle in its case is leaning against the bench. Gabriel gives it a friendly pat.

A look of pain spreads over Nigel's face. He looks as if he might burst into tears. The vicar puts an arm round him.

'What about if we paid you extra to let them go somewhere?' asks the vicar; 'Couldn't you bend the rules just a little?'

Gabriel purses his lips as he considers this option.

'Well,' he said, 'I suppose just this once I could take them the other side of the river Blyth and let them go on the Southwold side. That way they'll never find their way back.'

'How do we know you won't just kill them?' asks Nigel.

He is, evidently, a good judge of character.

'Well, I don't know...' says Gabriel, for once lost for words.

It was time for me to interrupt:

'I'll send you a picture of them being released,' I say. 'Nigel, give me your mobile number, I'll send you a photo each time we release one over the river.'

'That is *so* kind,' says Nigel, beaming.

'That's sorted, then,' says the vicar. 'No more squirrels need be killed, I'm so relieved. Just bill the extra charge to the diocese, I'll make sure you're paid promptly.'

'Thanks,' says Gabriel, putting his empty tea mug back on the tray. 'You'll have more birds in the garden when the squirrels are gone. I suppose you know they eat the eggs and young of every bird's nest they come across. That's why the number of birds has gone down since grey squirrels came into the area in nineteen-seventy.'

'Well,' says Nigel, 'That's nature. The birds on the Southwold side of the river will just have to take their chances.'

'Yes, they certainly will,' shrugs Gabriel. 'Ah well, I'll see that my young assistant here sends you an action picture of each one as it's released. There'll be a small extra charge for our travelling expenses.'

'I'm sure there will,' says the vicar, picking up the tray of empty mugs.

Soon we're careering through the countryside in the Scudo at breakneck speed on our way to yet another gruesome job. For my part, I'm relieved not to have been shown how to shoot the air rifle, or mix up squirrel-poisoning baits as Gabriel had promised earlier.

Gabriel is smiling. He has a cigarette in the corner of his mouth, and is blowing contented puffs of blue smoke out of his half-opened window.

'Releasing poor little squirrels back into wild!' he laughs; 'Whoever heard of such nonsense?'

'We've promised Nigel,' I say, 'So now it'll have to be

done.'

'Oh, it'll be done all right,' says Gabriel, making the cigarette in the corner of his mouth waggle as he speaks. 'You'll have to take a snap of each one as we let them out of the traps. Then those bloody squirrels will have to get up a tree pretty sharpish.'

'Why?' I ask naively.

'Because,' says Gabriel, 'little Nancy here will be right behind them, and she's absolute mustard when it comes to catching grey squirrels running across open ground!'

This makes him laugh so much that he half chokes on the remnants of his cigarette, sending puffs of smoke and showers of sparks into the air of the cab and out of his open window...

CHAPTER FOUR:
INSIDE THE LAIR OF THE BEAST

Thursday 17th July

It's six thirty in the evening, and I'm driving my ropey fifteen-year-old orange Ford Fiesta the two miles from my house in Middleton over to Fordley. I make my way slowly and carefully as I've only passed my test a month previously, and I am nervous as hell. I already had one accident a week ago, driving straight on at a sharp bend and ending up in a sugar beet field. This was caused by my dropping a vape on the floor and attempting to pick it up while driving. A grumpy farmer towed me back onto the road and said he might charge me for 'crop damage'. Fortunately the car and I were both okay, but my mother almost had a heart attack when she found out. Now she keeps reminding me of the fact that so many people my age have accidents shortly after passing their test, and says I have to drive slowly and carefully for the next *five years!* She's absolutely paranoid that I'm going to smash into a tree next, or drive over a cliff, and it's as much as I can do to stop her taking the car off me. It's a wonder she paid for my driving lessons in the first place, and then gave me her old car, when she bought herself a newer one.

After a hard day's work today Gabriel dropped me off earlier at my house for a shower and change of clothes, and now I'm travelling to his house for my evening meal. When I told him my mother was out for the evening he absolutely insisted that I go to his home 'and get stuck into a great big steak and kidney pie' that his wife Naomi was making. Can you imagine the look of disappointment on his face when I finally had to admit that I was a vegetarian? I asked him if there was any chance of some plain pasta with passata, which is my go-to meal when I'm ravenous after a hard day's work, and which I thought would be the least trouble for Mrs. Miller to make.

Gabriel said:

'I knew there was something wrong with you, but I couldn't quite put my finger on it'.

I think he was highly suspicious of me the time we stopped at a roadside cafe and I ordered the veggie sausage roll, then asked for soya milk in my coffee. Gabriel gave me a really funny look, then one of his enigmatic smiles. Today, after my admission, he keeps giving me the same strange little looks, as if he's been infiltrated by a Greenpeace activist.

Today, after contemplating his assistant's weirdness for a while, Gabriel said:

'I'll get Naomi to make you something proper. Do you eat eggs and cheese?'

I said that I did, as I was vegetarian but not vegan.

'Well then,' he replied, 'I'll ask Naomi to make one of her mushroom soufflés – she used to work as a chef at Westleton Crown, the best gastro-pub in the area, so you won't be disappointed.'

I said I didn't want to put them to so much trouble, but he waved aside my protest and said 'Call Naomi!'

into his voice-activated hands-free phone, and in a short while my supper was ordered.

After another of our awkward silences, Gabriel asked the million dollar question that had been playing on his mind.

'So, as a vegetarian, how do you feel about polishing off a few thousand wasps, mice, rats, moles and so on? Are you sure you're OK with all that?'

'Absolutely!' I said without hesitation; 'I'm only a vegetarian, for health reasons.'

I'd already rehearsed this little lie, and I think I delivered it pretty convincingly.

'Good,' he said, 'and I see you wear leather boots, so I guess you're not one of those weirdo vegans who throw red paint over butchers' shop windows...'

'Oh, I don't agree with any of that nonsense,' I said, 'and I'm completely OK with killing pests that mess up people's lives. In fact, I quite enjoy it.'

Another awkward pause. He glanced at me for a long moment. Then he broke into a broad grin.

'Good,' he said, 'We'll make a pest controller out of you yet!'

I was hugely relieved my little lies had gone down so well. I think the deciding factor hadn't been my acting skills, but the fact that I'd already earned my spurs earlier in the day by helping Gabriel with the mole trapping, setting a half-dozen of the nasty little things myself, under strict scrutiny and supervision. Later he'd dressed me in a full-body bee suit and laughed as I deposited permethrin dust into a wasp nest's hole in the ground on the edge of a lawn at Saxmundham and got more dust on me than in the hole.

Our other antics today involved digging up and disposing of three unfortunate rabbits in a garden in Framlingham, the coups-de-grace being inflicted by Nancy in a particularly gruesome way, then putting paid to some mice in a farmhouse roof by depositing a few dozen mouse bait cubes. Lastly, we'd fumigated a caravan for bed bugs at a holiday park near Leiston. It was a gruelling day, involving the deaths of innumerable small creatures, but I consoled myself with the thought that the burden of guilt fell on my boss rather than his reluctant apprentice, and that each day – I hoped - might reveal more clues as to the guilt of Gabriel Miller as the East Coast Killer.

As, back home, I soaked under the shower, I wondered how my mother was getting on during her date. This had taken the form of afternoon tea with the unsuspecting stranger, followed by a boating trip on the ornamental lake at Thorpe Ness. These things had been her own idea, perhaps thinking a man who was able to row a boat with a bit of skill would make her a good future husband. She's been out on a few weird and wonderful dates in the last year, but they all seem to end the same way, that is, by her phoning each unfortunate suitor and diplomatically revealing that he was not quite the person she was looking for. From what I can glean from our conversations, it seems she finds dozens of faults in the men she meets, of both the physical and temperamental kind.

My mother is an attractive lady of forty-five and has only very recently gone back into the dating scene. She is extremely intolerant of men that don't match up to her own high standards. Some friends and acquaintances who've known her a long while find this surprising when they consider what a scumbag my father was. He was a man of innumerable bad habits such as getting off with young women in his office, forgetting my mother's birthday, spending half of his salary on gambling, ignoring his only son, viciously kicking the family dog, getting drunk nearly every evening, and finally, as the piece-de-resistance, packing his bags and running off with his best friend's wife and going to live thirty miles away in Lowestoft.

Of course, the truth is that my mother doesn't want a new partner with *any* of the kind of faults my father had. In fact, she now wants a man with no faults at all, which is, I think, rather charming but completely mad.

People have sometimes expressed sympathy for the fact that my father left home, but my mother and I both agree it's the best thing that ever happened to us. Trying to live around my father was an extremely stressful experience. It was always very frustrating to see him promise to make amends then go off the rails again, and no matter how much we wished that he were a different person, in retrospect it was glaringly obvious that the leopard was never going to change his spots. The best thing he ever did was to bugger off as far away as possible and never bother to get back in touch. The funny thing is, he was my father but I don't even miss him. My mum and I have always been very close. She's the one who was always there for me, the one who taught me everything, gave me everything, provided me with all the love I needed. She even taught me to drive and gave me a car, so I guess I'm a lucky boy when it comes to mothers.

I continue driving very, very carefully, and soon I arrive in the single long street of Fordley. It consists of cottages on either side of the road, but apart from a red telephone box with a sign saying 'Not in use' there's no evidence this is a recognised village at all. There aren't even village signs at either end of the street.

Gabriel and his wife live in a detached farm cottage on the very edge of the hamlet. There are only about thirty houses in total, but the place does have a few acres of allotment (generously donated by the local land owner, Sir William Haslett, I'm told) which serves not only Fordley but also the surrounding villages. The fifteen or so plots have a main gate off the village's single street, but at the other end of the allotments another gate leads straight into the Miller's garden. So, when murder victim number four was found about fifty yards away from Gabriel's property in April, it was no surprise that he himself came under the scrutiny of the police.

Gabriel has said that even now he occasionally gets sightseers walking into the allotment, taking pictures and videos with their phones and cameras, most probably to post online. There's nothing like a serial killer to excite the interest of the public and stir up a social media frenzy. Try putting 'Fordley Suffolk' into a search engine like Google, and the first things that come up are *East Coast Killer, Fordley murder, serial killer, Fordley killer,* and so on.

It must have been horrendous to have the police and press milling around the small hamlet for days and days after the murder had taken place. Suffolk Constabulary detectives, I'm told, questioned every member of the village. My mother said that several men here in Fordley were interviewed, but so far as she knows, only Gabriel Miller was investigated as a possible suspect...

'Hello, Ivan,' says Naomi, opening the door of Hawthorn Cottage. 'Come through to the lounge, I've just about finished with the cooking. You and Gabriel can have a beer while you're waiting.'

Seeing the look of on my face she reads my mind and adds:

'Don't worry, yours is a non-alcoholic one, we knew you'd not want to drink and drive.'

I walk through the kitchen, noting that the Millers have a huge and expensive-looking electric kitchen stove, which has a few pots and pans perched on it. They're expensive copper ones, and there are also antique weighing scales and an old coffee grinder on a work surface crafted out of an old butcher's block. On shelves on the walls are vintage glass storage jars and a spice rack with about fifty different little pots. Evidently,

Naomi takes a great pride in her kitchen, and is, no doubt, a chef rather than a cook.

Naomi looks about forty, very pretty, slim and shapely with long, light-brown hair. She's wearing jeans, flip-flops and a grey sweat-shirt with 'RELAX! printed on the front. She smells vaguely of vanilla, and her smile is sweet, and, I think, quite motherly.

'Here,' take these through,' she says, handing me two ice-cold cans of lager from the fridge. The one for me promises '0% alcohol', but Gabriel's is a Kestrel lager with 9%, which seems an odd choice as an aperitif.

I step into the lounge and see Gabriel sitting in an armchair. He doesn't get up as I go in, but points to another chair.

'Park yourself over there young feller,' he says, taking his beer off me. 'I was just saying to Naomi what a good job you did today. But let's not talk about work.' He breaks into a smile. 'You can tell me first how you came to drive your car into John Hodgson's field the other day. I was talking to him on the phone when I got home this evening, and he says he's got a job for me. Anyhow, we were talking about this and that, and he said he had to pull an orange car off his field the other day, and the description of the driver and car fitted you and your old banger to a tee!'

I explain how I dropped my vape, then misjudged the corner and went up a bank, damaged some sugar beet, as well as the underside of my car, then got stuck on a ridge made by a tractor wheel.

Gabriel laughs again.

'When I was your age,' he says, 'I wrote off my first car when I drove into the back of a land rover. When I got out, I discovered I'd run into Walter Tranmer, the biggest and richest farmer round these parts, and he fairly tore me off a strip. But he ended up giving me a lift home as his vehicle was hardly damaged. Not only that, but he offered me a job on his pig farm, which I took up the next week.'

'So how did you get into pest control? It's a funny old way to make a living, if you'll pardon me for speaking my mind.'

'Ah, well,' laughs Gabriel, 'While I was working for Tranmer, up to my ankles in filthy muck and smelling like a pig sty, I met the local pest controller called Joe Sankey, and got talking to him. He needed an assistant, and as I was fed up smelling of pigs, I gave in my notice to Tranmer and went to work for Joe. I worked for him for five years till he retired, and he passed on all his contracts to me, and gave me a list of all his customers. Twenty-five years later, and I'm still doing the same job, and I even have some of the same contracts. Walter Tranmer is one of them – he's very old now, getting on for eighty, and everyone calls him Old Man Tranmer. He's Naomi's great-uncle, by the way, but he hasn't shared his wealth with her, worse luck. You'll probably meet him next week when we go to his farm – he's quite a character but gets on your nerves after a while as he never stops moaning.'

'Typical farmer, then,' I say.

'Exactly,' says Gabriel, 'Loads of money but never

shuts up about how hard things are for farmers like him.'

At this point a girl comes into the room carrying a big glass of white wine in one hand, a paperback book in the other. I just catch sight of the author, Virginia Woolf.

She is very slim and pretty, about my own age, with big green eyes, very full lips, long dark hair and an incredibly bored sort of look on her face.

'Oh, hello,' she says when she spots me, and sits down at the far end of the dining table. Then she calls out:

'Mum! When's dinner ready? I'm absolutely starving and it's nearly half-past six.'

'Almost there,' says Naomi, 'I've almost finished – you can help me carry it in if you like.'

The girl raises her eyes to heaven in a mock-exasperated kind of gesture, gets up and goes into the kitchen.

'That's our Fleur,' says Gabriel, 'She's just finished 'A' levels like you, but still doesn't know what she wants to do. I offered to give her a job in pest control, but she hasn't made up her mind yet.'

'Ha bloody ha!' says Fleur, returning to her seat with a big hunk of bread. 'I'd rather be dead than have a job in *pest control.*'

'Well, that's just rude!' laughs Gabriel, taking a big pull at his can of super-strength lager.

'Food's ready!' says Naomi from the kitchen; 'Everybody at the table, please.'

Gabriel sits at one end of the big dining table, opposite Fleur at the other end, and I take a place next to my boss.

'So you don't want to get rich killing pests, then?' he teases Fleur.

'It's a rotten job that everybody hates,' she sneers, tearing her piece of bread into pieces.

'Being rude to your father again, are we?' says Naomi, bringing in two plates of food. She sets the one with steak and kidney pie at the end of the table before Gabriel, and places a mushroom soufflé in front of me.'

'Hey, where's mine?' demands Fleur.

'Guests and senior citizens first, young, lady,' says Naomi on her way back to the kitchen.

Fleur raises her eyes to heaven again.

Presently, Naomi comes back with two more plates. She sets down one of them loaded with salad and a piece of pie next to Fleur, and takes her own place opposite me. Thus, Gabriel, Naomi and I are at one end of the table, leaving an empty seat between us and Fleur, who is reading her book as she eats.

'Now, Ivan,' says Naomi, 'Tell us about where you're going to study in September. Fleur got a place at Durham to study Law, but now she's decided to take a year out.'

'Wasting her time when she should be studying,' says Gabriel. 'But you can still get in, if you really want to go.'

'I already told you,' she snaps, looking up from her book, 'I'm not bloody going. Me and Beatrice are going to Australia to work for a year.'

'No you're not,' says Gabriel; 'We were paying for you to do 'A' levels to get you in college, not go gallivanting around bloody Australia.'

'You weren't *paying* for my 'A' levels says Fleur; 'Alde Valley Academy is free, in case you've forgotten.'

'But we were supporting you while you studied there,' says Gabriel, 'and the whole point was to get you into a decent college.'

'Well, it's my life,' says Fleur, resuming her reading, 'and I'm not going straight into uni. Lots of people have a year off.'

'Lots of *rich* people have a year off, you mean,' chips in Naomi. 'It would take thousands of pounds to get to Australia, and you don't have the money.'

'It costs six hundred and fifty quid for a return flight, and Beatrice's lending me the money. I'll pay her back from the wages I'll get working on a farm.'

'Working on a farm?' says Gabriel; 'You can do that round here.'

Fleur pauses reading long enough to raise her eyes to heaven once more. Then she bends her head and concentrates on her book, while cutting up her food and placing morsels of pie, bread and salad in her mouth.

After a long silence, during which we all make inroads on our food, Naomi says:

'So, Ivan, where are you going to study?'

'I'm doing English and Drama at Anglia Ruskin in Cambridge,' I say. 'I'm looking forward to it.'

'Oh, the famous university,' says Naomi, 'That's nice.'

Fleur scoffs, and does yet another eyes-raise.

'Anglia Ruskin isn't a part of Cambridge University,' she says. 'It used to be a technical college. Its entry requirements are really low.'

'Fleur!' says Naomi. 'That's a really insulting thing to say to our guest.'

'I wasn't talking to him,' she says, 'I was talking to you. Anyway, it's true.'

'Well, Anglia Ruskin is good enough for me,' I shrug; 'I still needed to get three grade B's, so it's not *that* easy to get in.'

'Of course it isn't,' says Naomi, 'I'm sure it's a really good course.'

There follows a long awkward silence while we eat. Gabriel, trying to change the subject, says with a wry smile:

'Ivan – how are you getting on with your driving lately? Are you keeping that little car on yours safely on the road these days?'

'Well,' I say, 'I didn't end up in a field on my way here, if that's what you mean.'

Fleur scoffs again, without looking up from her book.

'Fleur is taking her test in my car in two weeks' time,' says Naomi. 'It'll be her third time–'

'Thanks for making me out to be an idiot,' snaps Fleur.

'I took three tests too,' I say. 'Maybe it'll be third time lucky for you too.'

'I bloody-well hope so,' says Fleur, still not looking up from her book.

There is another long silence.

I decide to ask a question to solve a mystery that had intrigued me for a week or two. I had, more than once, heard Gabriel say when chatting to pregnant housewife customers that the birth of his son was the best day of his life. So I say to Naomi:

'What does your son do? I guess he's left home already.'

The three Millers all stop eating and look at me. I realise I've made a huge error of judgement, but though in a hole, I kept on digging:

'You said, Gabriel,' I begin, tentatively, 'that when he was born, it was the best day of your life...'

My voice trails off.

Finally Gabriel says:

'Yes, Ivan, it was the best day ever at the time, till Fleur here came along. But our son... he didn't survive. It was a cot death, you see, when he was six weeks old.'

I wish now, that the earth would open and swallow me up. Never in my life have I felt so ashamed and embarrassed.

'I'm so sorry,' I blurt out, 'I didn't realise...'

'Of course not,' says Naomi, 'How could you have known? But don't worry about it Ivan, it was a very long time ago.'

In the ensuing heavy atmosphere, the loudest noises are the clink of our cutlery touching on our plates.

Gabriel has a long, long drink of his beer, then says:

'Which school did you go to, Ivan? Fleur went to Alde Valley Academy, but she told me earlier she didn't know you, so I take it you went to Farlingaye High School at Woodbridge.'

'No,' I say, 'I've just finished at Thomas Mills High School in Framlingham.'

'Oh, the posh one where Ed Sheeran used to go to,' smiles Naomi. 'So you had to catch the bus and go all that way?'

'Oh it wasn't posh at all,' I say, 'and not too far. We used to do our homework on the bus on the way home.'

'Well, you must have done it well to get into uni,' says Naomi.

'Thanks,' I say.

'Did you ever meet Ed Sheeran?' asks Naomi. 'I heard he's in the habit of going back to visit his old school.'

'Yes,' I reply, 'A couple of times. I got him to sign my guitar. I was going to sell it on eBay to pay some of my university expenses.'

'It won't make that much,' says Fleur, looking up momentarily from her book. 'He signs so many they aren't worth more than about two hundred each.'

'How do you know?' asks Gabriel.

'Saw one auctioned off on a TV program,' says Fleur, standing up and walking towards the hallway.

'Where are you going?' asks Naomi; 'You haven't had your dessert.'

'Are you trying to make me fat?' snaps Fleur from the hallway. 'I'm going up to my room to phone Beatrice.'

'Get back up the table,' calls Gabriel.

'Let her go,' says Naomi, 'You should know by now she'll do whatever she wants.'

Gabriel exhales angrily, and took another long pull at his beer. Naomi tries to fill the silence:

'Got any brothers or sisters, Ivan?' she asks.

'Nope,' I tell her, 'I'm an only child.'

'But not as spoiled as our one, I hope,' says Gabriel.

'My mum says healthy teenagers are supposed to be stroppy and rebellious,' I say.

'In that case,' says Gabriel, 'we have a very healthy girl. Now, what's for dessert?'

'It's apple tart and crème anglaise,' Naomi says.

'You mean pie and custard,' he says.

'No,' she says, 'It's different. It's an open tart with cinnamon and nutmeg, and crème anglaise is similar to custard but thinner and with more egg yolks and vanilla.'

'If you say so,' he says.

'Sounds good,' I say politely.

Over our dessert the conversation turns to the subject of the recent murders when Naomi says:

'How did your mum get on, Ivan, when all this East Coast Killer thing was going on? Was she as scared as I was?'

'Well,' I say, 'We didn't have a murder right on our doorstep like you, but she was still living in a state of terror. Me too, come to that.'

'Oh, but you weren't in any danger,' says Naomi. 'The killer was only interested in women.'

'I was mostly fearful for my mum,' I say. 'She's still scared now, won't take our dog out in the woods any more.'

'That's understandable,' says Naomi. 'I think everyone around here has had a big shock.'

'That's for sure,' I say. 'If you don't mind me asking, who actually found the body on the allotments?'

Naomi and Gabriel exchange glances.

'Oh, that was our neighbour Cindy Mayhew,' says Gabriel. 'She lives just up the street. She was pretty hysterical. Carol Sansom was her friend, and she tended a plot next to her, you see.'

'And you must have known her pretty well,' I say.

'Of course, we know everyone on the allotments,' says Naomi; 'We have the plot at this end nearest our garden, we spend most of our Sundays there. We were the first ones to get a plot after Sir William Haslett donated the land for the project. Do you like gardening, Ivan?'

'I have to say I hate it.'

Naomi and Gabriel both laugh at the same time.

'You don't know what you're missing,' says Gabriel; 'It's very relaxing, really takes you out of yourself, if you know what I mean.'

'I bet it does,' I say, checking the time on my watch.

And that's about it, on my visit to the Millers' cottage. I ask to be excused on the grounds I'm meeting up with my friend Baz in Peasenhall to do some computer gaming. But before I leave, I politely thank my hosts for the meal.

Outside on their driveway, fumbling in my pocket for my car keys, I look up and see that Fleur is hanging out of a window puffing away on a vape. She looks down on me as she exhales a little cloud of vapour without changing the expression on her face.

Then, as I'm getting in my car, she says, in a loud whisper:

'Hey, Ivan, don't tell *them* you saw me vaping.'

'Why would I do that?' I say.

I see her shrug, just before I turn my back on her. Then I hear the window close behind me.

On the way to Peasenhall I reflect on how I found myself sitting and eating a meal in the very lair of the beast! I have to say, I feel like a monstrous hypocrite for taking their food, not to mention being paid and mentored by the man I intend to shop as the true serial killer. On the other hand my curiosity has been satisfied, having seen the home life of a man who, if my gut instincts are correct, is soon to be named Britain's most notorious criminal.

Perhaps I should consider myself lucky to have eaten a specially prepared soufflé, without being poisoned and buried in the garden. However, I bore in mind the serial killings all involved the slaying of women of a particular age and a particular type. One article I read online suggested that the serial killer was murdering women who reminded him of their mother, acting on some kind of deep-seated, uncontrollable anger.

Of course, though my gut feeling tells me that Gabriel is the killer, I'm acutely aware that others have already dismissed the idea. The Chief Constable himself, and the entire Suffolk police force do not think Gabriel Miller is the man they're looking for. My mother, having taken on board all their data and opinions, is convinced he's innocent. Even I have to admit that the evidence does, at the moment, point to somebody else completely.

And yet, having visited Gabriel Miller in his own home setting, and seen him amongst his slightly peculiar family, my instincts tell me – even more strongly – that the killer is still at large, still hiding in plain sight, and likely to strike again.

Chapter Five:
Old Man Tranmer Had A Farm

Tuesday 22nd July

Today Gabriel and I are on our way to sort out a mole problem in Kelsale Green, a small hamlet near Saxmundham. Along a small country road, we happen to pass one of those small vegetable stalls, common across the country now, where gardeners sell their excess produce to passers-by. This one consists of a table with an open cupboard attached to its top. Inside are deposited various offerings from the grower's garden in clear plastic bags, including new potatoes, runner beans, tomatoes, cucumbers, and several boxes of eggs. A biscuit tin with a slot cut in the top has the words *'HONESTY BOX'* written on it in white paint.

Gabriel drives up alongside the stall and presses the switch to wind down his window. He seems to be thinking for a good few seconds. Then he gets out and opens the side sliding door of the van. He takes out an empty cardboard box. Walking over to the table, he selects some bags of runner beans and one of potatoes, two cucumbers, and a punnet of tomatoes. He takes a couple of steps back towards the van and then seems to have a change of mind. He scratches his chin and looks at the eggs, then reaches out and takes all six boxes and puts them in his cardboard box. I watch him put this produce into the side door and close it firmly.

Then I distinctly see in the mirror that he reaches

into a trouser pocket and takes out a handful of change to put in the honesty box. I'm looking very carefully, and am somewhat surprised to see that he only slots in a few loose coppers, though the total cost of his produce must amount to several pounds.

Back in the van, Gabriel seems very pleased with himself.

'There was some nice stuff there,' he says. 'The eggs look nice and fresh, and you can't beat good home-grown runner beans. That gardener must have a knack for getting stuff ready very early – the beans and tomatoes I'm growing are nowhere near ripe yet.'

Half a mile further on, we slow down as a big, arrogant cock pheasant stands watching us approach from the middle of the road. Gabriel stops the van five yards away, and then I realise why he's got his air rifle at the ready in the cab with us. Its butt is in my foot-well, and the barrel is leaning against the dog's centre seat. In just about six seconds Gabriel takes up the gun, cocks it using the under-lever, places a pellet in the rotating breech, leans out of his window and gets his telescopic sight trained on the quarry. Gabriel's aim follows it as it walks to the side of the road. *Ping!* goes the rifle, and the pheasant, hit in the head, collapses flapping on the verge.

'Fetch it Nancy,' says Gabriel.

The Jack Russell leaps out of his side window and in a few seconds has hold of the big bird. Nancy half drags and half carries the pheasant to Gabriel's side of the van. Meanwhile, Gabriel hands me the gun and gets out to examine his prize.

'Good girl,' he says to Nancy, taking the poached bird, and puts it in the side door of the van. Gabriel and Nancy are both soon on board again in their respective seats, and then we're on our way.

'That's my Sunday lunch sorted out,' laughs Gabriel. 'There are always pheasants walking about on this road. Would you like me to get one for your mother? I'm sure she'd appreciate some freshly shot game.'

'No thanks,' I say; 'She doesn't, er, like pheasants very much.'

'She doesn't know what she's missing,' he says, with one of his funny little smiles.

'I take it you eat a lot of pheasants?' I ask. 'They certainly seem quite easy to get.'

'Oh, I like the odd one now and again. As for them being easy to get, they're buggers to catch in the shooting season. They get wise to the fact that guns mean danger pretty quickly, you see. But that one, he thought he was safe in the middle of summer – but as you saw, he thought wrong.'

'Ah, well,' I say, 'I guess the landowner would only have shot it himself in the hunting season.'

'That's right,' smiles Gabriel, 'and Walter Tranmer, who owns this land, he releases about five thousand more of them every year – so I don't think he'll miss that one.'

We drive on for another mile and enter a driveway marked with a sign bearing the words:

> RED HOUSE FARM
> NO SALESMAN
> NO TRAVELLERS
> BEWARE OF THE DOGS

Gabriel then stops, puts the air rifle back in its leather gun slip, gets out, and places the weapon out of sight in the back of the van.

'That's pheasant hunting over for the day,' he says. 'Too bad we only got one.'

'Yes,' I say, 'Too bad.'

'Now, when we get to the yard,' says Gabriel, 'don't open your door until Old Man Tranmer comes out and puts the dogs in a safe place. Otherwise you're likely to die a very early death.'

It's soon apparent what he meant when we reach the big red brick house. Two huge German Shepherd dogs come out to greet us. They don't bark, but circle the van like hungry wolves in search of prey. One of them comes sniffing at my side of the van, and I can distinctly hear its nose snuffling at the crack in the door. Nancy begins uttering low growling noises in her throat without actually opening her mouth.

Gabriel gives Nancy a reassuring pat,

'They're a bit too big for you to handle, my little pup,' he says, 'though I'm sure you'd have a good go at them.' He turns towards me. 'She absolutely hates those two dogs.'

'Yes,' I say, 'and those two dogs hate us too.'

'As I said, we'll have to wait here for Walter to come

out and lock them away,' says Gabriel. 'Those two buggers are really vicious. I wouldn't come here at all except for the fact I have a contract to keep down the rats round his piggeries, which are the big buildings you can see over there, but part of the deal is that I have to come here to the garden and sort out his moles once in a while. I get extra for it, but each time I come close to the house I run the risk of being savaged by those bloody dogs. And you'd be amazed how dangerous some of his pigs are, too. Walter has a shed full of wild boar crosses, and they're not very fond of humans.'

'Wild boar crosses housed in enclosed barns doesn't sound very nice,' I say.

'Ha! You don't know the half of it. He uses that Danish-invented 'Psycho-Dynamic' growing system that starves the weaning young piglets and feeds them automatically when they hear the sound of a buzzer. Then, as they grow, the buzzer is sounded more and more often, and the pigs stuff themselves with food, and fatten quicker than usual. None of the male pigs are castrated either, so the buggers fight and sometimes cause terrible wounds to each other. Whole hogs, as we call them, are a bloody danger to work with, but luckily our job is mainly to service the rat bait boxes on the outside of the sheds.'

Presently a tall, elderly man in blue overalls comes out of the front door of the house. He has grey hair slicked down with hair oil. His wrinkled face is pasty and white and covered in a day's grey stubble. He has a long walking stick with a piece of stag antler attached as a hand grip. He shepherds the dogs into the house, waving the stick in the air to hasten them along, and they slink heads-down inside the hallway, and he slams the door behind them.

Relieved to see dogs safely locked up, we get out.

'Hello, Walter,' says Gabriel, 'How are those pigs?'

'Well, you could say they're eating me out of house and home,' says Walter. 'The price of feed has doubled, but I suppose the greedy little sods are getting a little fatter each day, thank Christ.'

He focuses his gaze on me.

'What-ho young fellow,' he says, 'Now who're you, young whippersnapper? I haven't seen you before...'

'Ivan is helping me out for the summer,' says Gabriel. 'I'm teaching him a few tricks of the trade. He reckons he wants to be a student in Cambridge, but by the time I've finished he might want to be a pest controller and go into the business for himself.'

'I'm not sure about that,' I protest.

'Well,' says Gabriel with a wink, 'It would certainly be better than going off to some smoky polluted city and saddling yourself with thirty thousand pounds of debt, and ending up as a teacher with kids cursing you and parents beating you up in the playground after lessons!'

'Well, you'd earn a bloody good living in pest control if you charged half as much as this gentleman,' says Walter. 'Do you know last month he charged me fifty quid for clearing a few moles from my back garden?'

'It took me three visits and would have been ninety-five if you were a Londoner in a holiday cottage,' says

Gabriel.

'I've no doubt,' says Walter. 'I remember the time when I used to get old Joe Sankey to catch my moles. He used to charge me five pounds a mole, but I did let him go ferreting in my meadows as a perk. He's long gone now of course, so now I have to have Gabriel every month or two coming to stitch me up. How much are you going to charge me this time for catching a mole, Mr. Miller?'

'Oh, not much, I think you can afford me,' says Gabriel.

He turns to me and whispers loudly so that Walter can hear him:

'Walter here is the richest farmer in Suffolk. He's got two over two thousand acres and some of the biggest pig units in the country. I reckon he's got about ten thousand hogs fattening in his buildings – it takes me a whole morning to go around and check all the bait points.'

'Ten thousand? Whatever are you on about? I should think not! I've only got capacity for six thousand two hundred and fifty. There are plenty of producers across the country bigger than I am. I'll tell you another thing too – with the way prices are going. I'll be lucky to make ten pounds a pig. Ten measly quid for all that work! The stupid government's been letting pork in from all over the world for next to nothing, the price of feed has gone through the roof and don't even get me started on the cost of electricity. Ivan, if you ever start up a business, make sure it's not pig production, it's one big waste of time and too much bloody worry.'

'Moan, moan, moan!' says Gabriel, 'Typical old farmer, always moaning. But never mind the pigs, how are the pheasants doing this year?'

Walter's face changed in an instant, and he begins to smile.

'Oh, they're doing alright,' he says; 'I believe in releasing them nice and early so we can have the first shoot in October. We've got a team of American guns coming on the tenth. They're a bit trigger-happy but they pay cash on the nail. There were are nine of them, and last year they turned up in rented Range Rovers, and they tipped my gamekeeper fifty pounds each. Now what do you think about that? They're a merry old lot and they shoot at everything they see, even on the ground if we're not careful. The only trouble is, last year they shot one of my beaters. They only got him one pellet in the leg and we managed to get it out with a pen knife. He hollered a bit when I put the pig iodine on the wound, but that stuff will stop any infection in one second flat. Luckily, the pellet was just sticking in his skin – you see, those guns, they were a long way off when they shot him. Anyway, this year I'll tell them to be a bit more bloody careful.'

'If you fancy a day's shooting,' says Gabriel, 'Walter only charges forty pounds a bird, and the minimum number of birds per day is a hundred and twenty.'

'No, no, it's forty-eight plus VAT these days,' chuckles Walter; 'That's cheap compared to some of the big shoots down south that cater for the London City crowd. But we don't get in the caterers and serve smoked salmon and wagyu beef and all that nonsense, my cook from the village does a good lunch in the house here, and they get as much wine and cognac as they can drink, and that keeps them happy.'.

'That's half the trouble, I hear,' says Gabriel; 'Most of the guns who come shooting here are drunk as lords by the time their boozy old lunches have finished. No wonder they keep shooting your beaters.'

'Ah, well, we've got to do whatever it takes to earn a shilling these days,' says Walter. 'In my father's time, we just raised a few pheasants for ourselves and the neighbours, but these days we've got to do whatever we can to pay the bills.'

He turns to me.

'And do you know what the agent told me to do the other day?'

'I don't know,' I say.

'Well, he only went and told me I had to convert all the barns and outbuildings in the yard over there into holiday lets and have a bunch of strangers – bloody Londoners and foreigners – coming and going all hours of the night *on their nice little holidays in the countryside!* I asked the agent how much he reckoned it would cost to convert all the buildings and do you know what he told me? He said "Oh Mr. Tranmer, we should have it done for about *four hundred and eighty thousand pounds!*" Why, that's nearly half a million quid, just to have a load of strangers coming up my driveway, parking in my yard and making my dogs bark!'

'I don't think anybody would come to stay if your dogs were about,' says Gabriel. 'I'll tell you one thing though, Lenny Mills up the road at Grove Farm has three holiday lets, and he charges a thousand pounds a weekend each for them. Now, I should imagine that adds up to a good bit by the end of the year.'

'Yes, but be that has it may, it would still take a long time to make back four hundred and eighty thousand pounds – and the agent said my dogs would have to be tethered up round the back or locked up in kennels. Next thing you know I'd have the gypsies back round here – do you know, last year they made off with the sat nav off two of my tractors, and the CCTV round the piggeries showed two of them poking around there trying to get in and steal whatever they could bloody-well find.'

'Yeah, the thieving situation is getting bad these days,' says Gabriel. 'Only last week I had ten mole traps stolen out of Middleton churchyard. I thought they'd be safe there and put a stick to mark them, but some bloody tea-leaf took all ten traps and the marker canes as well. What a world we live in!'

'Yes indeed,' says Walter, looking at his watch, 'You can't trust anybody these days. Ah well, I can't stand around here talking to you all day. I'm off to sort out the pigs. My man Hubbard said he heard a couple of them coughing this morning. If they've got that bloody microplasma again it's got to be nipped in the bud. Newson the vet is supposed to be there in half an hour's time to take some samples. And last night we got seven pigs cut up badly in a fight, bloody things. They were the wild boar crosses we do for the restaurant trade. They taste good, but they'll take chunks out of you if you aren't careful. Now I suppose I'll get another huge bill from the bloody vets, Newson and Wright Associates, the biggest thieves in the country.'

Again, he turns to me, continuing his rant:

'Ivan, make sure you never go into the pig business, waste of bloody time. I'll tell you what, train to be a vet, that's where all the money's at. That bloody Newson has had thousands out of me this year. Charged me three hundred pounds for one small operation on my German Shepherd. Bloody outrageous!'

And then, with a dismissive shake of his head, Walter Tranmer walks over to his ancient Land Rover and gets in. The engine starts and he drives off, leaving a cloud of black diesel smoke all the way down his driveway.

'Grumpy old sod,' says Gabriel. 'He's as rich as hell, but he never stops moaning. You wouldn't think he was Naomi's great uncle, either. Never offered her a penny, and it's strictly business between him and me. So much for family! Naomi does come to see him once in a while, and they get on all right, so she tells me. Her grandmother was his sister, you see, but she died twenty years ago.'

I decide to be nosy, and ask:

'So Naomi didn't inherit any land or money, then?'

'Naomi has never received so much as a brass farthing from those tight-fisted Tranmers. The daughters in these farming families never get the farms or the money passed on to them, it all goes to the oldest son, and bugger-all to the rest of the clan. But, funnily enough, Naomi did at least inherit Hawthorn Farm and our cottage from her other grandparents when they died. But that was only because her dad was already dead and he'd been an only child. Naomi was also an only child, so she got some run-down properties. But all the land had been sold off to pay debts years ago, and now the farm house is derelict. We've spent thousands on our cottage, and I guess we'll do up the big house one day, when we get the money. But it'll take more than the fifty measly quid I'll get off Walter for this job. Ah, well, let's get those moles sorted and get out of here before *he* comes back and depresses the hell out of us all over again.'

'He's certainly a strange one,' I say. 'He's got millions and millions of pounds of property, but he looks like a tramp, drives around in a wreck and talks as if he's about to go bankrupt. He may be a good customer, but he's a miserable old git. I wonder how his wife puts up with him.'

Gabriel laughs.

'Oh, there isn't a Mrs. Tranmer any more,' he says. 'His first wife died of cancer, and his second wife, Katy, who was forty years younger than him, she disappeared without trace a year ago, and since then he's been under suspicion of doing away with her. I thought you knew – it's a well known story in this part of the world, and people do like to gossip.'

'Wow, that's quite a story. But surely the police would have got up a case to try and convict him – I mean to say, there's always something in the way of evidence to bring a case to trial.'

'Not in this case,' says Gabriel. 'Apparently Katie Tranmer disappeared along with her phone, her passport, some clothes and personal effects, and vanished into thin air. Old man Tranmer reported her missing the very same evening and said he was completely baffled by her going. Over the next few days and weeks no sign of her was ever found, no financial transactions made on her bank cards, no record of her using public transport or taxis, no hotel, airport or other sightings of her whatsoever.'

'That's a real mystery story.'

'Not a story, Ivan, that was what really happened. But one thing is an absolute certainty – you can bet your boots the police have him down as the chief suspect in an open case.'

'And what do you make of it, Gabriel?' I ask. 'Do you think he did away with her and disposed of her body?'

'Well, if he did, if he really is guilty, he's one hell of an actor. You see, when he first told me of his wife going missing, he cried his eyes out. I felt really sorry for him, ended up sitting in his kitchen drinking tea, listening to half of his life story, hearing about how much he missed Katy. And all the time those two bloody dogs were lying down at his feet giving me the evil eye.'

Gabriel then points to an open cart shed on one side of the yard.

'Now I'll tell you something really odd. Do you see that little white Citroen over there in the barn? Well, that's Katy's little car, the one she used almost every day. If she were really going to run away, why didn't she take her car with her? That's something I've always wondered about. But, hey-ho, it isn't up to me to speculate. That's not going to help poor little Katy, I'm afraid.'

'Did you know her, Gabriel?' I ask him.

He looks at me strangely, as if I'd accused him of something.

'Yes,' he says very quietly, 'I knew little Katy very well. She was a lovely woman. She deserved someone much better than Old Man Tranmer, in my humble opinion. Now, that's enough talk, let's get on with the job in hand, or we'll soon end up finishing our day completely on the drag.'

The conversation over, we go to find the offending moles in the garden. As we work, we can hear in the distance the muffled sounds of pigs roaring and squealing in the fattening units. There are seven buildings, side by side, each one a hundred yards long and forty wide. I hate to think what horrors are taking place inside, where small piglets are grown to the required size in small, overcrowded pens in a few short weeks. I'm grateful not to have to visit these units for the time being, our brief for this trip being only to deal with a few moles, rather than the rats inevitably drawn in by the stench of the unfortunate animals.

Within ten minutes, we have six traps placed all around the back garden. After washing our hands and drying them on squares of paper towel, we get back into the van, and soon we're speeding through the lanes toward Sternfield, our next port of call, where a nest of ants has undermined a kitchen wall and invaded a beekeeper's larder full of honey.

Then, after a few miles of driving along without a word of conversation, Gabriel says the most unexpected thing:

'Hey, Ivan,' he says, with another of his wry little smiles, 'You know how some people round here like to gossip.'

'They certainly do,' I say. 'What of it?'

'Well,' he says quietly, his left hand stroking Nancy as he drives, 'Some people have been saying that Walter Tranmer might be the East Coast Killer... what do you think about that?'

At first I am speechless – because, of course, I don't think it's the sort of thing that the *real* serial killer would say – if, indeed, Gabriel really *is* guilty.

I become aware that my boss keeps glancing sideways to study my reaction. Eventually, I hear myself say:

'I'm not surprised that people have said that. After all, he lives alone, he's weird as hell, and he already has suspicion hanging over him. Maybe he really did kill his wife, and that somehow gave him the urge to do more murders.'

There are a few seconds silence, then Gabriel says:

'Well, as far as the police are concerned, we're *all* under suspicion. They gave me a right grilling when that body turned up the other side of my garden fence in April. I'm surprised they haven't taken you in, as well. They've already interrogated half the male population round here.'

'I did speak to some officers two months ago, when they did the rounds of door to door enquiries in Middleton.'

'Yeah? And what sort of stuff did they ask you?'

'Well, they saw my car with 'L' plates and asked if I'd ever driven it without passing my test.'

'On the way to a murder, perhaps?'

'I suppose that was what they were thinking.'

'And what did they ask you, Ivan?'

'Well, it was just after the May 16th killing. That's the one that was done in Yoxford, only two miles away. They asked me my name, where I went to school, if I'd seen anything suspicious, that sort of thing.'

'The May one was the murder near the Yox Man statue next to the lake, wasn't it?'

'Yes,' I say, 'That's the one. That was horribly close to us, and my mother was petrified.'

'Not as horribly close as the one we had outside our back door. Naomi says even though that Hadiscoe bloke has been charged, she's still nervous every time she leaves the house on her own. Even when driving her car, she hates to be alone, in case it breaks down. She won't even go for a walk in our village now. She goes to an area where there's loads of people about when she takes Nancy for a walk.'

'Yeah, my mother is the same. She only takes our dog along the village street, or sometimes she goes to that 'Dog Orchard' place at Saxmundham where you pay three pounds a session to exercise your dog in what is advertised as "a safe space". The safety was supposed to refer to the dog because it couldn't run off, but now the owners flock to places like that because of all the murders. Yet, there are some people – I mean women – who don't seem bothered and are going out alone again to exercise their dogs, or are even walking about the countryside completely on their own.'

Just as I say that, we drive round a bend and there is a woman with two spaniels on leads. Gabriel slows down, and the woman moves onto the grassy verge and reins in her dogs as we pass. Gabriel has a long look at her, raises his hand in acknowledgement, and the woman smiles and waves with her free hand.

'Amazing,' he says, 'how careless some women are, considering we've had a murder every month for six months.'

'But at least there hasn't been one for almost six weeks,' I say, 'not since that Hadiscoe bloke was locked up.'

'Touch wood,' says Gabriel.

I begin looking around for something made of wood, even fumbling in my trouser pockets for something to fit the bill. But, try as I might, not a scrap of wood can I find anywhere in the cab, not even a wooden pencil.

'Ah, well,' I say, 'It's just a silly superstition. Anyway, they've got Hadiscoe in custody, let's hope he turns out to be the real killer.'

'Yeah,' says Gabriel, with lips pursed as if he were deep in thought, 'Let's hope.'

Chapter Six:
Another Visit To The
Scene Of A Murder

Sunday 27th July

Today is the last Sunday in July, and it's a fitting time for me to exercise my detective skills and visit an area known as Saint Botolph's Meadows in Iken on the banks of the river Alde. I have a vague idea that visiting some of the murder sites might lend me a clue, a piece of information that would confirm the guilt of Gabriel Miller. But I'm not really sure what I'm doing there, or what exactly I'm looking for. I am hardly likely to find a hatchet with Gabriel's name on it. Perhaps I am just looking for an excuse to indulge my morbid curiosity. On the other hand, you never know, there just might be something here that will give me that one, single, all-important shred of evidence I need to nail the guilty person.

Although it's midsummer, the sky is grey and the air is flecked with rain. A breeze is blowing north-easterly across the mudflats which are made visible by the low tide. The air has the salty aroma of the estuary mud and brackish water. An occasional call of a curlew adds to the atmosphere of lonely gloom.

Here, on Thursday 13th of March, at about ten in the morning, a riding instructor named Mary Sommersby was brutally murdered, the third of the East Coast

Killer's five victims. The killer, as usual, chose a lonely spot, delivered the same single blow to the head, and ended the life of a woman of the same age group as the others. Mary Sommersby was thirty-nine, blonde-haired and, according to the newspapers, an attractive single woman. She had just entered a field to bridle a horse, when the killer approached her, and struck her with a fatal blow.

But how was this possible without a struggle, with her making no apparent attempt to run away? Did she see the attacker approaching? Did she know him and therefore assume she was in no danger? Perhaps the geography of the meadow where she died will lend a clue. The newspaper cutting in my pocket has a little plan of the area, with the murder sight clearly mapped, so finding the exact spot is going to be easy enough.

As I enter the long, gravel-strewn lane that leads down to the meadow, I am pondering the mystery of why she died like that without putting up a fight or trying to get away. The first thing that comes to mind is that, as my boots scrunch the gravel underfoot, approaching the area is relatively noisy. Then, reaching the muddy area around the five bar gate leading on to the meadow, it is possible to walk more or less silently. But the big field – today it has four horses quietly grazing in it – is open and without cover. The murder happened only fifteen feet from the gate, which Mary Sommersby presumably opened to enter the field, then closed behind her as she made ready to catch up her horse and put on the bridle.

Two thoughts now enter my head: either she knew her killer and sensed no danger; or, perhaps, the killer looked harmless so that she felt no sense of threat.

I imagined the sight of Gabriel Miller approaching her, a little smile on his face, the hatchet maybe still tucked in his big cargo pants pocket as he quietly closed the gate behind him...

But I can't believe either that his presence would be undetected as he stalked across the grass towards her, or if he was seen, that Mary Sommersby just calmly waited for him and stood there as he drew back his arm to strike.

I am in the field, having climbed the gate and jumped down close to the murder's position. It is an eerie feeling, just to look across the grass to where it happened. I spend a long few minutes just looking down at the ground contemplating how and why it all took place.

The harsh cawing of a carrion crow sitting on a distant fence post causes me to look up, and scan the meadow. One of the horses is staring at me, the others continue to graze. A more picturesque place for a murder is hard to imagine. The meadow sits on a low sandy cliff on the edge of the river Alde. From where I'm standing, looking north, it's possible to see right across the river which at this point is about a quarter of a mile broad. Patches of brown mud flats are visible, with flocks of waders milling about on them: low tide. Away to my right in the far distance, St Peter's church tower is just visible above the roofs and garden trees of Aldeburgh.

Iken's own church, dedicated to Saint Botolph, is on my side of the river about a quarter mile away to my left, just visible between the gently stirring oaks, ashes and sycamores of a little wood that borders the western edge of the meadow.

According to the newspapers, riding instructor Mary Sommersby worked at a nearby riding stable. One account described how she died with a bridle still in her hand. Struck down the by the killer's trademark blow to the skull, felled as usual, by a small sharp blade such as a hatchet, the poor woman lay in a pool of her own blood until she was discovered by her boss, the owner of the nearby stables known as Howard's Riding School. According to the information released by the police, a man in a brown Barbour-style waxed cotton jacket was seen walking along the country road back towards Snape. After five murders, this is the only known sighting of a suspect.

Keith Howard, owner of the riding school, is reportedly the one who saw the suspect walking back along the main road, presumably to a parked car. The man, of medium height (like Gabriel Miller) had his collar turned up, and his face was partially obscured by a floppy green combat style hat.

Howard saw this stranger a half hour before he discovered Mary's Sommersby in the field. At the time he spotted him, he had no reason to look at him too closely, not knowing yet anything untoward had happened to his riding instructor. It was only later when he couldn't find Mary Sommersby in the yard that he decided to go to the meadow and see if she had somehow been delayed, perhaps having difficulty getting a bridle on one of the ponies needed for a ride later that morning.

The fact that the man in the brown coat was walking down the road, westwards, in the direction of nearby Snape, means that he had probably parked a car in a field gateway; but, according to the newspapers, Howard had no recollection of seeing any vehicle and had assumed at the time the man was just another hiker, this road being very popular with walkers.

He discovered Mary Sommersby in the horse meadow lying on her back. Her jacket had been pulled open with enough force to pull some of the buttons off the garment and her jodhpurs had been pulled down to her thighs but not removed, thus revealing her underwear, which apparently had not been disturbed. When leaving the meadow the murderer had left the gate open, though the horses hadn't strayed into the lane by the time Howard arrived.

Subsequent police enquiries discovered no other witnesses who had seen either the man or the car. The murderer must have made his way back either towards Snape and Saxmundham in a northerly direction, or south towards Orford. Whichever way he went, the roads have only the very lightest of traffic, and there are no CCTV cameras for miles and miles around.

After so many killings it has became apparent that the murderer is very adept at avoiding detection. By the time murder number five had taken place it was obvious to anyone living in the area that the police were making some attempt to show everybody that they were present in the area, with patrol cars being seen for the first time even in the most remote areas. Furthermore, every town and village had been visited at some stage by plain clothes detectives making door to door inquiries. The manpower involved in the operation must have been immense, and yet in the midst of all the activity the murders were still taking place, and people, especially women, were in a state of fear.

However, with the arrest and confession of Gerald Hadiscoe on June 10th, things suddenly changed. The patrol cars ceased to be seen on country roads. Door to door enquiries were curtailed. Newspapers and TV reports now focused on Hadiscoe and seemed convinced that he was, in fact, the East Coast Killer.

The scrunching of the gravel behind me makes me turn, and I see coming down the lane a man in a green tweed jacket, the kind worn by game shooters and racehorse trainers. On his head is a flat tweed cap of a similar colour. He is carrying something in his hand, and I feel a wave of fear pulse through me, until I see that all the man has in his hand is a bridle.

The fellow is extremely tall, maybe six feet six, and is wearing tall riding boots. As I stop and watch him approach, I can already see his hostility, as he's staring angrily in my direction. His stride is quick and determined. At about five yards' distance he stops and tilts his chin in my direction.

'Yes, can I help you?' he says, with as much unfriendliness as he can muster.

'I just came to see the meadow,' I say stupidly.

'Oh, and why on earth would you want to do that?' he says.

'Well,' I say, 'I was out for a walk and just got curious and wanted to see the place of the crime.'

I just couldn't think of anything else to say. The man looks at me with contempt and slowly shakes his head from side to side.

'You're the third person this week who's come trespassing on my property, and I'm going to tell you the same thing I told the others. There's no public right of way along this lane.'

'It looks like a footpath down to the river.'

'Oh no, it doesn't,' he counters; 'It *looks like* a private drive to my meadow. It has a sheer drop off to the foreshore just behind that far hedge, and if you want to take a run and jump off the cliff go ahead and be my guest. Otherwise, bugger off and get back on the public roads, the footpaths, or wherever the bloody-hell you're supposed to be.'

'All right,' I say walking past him, 'I'm sorry to bother you.'

Possibly softened by my apology, he calls after me:

'There's a public footpath further along the road that leads to the church if you want to go hiking. Or you can take the other footpath to Sudbourne, they're both clearly marked.'

A few yards past him, I stop and turn, watch him unfasten the gate.

'Are you Mr Howard?' I ask boldly.

He looks up, and is so surprised I haven't gone that he doesn't speak for several seconds.

Eventually he says:

'I am, and who are you? I might as well have *your* name, the police asked me to keep an eye on the lane and tell me of anyone coming along here. They might be quite intrigued to make your acquaintance, as I'm told murderers often return to the scene of the crime.'

'I'm Ivan Salter, I live in Fordley and I've got nothing whatever to hide from the police.'

'Well, Ivan Salter from Fordley, I'll take a wild guess that you're some sort of vlogger or blogger or internet sleuth come here to try to get the reward money!'

'Well obviously I came to have a look at the murder site, there's no law against that.'

'Well, my nosy friend, now you've had a look and it's time to go, and I'll tell you one thing for free. The police sent a team of about fifty trained and highly experienced officers down this lane and across the meadow, under the cliffs and everywhere around this area. In fact, they combed and re-combed it for days and days, going over it thoroughly for every tiny bit of evidence, and if you think they left any big fat clues that you might discover I would suggest you're living in cloud cuckoo land. Now, take yourself off and don't come back.'

He puts his hands on his hips and raises his eyebrows in a theatrical gesture of impatience, waiting for me to leave.

'Just tell me one thing,' I say, standing my ground, 'I read that you got a glimpse of the murderer. Could you tell me roughly how tall he was, was he well-built or slim, and did you happen to see what colour hair he might have had?'

The man's eyes open wide with annoyance, but he says nothing.

'And the car,' I persist, 'The murderer must have had a car – are you sure you didn't see anything significant before or after the crime?'

'I'm sorry, I'm not going to tell you *anything!* Any information I have is strictly for the police. And I'm certainly not going to waste more time talking to *you*. Have you ever considered you might be the world's very worst private detective?'

'That's very rude,' I say, as I walked away.

He calls after me:

'I didn't ask you to come walking onto my land. If you really are one of those stupid get-rich-quick internet vloggers, I suggest you get yourself a proper job and stop wasting your time coming to places like this.'

I laugh out loud, hoping that he'll hear me and get even more annoyed, but I'm already too far off for him to hear me. When I get to where the lane joined the road I turn around and can see him beyond the five bar gate trying to catch one of the horses. I watch him for a few seconds. To my great satisfaction, every time he walks up to the horse, it trots off.'

'Ha-ha!' I shout, 'Serves you right, you bad-tempered

old fool!'

But I'm pretty sure he doesn't hear me through the wind and the rain and the lonely call of the curlews and plovers down below us on the muddy edge of the river.

So, after this rather unsatisfactory visit to the crime scene I walk back to my car. In the field gateway where I'd pulled off the road, I have a good look at the ground and the surrounding bushes, as if after four months there might still be a tyre mark or a cigarette end, or – if I were really lucky – a calling card with the guilty person's name and address on it to give me confirmation of where I might find the murderer and so claim my fifty thousand quid.

So far, today, or any other day, I haven't found or seen anything linking Gabriel Miller to the murder of Mary Sommersby. On the other hand I haven't seen anything to dissuade me of his guilt either. I know for a fact that Gabriel has a waxed cotton Barbour-style jacket hanging on a peg inside his hallway. But, there again, there is one in my own household too, left behind when my father left home. There are thousands of other similar jackets owned by men and women up and down the country. As for the floppy hat, I have never seen Gabriel wear one, but that doesn't mean he hasn't got one somewhere, hidden away with his killing hatchet and size twelve boots.

But why, I thought, as I got back into the car, why murder this sequence of seemingly innocent women? Are the murders carried out purely for the primitive thrill of killing? Every day I see Gabriel smile as he cheerfully slaughters his squirrels, rabbits, rats and mice. I don't think there is such a thing as a pest controller who wouldn't secretly enjoy killing. Sure, they'll tell you over and over again that they do it for the money, that it's a job that has to be done and they regret having to kill wasps, bees, pigeons, rats, mice, flies, squirrels, rabbits and any other innocent creatures they can get their hands on. But, as far as I'm concerned men like Gabriel Miller or all cold-blooded killers, and the step up to murdering a human being with them is not so great. For them, I believe, it's just a higher sort of thrill.

As for 'sportsmen' like Walter Tranmer who enjoy blasting pheasants and partridges out of the air, how much greater for them would be the thrill of seeing an innocent woman die right before their eyes! Perhaps killing is also an act of revenge or hatred or frustration for all the perceived wrongs females have inflicted on them since birth – a neglectful mother, an unfaithful wife, a potential lover who spurned their lecherous advances...

Who knows what twisted thoughts pulse through the minds of men who wantonly take life after life and leave behind them a trail of misery and terror.

Driving back towards Snape, I think of Gerald Hadiscoe, the man who came forward and willingly confessed to the murders. I decide there and then to look through my mothers work papers and access her online police PDCS account to see what Hadiscoe's told the police so far. Come to think of it, it was neglectful of me not to have investigated him before.

I am fully expecting details of his confessions to give indications he really is some kind of nutter who is falsely claiming to be the East Coast Killer. But, as it turned out, I was in for more than a few surprises.

CHAPTER SEVEN:
GERALD HADISCOE

Thursday 7th August

It's a Thursday evening at 7 p.m. and my mother is out on a date, giving me the opportunity to snoop in her office a little earlier than usual. The door of the room is invitingly slightly ajar, and tonight after my spaghetti and passata I have only one aim to fulfil, namely to learn as much as I can about Gerald Hadiscoe, the man presumed by many – including the local police – to be the East Coast Killer.

I switch on her computer, and, when prompted I put in her password of IVAN, and then log into her Police Data and Communications System account by typing in my birth date of 30 03 07 which is her six figure code. But wait! I haven't yet checked out her briefcase, which is usually stuffed with all kinds of confidential stuff.

The first buff-coloured folder I find in the briefcase is handily marked *Confidential/Chief Constable's Communication.* It contains several sheets of A4 sized paper with hand-written notes on them, ready for her to type up, which I know from previous snoops are items from the Chief Constable himself that he requires to be organised into online memos, emails and letters. These things that come from the top to be distributed downwards through the chain of command are of little interest to me. It is the information the Criminal Investigation Department send *to* him that makes the most interesting reading, since these briefs invariably mean newly discovered facts and the results of recent interviews are being reported. The Chief Constable gets these briefings in summary form, making it quick and easy for him – and me – to get the gist of all the latest developments.

I soon find what I'm looking for, another buff folder, headed: *'Summary for CC/Latest developments/East Coast Murders'*. Inside are several sheets of neatly typed and printed paper which my mother must have been working on earlier in the day.

My heart drops like a stone as I read:

`'Suspect no. 1 Gerald J. Hadiscoe's shoeprints, size twelve were confirmed at Yoxford Yox Man scene of crime number five, although this treaded shoe is not of the type present at murder scenes of crime 2 and 3.'`

Confirmation that Hadiscoe was present at scene of crime number five could, of course, be taken as proof that Gabriel Miller is *not*, in fact, the East Coast Killer.

However, I am a little cheered to read:

`'DCI Smethurst points out that Hadiscoe, while definitely present at the Yoxford scene of crime, may have arrived after the crime took place'.`

The report reveals that on May 16th several members of the public were found milling around the body of victim Wendy Banister lying in fairly long grass when police arrived at 2.20 p.m., but unfortunately the uniformed officers first on the scene ushered these people away, believing for the first few minutes that the woman had collapsed with possible heart failure. It was only when they turned her over, with the intention of administering CPR, that they spotted the pool of blood and deep gash in the back of her head.

The page continues:

```
'There    is,    however,    some    doubt    that
Hadiscoe was one of the milling crowd because
there is no sign of him on the uniformed PC's
BWV's.'
```

BWV stands for Body Worn Videos, the cameras clipped to the lapels of their uniforms. So, the fact that these devices failed to spot Hadiscoe in the 'milling crowd' has led the police to believe Hadiscoe's footwear imprints may well have been laid down earlier, as he murdered Wendy Banister.

But DCI Smethurst isn't convinced Hadiscoe is the killer, and nor am I. What if Hadiscoe simply found himself close to the scene of crime as he visited the popular tourist attraction at Yoxford where the giant Yox Man statue stands gazing over the man-made lake?

Perhaps, after the murder was committed and the East Coast Killer slipped away, Hadiscoe was among the tourists standing around the statue. Then, having seen the body, he approached the scene of crime, along with other onlookers, who were later ushered away by the uniformed police. It is possible, in fact very likely, that Hadiscoe remained out of sight of police BWV's, as the officers were not interested in gathering up and questioning members of the public at this time. Presumably these uniformed police had arrived on the scene very swiftly because the busy A12 road runs within a hundred yards of the lake and statue. This road has regular patrols of police, and in any case the market towns of Halesworth and Saxmundham are fairly close by, at 6 miles and 5 miles distance away respectively.

Hadiscoe, having seen the body, may then, or at a later time, have hatched the crazy idea of taking on the identity of the serial killer. On June 10th he acted on this bizarre notion and came forward, 'confessing' to all five murders.

Why anyone would do such a thing, is something only the psychologists and psychiatrists might try to explain; but such things have happened before, and will no doubt happen again.

The next sheet of paper in the file is equally relevant to the guilt or innocence of Gerald J. Hadiscoe. It is headed: *'Summary of Interviews to date with Suspect No.1 Gerald J. Hadiscoe'.*

It reveals how Hadiscoe knew details of every single murder scene, said that he killed each of the victims with a small axe, that a different axe was used for each victim, the axes being disposed of by throwing them into the *'deepest part of the River Alde near Aldeburgh'*. He stated that he killed the women because he was urged to do so by *'a heavenly voice in his head'*, and that he turned himself in because he knew he would have to *'kill again and again'*.

The report on the Hadiscoe interrogations ends by saying that in the opinion of Detective Chief Inspector Robert Kepler, the confessions were *'very plausible'*, but were as yet uncorroborated by digital forensic evidence linking his movements at, or nearby, the murder scenes of crime.

This lack of digital evidence was, according to the report, because Hadiscoe had the habit of travelling away from home with his mobile phone switched off. His car, an older type of Volvo hatchback had no tracking device. His online digital footprint was still under assessment, but it was already proven he had accessed numerous websites after googling phrases including 'serial killer', 'how to commit a murder' and 'how to kill quickly.' However, these gruesome searches only began in March, three months *after* the first murder had taken place.

One footnote says that recovery of the murder weapons from the tidal River Alde at the point Hadiscoe indicated was *'extremely difficult and may never be accomplished'.*

Another footnote states that Hadiscoe's mobile phone was still being examined, but early indications were that there were no photo or video images of any scene of crime. He had, however, *'collected over five hundred newspaper photographs and articles pertaining to the East Coast Murders.'*

Well, thanks to the very brief but very inclusive summary intended for the top man of Suffolk Constabulary, I am now as well informed as he is concerning the likely guilt of Gerald Hadiscoe. But, despite the several types of evidence put together for their boss, I still don't think the plain clothes men have a watertight case against their *'Suspect No. 1,'* as they like to call him. The shoe print at the Yox Man site, while it is the correct size, isn't the one with the defective heel. In any case, the police admit Hadiscoe may well have turned up *after* the murder. The digital stuff is inconclusive, proving nothing either way, and while switching off your mobile phone when leaving home is unusual, even suspicious, it could just be the nutty habit of a man trying not to run out of battery power. What I do find odd is that Hadiscoe's phone had no trophy images of the murder scenes, or of the deceased victims for that matter.

Could it be that Suffolk Constabulary's decision to charge Gerald Hadiscoe is an extreme case of wishful thinking? After all, the pressure on them was intense, when suddenly a very cranky man walked into their office and confessed to all of the murders. With no further murders taking place (touch wood) and their team still working on the assumption Hadiscoe is their man, I suppose their approach makes horse sense. The newspapers, TV and online news programmes were jubilant when Hadiscoe was charged. You can just imagine the critical backlash the police would receive if they announced they were not quite certain they'd got their man...

My train of thought is interrupted by a vehicle approaching outside. I have a quick glance out of the window, which gives a good view of our driveway, and am relieved to see that the noise was made by a car that passes by our house. Returning to Mum's desk, I make photocopies of the briefs for the Chief Constable on her printer for me to keep, and put all her stuff back exactly as I found it.

As I'm already logged into the constabulary's confidential system, I decide to have a quick look through Mum's work emails. The only one of interest is marked *'Memo for the CC'*, and has an attachment tagged *'Latest update from DMI's'*, which I soon discover stands for *'Digital Manager Investigators'*. Scanning through it, I discover it contains two significant pieces of information. The first is that Hadiscoe's car was filmed by a CCTV camera at a petrol station only five miles from the scene of the Iken murder, on March 13th. This occurred at 9.26 a.m. on the day the crime took place, thirty-four minutes before the predicted time of death. It left in the general direction of Iken, though the car *could* have been going on to any one of the nearby villages.

Secondly, Hadiscoe's car was filmed on January 18th going over the automatic level crossing at Darsham, thirty-three minutes after the murder at Walberswick. Darsham is only twenty minutes from Walberswick, furthermore, Hadiscoe was driving in the general direction he would be heading if he were fleeing the scene of crime and on his way back towards Framlingham.

This is tantalizing, but strictly *circumstantial* evidence! Hadiscoe could have been in these two locations purely by chance. But, presented to a Crown Court, these accounts of Hadiscoe's movements, when combined with his confessions, and the Yoxford footwear evidence, would most probably be persuasive enough to put all doubt out of the minds of a jury and secure for Gerald J. Hadiscoe his twisted heart's desire of a guilty verdict.

Another car approaches the house, and I am horrified to discover that it is my mother coming home early. I just have time to log out of the Suffolk Constabulary website, switch off her laptop and put her briefcase back on the floor in the place I found it before the back door opens. I slip out of her office and go upstairs into my room, dumping my freshly printed confidential pages in the top drawer of my desk.

Mum knocks on my door and comes in.

'Why is the light on in my office?' she asks.

'Oh, I ran out of A4 paper, so I just went in and nicked some from your printer,' I say nonchalantly.

'I'll order you more paper on Amazon,' she says.

'How was your date?'

'Don't ask,' she says with a sigh, and goes back downstairs.

Alone in my room I lie on my bed and turn over in my mind the things I learned this evening. The barrage of circumstantial evidence ranged in favour of a guilty verdict against Gerald J. Hadiscoe has depressed me a little. What if Suffolk Constabulary is right, and 'Suspect No.1' is indeed the East Coast Killer? Surely the best and most experienced Criminal Investigation Department officers can't all be wrong... can they?

But still my gut instincts and reasoning tell me that the focus on Hadiscoe is, indeed, nothing but wishful thinking, and the women of East Suffolk are in as much danger as ever, as a sinister figure plots how to carry out his next shocking crime. And when this finally happens, Suffolk Constabulary are going to look very silly indeed, as the British press and media fall on top of them like a ton of bricks...

CHAPTER EIGHT:
THE MAKING OF A THIEF

Tuesday 12th August

On the way to our first job of the day, Gabriel informs me we have to visit his 'storage barn' which turns out to be a big brick farm building next to a derelict farmhouse, about half a mile from his house in Fordley.

We pull up in the van on a concrete roadway that runs past this big barn that might once have been a stable or a feed store. The old farm house, overgrown with trees, bushes and weeds is further along the driveway.

'We actually own the old house and yard,' Gabriel tells me. 'This is the place I told you about, that belonged to Naomi's grandfather, and he left it to her in his will. As I said before, we plan to have it done up and maybe live in it one day, but we don't have quite enough money yet to pay the builders. The house is in a pretty poor state, but the barn is still in good condition. Naomi comes down here nearly every day to sort out the stuff we sell on eBay.'

Inside the barn, Gabriel flicks on the four big strip lights, and I'm immediately astonished by the sight before me.

Talk about an Aladdin's cave! There are boxes stacked everywhere, overflowing with books, vinyl LP's, clothes and fabrics, shelves of porcelain and china, dolls, teddy bears, glassware, ornaments, clocks, tools of all description, car and motorcycle spare parts, vintage radios and at least three old gramophones. Leaning against the walls are several old prints and pictures, some of which are oil paintings and watercolours. There is also a stack of old enamel advertising signs, a stash of vintage oil cans and dispensers, and a clothes rail hung with various items of clothing neatly enclosed in clear plastic bags.

But that is just what I can see from the door. The building is about fifteen by thirty feet, and some boxes are stacked above head height.

'Where on earth did you get all this stuff?' I ask.

'Oh, car boot sales and auctions mainly, but also farm and garage sales, that sort of thing. It's just a hobby, but it brings in almost as much as a full-time job.'

While Gabriel is uncovering two twenty-five litre jerry cans of woodworm fluid, I cast an inquisitive eye around the room. A thought comes to mind, a question I need answering. I am in two minds whether I should ask it, but then I throw caution to the wind, and say:

'I bet the police had a high old time searching this place back in March.'

'No, they didn't,' says Gabriel, turning to look at me. 'They looked through all my sheds at the cottage, even in my loft at home, but they didn't even ask if I had another place for storage so I didn't bloody-well tell them, the nosy buggers. Besides, there's nothing here of interest to them.'

He turns back to his task of pulling the jerry cans clear of all the boxes and junk.

Gabriel and I each carry a can of woodworm fluid the short distance to the van. Then Gabriel goes back to the thick oak doors of the barn, and I am careful to see which keys he uses to lock it up. He uses a brass chub key to close the deadlock, and a long silver one to close the huge steel padlock that secures a massive bolt into its mounting on the jamb for added security. The only window I can see has been bricked up. All in all, it's a pretty safe place in which to hide a bunch of merchandise for sale on eBay... but what other secrets lie hidden in the barn? A hatchet and a pair of size twelve boots, perhaps. I have already decided I need to 'borrow' those keys and have a good look around the barn, but getting hold of them won't be easy.

By nine a.m. we're way up in the loft of a 16th century farmhouse, spraying the beams for woodworm, or at least we're supposed to be. We're wearing dust masks, blue overalls, yellow hard hats and disposable latex gloves. Gabriel is sitting on a cross beam reading the Daily Mirror using one of our inspection lamps to illuminate his paper. Meanwhile I'm carrying out my orders to spray all the upper beams, trusses, roof supports and miscellaneous timbers with boron insecticide from my ten litre pressure sprayer. The area involved is huge, for we are above the upper story of five bedrooms, yet Gabriel makes no attempt to help me. I have to stoop and crawl into the corners and edges where the roof pitches down to the floor. Gabriel looks up gives me a nod and says:

'You're doing a good job there, Ivan,' before reaching inside his overall pockets for a packet of sandwiches. He removes his dust mask and tucks in.

I have to go down the ladder to get refills from the twenty-five litre drums in the van three times before Gabriel does a stroke of work. Then, finally, after an hour of sitting on his beam, Gabriel rises to his feet, stretches and yawns, then picks up his own pressure sprayer and slips the support strap over his shoulder. He walks over to the far side of the attic and begins lightly spraying the dusty floor, which is an easy job compared to what he's asked me to do. I'm getting drips in my face and all over my overalls, my arms are aching and I badly need a break. I have been spraying for an hour and a half.

'Great job, Ivan,' says Gabriel, still without his mask on, looking at his watch. 'We're halfway there. I'm billing the owners for six man-hours, and they're sitting below us waiting for us to finish, so even if we finish spraying early we'll have to stay put till twelve o'clock.'

I nod and continue my work. Gabriel stops as he backs into a big tin trunk with a domed top. There are other boxes and tea chests too, which have to be shifted about so that Gabriel can spray under them. But this big trunk arouses my boss's interest, so he stops and lifts the lid to have a peek inside. I can see from my position that it's full of old books. Gabriel puts down his sprayer and begins sorting through the trunk, putting on one side on a patch of dry floor a pile of books that take his interest. He then takes out his i-Phone, and seems to be scrolling through some web pages.

'What are you looking for?' I call across the attic, curious as to what he's doing.

'Oh,' he says, 'I'm just checking for first editions. I'll ask the owners if they want to sell these ones. Naomi sells a few books on eBay – she tells me to watch out for the first edition ones on my travels, you see.'

Half an hour later, he's selected about ten books. He

places the other unwanted ones back in the trunk and put the selected ones on the top of it. He calls out to me:

'Don't get any drips on these ones, Ivan, there's one or two might be worth a few bob.'

Then he carries on spraying the floor. Thirty minutes and one refill later, he's finished covering the floorboards with boron solution. He returns to the trunk, sits on a crossbeam and begins reading one of the books. As I get closer, spraying the upper timbers, I see the title of the leatherbound book: 'Vanity Fair'.

'Is that a first edition,' I ask.

'Apparently so,' said Gabriel, 'I looked it up on my phone. There's a Charles Dickens one, too, dated 1857. It's called *Little Dorrit* – I've never heard of that one, so I didn't bother to look it up. I doubt it's worth much.'

By the time our three hours are up, I've finished spraying all the upper timbers. I had only five minutes idling time left at the end. I'm exhausted but Gabriel has a last little job for me.

'Take these,' he says, and, unzipping my overalls and unfastening the top buttons of my shirt, he stuffs in six books and, arranges them so they're sitting pretty flat next to my skin.

'Gabriel!' I say reproachfully, 'You said you'd ask if the householders wanted to sell them.'

He just laughs, and puts the other six inside his own shirt.

'We'll take these down and put them under the boxes in the back of the van for now,' he says. 'These dusty old books have probably been up here for a hundred years, so I don't think anyone's going to miss them.'

Fifteen minutes later, down at ground level, Gabriel has presented his invoice to the owners and been paid in cash. Meanwhile, with overalls, hard hat and mask removed I'm waiting patiently with Nancy in the front of the van.

Gabriel returns from out the house, and he has a satisfied little smile on his face.

'Not a bad morning's work,' he says, as he gets in the driver's seat.

'How much?' I ask.

'Oh, it was three hundred for the labour and three fifty for the woodworm fluid, plus VAT, which makes seven hundred and eighty.'

'Wow,' I say. A thought enters my head and I ask: 'Gabriel, are you actually VAT registered?'

'Not currently,' he says with a wink. 'You see, the pest control is one business, and the woodworm treatment is another. Neither one of them quite reaches the VAT threshold. But customers don't know that. If they got in Dial-a Kill or one of the big national companies they'd be charged even more, and pay VAT on top of it too. So, all in all, they're much better off getting in a local firm to do the work.'

'I see,' I say.

'Here,' he says, as we drove off into open countryside, 'I've got a present for you.'

He reaches overhead to the parcel shelf and takes down a book. *'Little Dorrit'* has a leather-bound spine and corners, and the front and back cover have a funny marbling effect. When I look inside, I see printed on the title page: 'London,

Bradbury and Evans, 11 Bouverie Street. 1857.

Well, I could hardly give it back to the owners, and I'm ashamed to say, it was the first item I ever placed on eBay. *Little Dorrit* took seven days to sell, and an American buyer in New York made the final bid of one thousand, six hundred and eighty pounds, no VAT payable. That's enough to pay my university hall of residence fees for four months. Or get me locked away in prison for selling stolen property, depending on how you look at it. Needless to say, I didn't dare tell my mother. Nor did I tell Gabriel how much it made. Had he known its true value, of course, my boss would never in a thousand years have gifted it to me.

Thus, in the pursuit of a serial killer, I have myself become something of a criminal. I have hacked into the local constabulary's confidential website, failed to report crimes I witnessed against people and wildlife, and ripped off an elderly couple for a large sum of money. But I have a funny feeling, these are just minor considerations compared to the whole heap of trouble and danger I am about to enter into, before I finally manage to bring my own 'Suspect No. 1' before a court of law.

Chapter Nine:
Fleur

Saturday 16th August

Driving from Saxmundham towards my home village of Middleton in my beautiful old Ford Fiesta, I'm surprised to see, just on the outskirts of the town, none other than Fleur Miller standing at a bus stop. She's dressed in jeans, red Doctor Marten boots and a white t-shirt, with a brown leather bag slung over her shoulder. Parked just past the bus stop is an old green Land Rover with the engine running. Puffs of black smoke are being coughed out of the exhaust pipe. I recognise it immediately as the vehicle I've seen at Red House Farm, owned by Walter Tranmer.

An instinct deep within me tells me that something is not quite right, so I pull up about fifteen yards past the Land Rover. In my rear view mirror I can see that Walter Tranmer is standing next to Fleur, talking to her. I can plainly see, too, by the uncomfortable expression on her face that she doesn't want to talk to him.

I glance at the clock on the dashboard of my car. The time is 5:25 p.m. and I happen to know that the last bus to Southwold that travels through Fordley and Middleton leaves each Saturday at 5:20. How did I know this? Because, before I had a car, I'd used the same bus service many times myself. In an instant I realise that Fleur has most probably missed the bus and either she has flagged down Walter to give her a lift, or, more likely, he saw her beside the road and offered to take her the five miles to Fordley. Either way, the situation gives me a very uneasy feeling. Of course, I know that Tranmer and Fleur are, in fact, related, but I can't ignore a strange sense of foreboding upon seeing this vision of 'beauty and the beast.' So, rightly or wrongly, I decide to step in.

I get out of the car and walk up to the bus stop.

'Oh hello Fleur,' I say, casually, 'Have you missed the bus?'

She turns around and looked me up and down. Tranmer also turns toward me, regarding me with mild surprise.

'Oh, it's *you,*' she says. 'What are you doing here?'

'I've just been to Saxmundham, and I'm on my way back to Middleton. I was wondering if you wanted a lift.'

'Well... yes,' she says, 'but Uncle Walter here has already offered to take me home.'

'But he lives at Kelsale Green,' I say. 'It's a bit out of his way.'

'Oh, I don't mind,' says Tranmer, 'It wouldn't take me long.'

'You can go with him if you like,' I tell Fleur, 'but I've got to go right through Fordley on my way to Middleton.'

Fleur looks at Walter Tranmer, then looks at me.

'Thank you for the offer,' she says to the farmer, 'but I may as well go with Ivan.'

'Suit yourself, young lady,' says Tranmer.

Fleur walks off towards my car.

'Ah, well,' says Walter Tranmer, to me, 'That's saved me a bit of a detour. Anyway, I'm sure she'd rather be taken home by a handsome young fellow like you.'

He walks back toward his Land Rover. I notice he's wearing green wellington boots, though the weather is hot. He's a big man, maybe six feet tall, and his boots, I note, look huge, maybe even size twelve.

When I get in my car, Fleur has already put on her seat belt.

'Do you think you can get me to Fordley without hitting a tree or ending up in a field this time?'

'I should think so,' I say.

There's a long silence. We turn off the main road, into the lane for Fordley, which is overhung with oak and ash trees. A signpost informs us: 'Fordley 5'. I'm driving very slowly and carefully.

'Do you mind if I vape?' she asks.

'Not at all,' I say.

'What about you,' she says. 'Do you vape? Or smoke maybe?"

'Used to vape a bit,' I tell her. 'It got me through exams. So what brought you into town?'

'I just met Beatrice to go for a coffee,' she says. 'Then we had a walk around the shops, which is a complete waste of time in Saxmundham because there's absolutely nothing worth buying.'

'My sentiments exactly,' I say, 'but I had to go for a haircut.'

'I thought you looked a bit different,' she says. 'You looked better with it long.'

'Thanks.'

There followed a fairly long silence, until I say:

'How come Old Man Tranmer stopped to pick you up from the bus stop? Did you see him pass and flag him down?'

'He saw me running to the bus stop with the bus disappearing up the road and stopped to offer me a lift. He was laughing his head off because I'd been running and still missed the bus and I was all hot and out of breath. It's the last one of the day going through my village.'

'I know,' I say, 'That's why I stopped.'

'That was very sweet of you.'

'I wasn't being *sweet*,' I say. 'It was just that...'

I hesitate, embarrassed to go on.

'Well?'

'To tell you the truth, I thought something wasn't quite right.'

She looks at me curiously.

'About what, exactly?'

'Well, if I were you, I wouldn't want to get in a car with *him*.'

'And why not?'

'Don't you know the story about his wife disappearing? He strikes me as rather a strange old man. Sinister, even.'

She laughs, looking at me with slightly mocking eyes.

'You think I may have been in danger, then?'

'Probably not, but I had a funny feeling.'

'You think he meant to kill me, and feed me to his

pigs?'

'You never know,' I say; 'He *is* a bit weird.'

'Well, I was about to take my chances until I saw you. He is my mother's uncle, after all.'

'Didn't you think of phoning up your folks to get a lift back? It wouldn't have taken them very long to come and pick you up.'

'I tried, but they're probably both at the barn. There's no phone signal there.'

'Lucky I was passing then.'

'Yeah, lucky.'

Our route takes us through an area of woodland, the canopy of leafy branches throwing patterns of sunlight and shade on the road before us. Fleur is drawing on her vape with the window open, but I can still smell the heady aroma of menthol flavoured vapour.

'Want a puff?' she offers, holding out the vape in front of me.

'The last time I vaped in a car I ended up driving into a field,' I say. 'I dropped it onto the floor, looked down to pick it up, and ended up in the sugar beet.'

'That was pretty dumb of you,' she says withdrawing the vape and putting it in her mouth again. She sits back in the seat, placing her feet up on the shelf just below the glove compartment, making herself at home.

'You looking forward to Australia?' I ask, trying to fill the silence.

She doesn't answer for a while.

'Kind of,' she says. 'But it's going to be hard going there with no money.'

'Won't your folks give you some to tide you over, for when you first arrive?'

She scoffs, making the vape come out of her nose.

'You heard what they said the other night. They want me to start at Durham immediately. They're trying to make the Australia thing so hard that I give it up.'

'Even your mum?'

'Especially my mum. She can be a right cow when she puts her foot down. She bloody hates Beatrice, too. Says she's *'leading me astray',* as she puts it.'

She takes another deep lungful of menthol vapour and blows it out straight in front of her.

'I hope you don't mind me asking, but why didn't you take a summer job?'

'Because there was absolutely nothing available round here except the fish restaurant at Dunwich, which I tried for a week before they sacked me for swearing at a customer. I had to cycle all the way there and back, seven miles each way, and they bloody-well sacked me...'

She puts the vape back in her bag, pouting as she ruminates on her misfortunes. Then she says:

'And then you took my other job – working with dad.'

'But you said you'd rather be dead than work for him.'

She looks at me accusingly.

'I was still thinking about it when he took you on. I didn't really want to spend the summer getting stung and murdering animals, but I suppose it would have got me to Australia.'

'Could you have stuck it out? It's a pretty horrible job sometimes. The other day we had to catch squirrels in

Walberswick and–'

'Don't tell me!' she says, holding up her palms in front of her protectively. 'I hate to think of what he does every day in his work. He can be pretty hard-hearted when it comes to animals.'

'That's for sure,' I say. 'Seems to me, you made the right decision not to work with your father. Now you can die with a clear conscience.'

'Not that clear,' she says, reaching for her vape again. 'When I was younger I used to help dad mole catching. I know all the tricks of the trade, setting the traps and all that. He used to pay me for raking over the molehills too, acres and acres of them sometimes. One year we did the whole of Henham Park before the festival in July, dozens and dozens of poor little moles we caught, just so's the bloody hippies at the festival didn't trip up on the hills, or pitch their tents on a bit of a bump.'

'Yeah,' I say, 'I hate mole-catching too. I tried to set my traps all wrong so's I wouldn't catch any, but your dad was watching me, and made sure they were all positioned in the best possible way to cause the most mole-havoc.'

'That's my dad for you,' she says gloomily. She takes another draw on her vape, and exhales slowly.

Then she brightens, and looks straight at me.

'Tell you what,' she says, 'You can come to Beatrice's leaving party next Saturday. 'It's at Rowan Tree Farm in Minsmere, next to the Bird Reserve.'

'What, in the farmhouse?' I ask incredulously.

'Of course not,' she says; 'It's in the big barn on the

driveway before you reach the farm. Bring a bottle – proper booze, of course. Bring some friends too, good looking ones if possible.'

'All right, I'll see who what I can do. What time does this shindig start?'

'Oh, anytime after eight. Most of my friends won't turn up till later, as they'll probably be in the pub till then. Some of us sleep in the barn all night. It's perfectly comfortable on the hay bales, especially after a few drinks, if you know what I mean.'

'It sounds all right,' I say.

'The police turned up at the last one,' she laughs, 'after someone complained of the noise, probably the warden of the RSPB centre up the road. They told us to turn down the music in case it disturbed the wildlife.'

'And did you?'

'Yes, of course, then we turned it up again after the police had left. We had a live band at ten, you see, you can hardly tell them to play quietly.'

'Who were the band?'

'Oh, it's just four boys from our school, but they're pretty good – they've sold quite a few copies of the album they've just recorded. They're called 'The Catastrophe', and they've got some videos on U-Tube, I guess it's a sort of *Indy* vibe. They'll be playing again on Saturday.'

'That's my Saturday night sorted out. I'll bring my friends Baz and Freddy along, you'll like them. They were talking about going back-packing in Indonesia if they could save up enough money.'

'And you don't want to go with them?'

'I've got my drama course, which starts on September 10th. When that's finished I'm going to try to get into RADA. I'm going to be an actor, you see.'

She turns to look at me.

'An actor?' she laughs, 'Are you any good?'

'I was Hamlet in our end of year play. It gave me a taste for having a go.'

'Well, good luck with that,' she says. 'It's a bit better than pest control.'

'Anything's better than pest control.'

'Yeah,' she says, putting away her vape, 'That's for sure.'

We're nearing her house in Fordley, and travel past the derelict Hawthorn Farm. The red Renault car of her mother is parked on the driveway.'

'Just as I thought,' she says, 'They're in the old barn, sorting out junk for eBay. Making money, it's all they think about – but they never give any to me. Twenty stinking pounds a month, that's all they give me.'

'That's not much,' I say. 'My mum gives me fifty, for doing all the housework.'

'Lucky old you,' she says, as we pull up outside her house. She gets out and holds the door open for a few seconds, looking at me.

'Thanks,' she says, before closing the door.

'See you at the party,' I call out, rather loudly and foolishly. But, as she walks away, she gives me no indication whatever that she's actually heard me.

I watch her shapely rear end waggle as she walks

away, goes into the house, and closes the door behind her.

I give out a long sigh, and remind myself that this is the offspring of a terrible serial killer, before driving very carefully away.

.

CHAPTER TEN:
GABRIEL MILLER, DEER KILLER

Tuesday 19th August

'I heard,' says Gabriel, 'that you gave our Fleur a lift back from Saxmundham on Saturday afternoon. That was very thoughtful of you.'

'Not at all,' I reply. 'She was about to get a lift with Walter Tranmer, but I told her I was going right through Fordley, so she came with me.'

He glances across at me.

'Did you think there was something wrong about Old Man Tranmer giving her a lift, then?'

I think for a few seconds before answering:

'No, not really, it was just that I had to go straight past your house.'

'I see,' says Gabriel. 'I'm surprised you stopped to pick her up, after the way she spoke to you when you came round for supper the other day.'

'Oh, she was just speaking her mind,' I say, 'I didn't think anything of it.'

Gabriel drives on, but he glances at me a couple of times as if he wants to say something, but then thinks better of it. Finally he says:

'Tell me something, Ivan, you must have talked to her on the way back... do you find anything *odd* about her?'

I'm not quite sure what to say in reply to this extraordinary question about his own daughter! What does he have in mind? Surely, if she's 'odd' he would know more about that than me. What on earth is he trying to find out?

'What do you mean by *odd?*' I ask.

''I probably shouldn't ask you,' he says, 'but does she come across as a *normal* sort of girl?'

'Well... yes,' I say. 'Why do you ask?'

'Naomi and I are a bit desperate to find out,' he says, 'if she's on some sort of drugs, or about to join a cult or something. Naomi thinks that maybe she's picked up some dangerous ideas online – you can never tell what people are looking at on social media and all that.'

'I didn't get the impression she was on drugs, as you put it, but I didn't talk to her long enough to learn anything much about her, except that she has a friend called Beatrice and wants to go travelling with her this autumn.'

'Bloody Beatrice is a pain in the butt,' he says with a sneer. 'It was her who talked Fleur out of going to do Law in college. Bloody queen bee Beatrice has a lot of spoiled snobby friends whose parents give them money to do whatever they like. But Naomi and me reckon it's not safe for any of them, going off with a rucksack to all ends of the earth where they could get robbed or raped or murdered.'

'Lots of people do go travelling, though,' I say; 'Girls too, and they come home safe and sound...'

'But the risk is always there,' says Gabriel, 'It's just so bloody *dangerous.*'

'Girls tend to go with a group of friends, and they usually keep each other safe.'

'That's easy for you to say,' says Gabriel, 'You don't have a daughter.'

'Well, that's true,' I shrug.

He's making me feel really uncomfortable, and I really wish he'd just shut up. But, rather than let the matter drop, he continues his ranting.

'And do you know what she wants to do this Saturday? She wants to go to Beatrice's bloody barn party and get drunk and drugged up like she did last time.'

'Drugged up?' I query, 'Are you sure?'

Gabriel turns to look at me, and his face is slightly contorted, as though he's in pain.

'Her eyes were all sort of funny,' he says, 'when we picked her up after the last party, and she was so drunk she could hardly stand up. And that was at ten in the morning the day after. She persuaded us to let her stay the night, by lying and saying she'd be sleeping in Beatrice's house, when in fact the little monkeys slept where they dropped down in the barn. We found her in such a state that Sunday morning, we almost took her to A and E in Ipswich.'

Gabriel's eyes are now wide and angry, the first time I've seen him like this. I think of saying something to try and calm him down, but before I can speak he continues his rant:

'I've a good mind to stop her going to this one next Saturday. I know she's going to do the same thing as last time. Naomi says we shouldn't give her a lift so she misses it. That'd stop her getting out of her head and going off the rails again! And once bloody Beatrice buggers off to Australia, then maybe we can talk some sense into her.'

'Well,' I say, 'She's your daughter, but don't you think that if you try to stop her going to the party she'll be really angry with you, and that will only make her more determined to do what she wants? After all, she is eighteen, and–'

'She's not eighteen!' shouts Gabriel, his eyes now full of rage, 'She's still seventeen till the end of the month, and while she's living under my roof she'll bloody-well have to live by my rules! I'll tell you something else, too, if we don't take her to bloody Beatrice's party, and she phones you up and asks for a lift, don't you go picking her up, do you hear? I absolutely *forbid* it!'

'All right,' I say, 'But I'm sure she wouldn't ask me. Anyway, she doesn't even have my number.'

'Good, let's just keep it that way, shall we?'

'Sure,' I say, squirming in my seat. Nancy has woken up to observe the disturbing atmosphere that's brewed up on our way to the very first job of the day. She looks at Gabriel, then at me, then lays her head down on her seat, but doesn't go back to sleep again.

'What's our first job?' I ask.

'What?' says Gabriel, still distracted.

'Our first job of the day – what are we supposed to be doing?'

Gabriel seems to be thinking for a few moments, then he looks at his watch and says:

'At nine o'clock we're supposed to be at Seamark

Cottage, Dunwich.'

'Wasps again?' I ask with slight trepidation.

'Not this time – apparently, the kitchen's infested with mice and the holidaymakers staying there had to be moved to another house by the Suffolk Coastal Cottages agency. It'll be a doddle, and the agency don't care how much I charge, as it just gets passed on to the owners, and they're all raking it in.'

'Good,' I say, noting with relief that Gabriel's voice and eyes have almost returned to normal.

We drive along the straight stretch of road that crosses Westleton heath, the purple heather and yellow gorse clumps very picturesque in the bright early morning light. A big red deer stag, bold in the broad daylight, runs right across the road in front of us on its way back to the haven of Minsmere Bird Reserve a mile over to our right side.

'Should've brought my big rifle,' grumbles Gabriel when he saw it. 'My freezer's almost out of venison.'

I imagine the horror of slaying the great animal, and the near-impossible task of getting the bloody corpse into the back of the van.

'But what if somebody passing saw you and reported you?'

Gabriel laughs.

'I'd just say it'd been knocked over on the road. And it's not illegal for me to put one down that's injured by traffic, either. I'm on the police's list of authorised deer cullers who they call out at any time of the day or night to deal with crippled deer. That big one there, that's an opportunity lost, about five hundred pounds worth of meat that got away. I could have shot it, bled and gralloched it, and laid the meat on cardboard in the back.'

He seems genuinely upset to have lost the opportunity of getting that stag. Then he perks up, and taps me on the shoulder.

'Tell you what,' he says, 'We'll come back and get one tonight. There always a stag or two on the heath here, it'll be a bit of overtime for you.'

I am ashamed to hear myself say:

'How much?'

Gabriel thinks for a second.

'Forty quid if we get one,' he says. 'Ten if we don't.'

As that's half a day's wages, I stupidly agree.

'Oh, and you get a joint of venison, too.'

'I'm vegetarian, remember.'

'What about your mother, then?' he laughs, 'Does she eat meat?'

'Well... yes.'

'All right then,' he says, 'I'll pick you up at ten o'clock sharp.'

'Why so late?'

'Deer don't usually come out till dusk,' he smiles. 'Besides, there won't be too many people about. With a bit of luck we'll be finished by midnight.'

'My introduction to deer poaching,' I say, 'like Robin Hood in Sherwood forest.'

He punches me lightly on the shoulder.

'That's the spirit,' he says, 'Only don't ever call it

poaching – that's a horrible word, Ivan. It's *culling* from now on.'

'Got it,' I say, both horrified and excited at what I was getting myself into.

The cottage at Dunwich turns out to be a huge flint-walled house close to the seafront. We let ourselves in after getting the key from the key safe and walk through the hall into the kitchen. There are mouse droppings all over the floor, on the larder shelves and in the drawers holding the cutlery, pots and pans. Gabriel sends me out to the van for a dozen plastic mouse bait boxes loaded with difenacoum bait, and a tub of ready-mixed filler paste. First we fill all the spaces around the water and waste pipes at the points they emerge from the walls, then check the gaps under each external door to make sure mice can't enter from outside. There are two chinks in the external wall of the kitchen too, which get filled with paste. Finally, Gabriel tells me to fetch the telescopic ladder so that we can check the loft for rodents.

'Lofts are often infested,' Gabriel explains for the umpteenth time, 'and mice then make their way down through the cavity walls and sneak out where the utility and radiator pipes come out of the walls. You have to deal with the sources of the mice infestation if you want to stop it for good. Check doors, windows and air vents for gaps large enough to let a mouse through, then make sure all climbing plants on outside walls don't reach up to the gutters. If so, they must be cut away at least a foot below the roof. Otherwise mice – or rats – climb up and squeeze under the roof tiles. Can you remember all that?'

'I think so,' I say.

'And remember, if ever you go into this business on your own, tell the holiday agency, or the owners or whoever, it takes a minimum of three visits to sort out a mouse problem. That way you can bill them for one ninety-five a house, instead of seventy-five for a single visit.'

'I know,' I said.

'And lastly–'

'Don't ever leave bait where pets, children or crazy people will find it and eat it,' I say.

Gabriel smiles.

'So you have been listening,' he says. 'Half the time you look so bored, I wonder if you're taking it all in...'

After a hard day destroying seven wasp nests, spraying a garage roof for woodworm and setting about fifty mole traps, Gabriel drops me off at my house at six o'clock.

'Be ready at a quarter to ten,' he says, through the open window, 'Wear some old clothes in case you get blood on them.'

'Charming,' I say, as I walked away.

'What's that?' asks Gabriel.

'I said I'll be ready,' I call out.

'Good,' he smiles, 'It'll be an experience for you.'

'I bet it will,' I say.

At exactly a quarter to ten I see the lights of Gabriel's van outside shining through our curtains.

'Goodnight, Mum,' I call out to her room, 'I'll be back soon...'

There's no reply, as she's already in bed, having an early night's rest and most probably knocked out by the pills she takes, which have the double action of keeping her moods stable and staving off insomnia.

In the cab of the van I share my space with a leather gun case. On the seat next to Nancy, who for once is wide awake, is a long metal tube, about a foot long.

'What's this,' I say stupidly,' holding up the tube.

'That, my friend, is a *sound moderator.*'

'A silencer?'

'No, a *sound moderator.* The Winchester .243 still makes a sharp crack, even with the moderator screwed on. There's no such thing as a silencer.'

'Where are we going?' I ask innocently.

'There's a long sandy track that runs across the heath at Westleton, leading to Orchard Farm. I have permission to shoot rabbits on the meadows at the end of the driveway.'

'Only rabbits?'

'Rabbits, deer, it's all the same thing. So, if we don't get a stag on the heath as we drive across it, we're bound to see deer on those meadows. They're there every night.'

'What if we get caught?'

'*Caught? Caught?* Never say that again! We're out to

shoot rabbits at Orchard Farm, so if we see an injured deer beside the road, that's just our good fortune. You got that?'

'Absolutely.'

'Now, unzip that gun, and screw on the sound moderator – we're getting close to the heath. Let's hope the deer are playing ball tonight and we don't have a wasted journey.'

Ten minutes later we're parked up in a gateway next to Westleton heath. The big rifle, now unsheathed, moderated and loaded, is lying across our laps, the butt resting on Gabriel's thighs, the dangerous end on my knee pointing at the door. Gabriel takes a hunter's spotlight with a long lead off the parcel shelf above our heads and plugs it into the power socket of the dashboard. It has red glass, so that the beam will be invisible to animals with poor colour vision, such as deer.

'This is a ten thousand lumen spotlight that lights up a deer at half a mile,' he says. 'I'll show you how to use it. The on-off switch is on the back, you use your thumb to switch it on. Now, we'll both open our windows ready.'

We open our windows, and Gabriel points the lamp out towards the heather and clicks the switch. He scans the heath by sweeping the beam to left and right, gradually increasing the distance, till two bright eyes appear in the distance, shining like two tiny mirrors.'

'What's that?' I ask.

'Just a little muntjac,' says Gabriel. 'We'll drive on a bit further, then take the road to Orchard Farm.'

He switches off the lamp and hands it to me. We drive off up the road towards Dunwich, close to where we'd seen the stag in the morning. Just then, a big deer crosses the road in front of us, its huge antlers and dark brown flanks showing up plain as day in the headlamps. Even before Gabriel can stop, another deer crosses the road behind it, followed by about thirty more.

Bloody hell!' whispers Gabriel, slamming on the brakes and switching off his headlights. 'Switch on the lamp, Ivan, try to keep the lamp on one with antlers. Shine it in his eyes.'

Gabriel switches off the engine, clicks open his door, and gets out. I feet the rifle slide across my lap towards him. I switch on the lamp and scan the heath on my side of the road. At first I can't see any deer at all, then suddenly the beam falls on a group of them, only thirty yards from the van. I dazzle a big one, till its glassy eyes shine back at us, but I hear Gabriel whisper:

'Not that one, Ivan, it's a hind! Find one with antlers.'

I move the lamp around, and rest it on a stag, this one definitely with antlers, though they're smaller than the ones on the stag we'd seen this morning.

'Perfect!' I hear Gabriel say, as the next second the rifle goes off with a muffled *crack!*

The deer is knocked off its feet and lays there kicking, and I keep the light on it, mesmerized by the horror of it all.

'Another one!' hisses Gabriel, 'Shine the light on another one!'

I hear the rifle bolt click as Gabriel chambers another

bullet. Waving the lamp to and fro, I search for another deer.

'To the right!' says Gabriel, 'There's a whole bunch of them to the right!'

I swing the lamp to the right, and there they are, two stags, no more than twenty yards from the road. I focus the red lamp on the biggest one, but it takes a few steps forward, looking as if it might cross the road. Gabriel swears.

'Put the lamp on its eyes!' he whispers.

I adjust my aim a little, and the stag's eyes show up huge and glassy. At the same instant the rifle cracks. The deer seems to disappear for a second. Then we see four hoofs sticking above the heather, making a running motion, as if the poor beast is trying to escape while lying on its back.

Gabriel unloads the rifle, unscrews the sound moderator and hands them to me.

'Put the rifle in the case without scratching it or knocking the sight,' he says. Then he climbs back in the driving seat, switches on the engine and headlights and pulls the Scudo onto the grass verge on the side of the road.

'Now, get a spade from the back and come with me,' he said, handing me a torch, 'The easy part's over, the hard work's about to begin.'

All I could think of was that forty quid was too small a wage to compensate for the horrors of deer poaching. And what happened next only reinforced that feeling.

By torchlight, Gabriel hacks off the head of the first

deer with his hatchet, then slits open its belly and pulls out its stomach and entrails.

'Dig, Ivan, dig!' says Gabriel, 'We need a hole big enough to take all these guts.'

I chop and hammer at the soil, and though it's dry and hard, within twenty minutes I have a hole about two feet deep.

'That'll do,' says Gabriel. He pushes all the offal into the hole and I cover it up. There's a conspicuous mound, but at least the disgusting stuff is out of sight.

'Now, grab a leg,' he says, 'and we'll drag the carcass into the van.'

It's very, very heavy, and as much as we can do to drag it towards the van. Just as we get near the edge of the road, some headlights appear over a low hill from the direction of Dunwich.

'Bugger,' says Gabriel, 'Keep your head down till it's passed.'

The car drives past us without slowing down, and we get the stag to the rear doors. Gabriel opens them wide, to reveal, most happily, he's earlier shifted all the boxes and equipment and neatly stacked it against the bulkhead at the far end to make a nice, deer-sized space. There's even a sheet of clear polythene duct-taped over the floor to prevent the plywood lining getting bloodstained.

Then, by a herculean effort we get the very smelly, headless torso inside.

'Now go back and get the head,' says Gabriel, 'Be quick, we're a bit exposed here on the road.'

Obedient to the last, I retrieve the bloody deer's head, antlers and all, and put them next to the deer's neck, for all the good it will do it now.

There doesn't seem to be enough room for the second one, but after a long bout of hacking, disembowelling, digging another pit, dragging torsos and retrieving another bloody head, we have the second one safely on board, slung on top of the first victim.

As we stand like two blood-stained murderers by the back doors of the van, Gabriel gives me a heavier than usual punch on the shoulder.

'Bloody good work, Ivan,' he says. 'I never expected to get two like that. Now let's nip off back to the barn and get them unloaded.'

It takes a while to wash the gore off our hands, wrists and, in Gabriel's case, arms, as well. However, we still have incriminating smears and spots of blood on our clothes and boots. On the way back to Fordley we pass a police car, an unusual sight since the day Gerald Hadiscoe was charged.

'I wonder what he wants,' muses Gabriel.

'Probably after deer poachers,' I say, rather unwisely.

'I told you before,' snaps Gabriel, 'Don't talk about poachers. We're just legitimate cullers, who found two poor suffering deer, and had to put them out of their misery.'

'Two deer, on the same night, on the same stretch of road?'

'Maybe somebody struck into a herd,' he says. 'It happens.'

'And you just *happened* to have that big rifle with you?'

'That's right,' says Gabriel, 'We've got the air rifle for rabbits and this one for foxes. I have written permission to control rabbits and vermin at Orchard Farm, and about thirty other places in Suffolk. Nobody questions a legitimate pest controller. We're always well known and trusted by the local police – otherwise we don't get permits for shotguns and rifles, and other stuff like gas.'

'I see,' I say.

'But remember,' says Gabriel, 'You signed an agreement to keep all my business secret. I've explained everything to you as we go along, and why we do the things we do. Every trade has its code of conduct, and it's very important that what you learn from me, under no circumstances, gets passed on to anyone else.'

'No problem,' I say, 'You can rely on me.'

Then Gabriel looks across at me, fixes me with a piercing look for so long that I fear he will crash the van.

'Are you sure about that, Ivan?' he says, holding one of his inscrutable little smiles.

'Oh yes, completely sure,' I say. 'If I'm lucky enough to be shown trade secrets, and be well-paid learning them, I can honestly say, Gabriel, that I'm very grateful, and what I learn from you will absolutely go no further.'

'Good,' he says, focusing on the road again, 'very good,' and he reaches across and touches me lightly on the shoulder. 'I knew as soon as I saw you that you were the dependable sort. And from what I've seen of you tonight, I'm really glad I took you on.'

Chapter Eleven:
The Reverend Alan Clitheroe

Thursday 21st August

After work today I arrived back at the house at five o'clock and discovered my mother had gone out, obviously having finished work in her home office early. At first I thought she must be on one of her dates, though she hadn't mentioned this to me earlier, but then I saw that the dog's basket was empty and the lead off the back of the door had gone, indicating that she had taken Tilly for a walk.

I was about to make some tea, when at five-thirty, my mother arrived back home with the dog. I knew immediately that something was not right. Mum's face was looking white as a sheet. She sat down at the kitchen table, letting the dog's lead drop to the floor, her hands shaking.

'What on earth's the matter?' I said, disturbed to see her looking so frightened and flustered.

'The most *horrible* thing just happened to me,' she said, her eyes staring straight ahead.

I moved closer to her take her hand in mine.

'You'd better tell me all about it,' I said.

Slowly her eyes began to lose their look of fear and she focused on me.

'I was just taking the dog for a walk in Walberswick,' she began, 'when something really creepy happened. Maybe I'm being overdramatic, but I had the most horrible feeling I've ever had in my life, that I was in real danger.'

'Hadn't we better call the police? I asked.

'No, don't do that,' she said. 'They'll probably just say I'm being hysterical, and maybe I am.'

By this time I was *really* worried.

'You'd better tell me exactly what happened,' I said, eager to know the details of what had made her so upset.

'Make me a cup of tea,' she said. 'I need a few seconds to get my head together and have a good think about what happened. Maybe I was just having a panic attack or something like that. After all, it was *Walberswick* churchyard, where that poor woman was killed back in January...'

'Walberswick churchyard? What on earth were you doing there? I thought you said you'd stick to the main street here for dog walking, or go to that safe dog Orchard place in Saxmundham.'

'Make the tea first,' she said, 'and then I'll tell you all about it.'

A few minutes later we were both sitting with steaming mugs of tea. My mother was beginning to look more herself again, much less frightened and her face was no longer quite so pale.

'It was the dog, you see, she was whining because she wanted to go on a walk, and she knows I always take her on a long one after I finish working at home. I wanted to take her somewhere different, I'm fed up of just walking up and down the village street, nodding to the same people and seeing the same old things. Obviously, after all that's happened lately I didn't want to go out to the woods, so I had the idea of going to Walberswick. There's a nice long street with lots of interesting houses and buildings to look at. I love seeing all the cottages and then going down to the harbour or onto the sand dunes. So I drove into the village and just past the village sign I found a safe place to leave the car on the side of the road. I got Tilly out of the back of the car, and made sure I had my purse in case I felt like going into the tea rooms. They're very dog friendly, so I could have treated myself to some Earl Grey and scones, which I've done once or twice before. Anyway, I set off towards the sea, noticing what a beautiful sunny afternoon it was. Now that they've got that Gerald Hadiscoe under lock and key it feels so much safer, walking out as a woman on my own – at least it *should* have felt safer, until I met that weird man in the churchyard.'

'*The churchyard?*' I said, 'What on earth were doing in there?'

'I'll get to that in a moment. First I want to tell you what I did on my walk. I took Tilly right along the street by the church, and then went past the village shop and the delicatessen, and walked right the way down to the village green. That's where the tea rooms are, and I thought of going in, but then as I got the salty smell of the sea in my nose, and I thought I'd walk down to the dunes. There were plenty of people around – there are always hundreds of holidaymakers this time of year – so even for a slightly nervous lady dog walker there was no reason to be afraid. And I wasn't, either, not until I got back up the High Street as far as the church gate. I'd decided not to go for that tea after all, and I was only thinking about going back to the car. But then, as I got to the churchyard wall I noticed several bunches of flowers over by the church door and I decided to go inside and read the messages which had been left on them as a way of showing my respect for that poor lady who'd been murdered back in January. There'd been people walking up and down the street, but the time I went into the churchyard I found myself completely alone. I was just having a look at the flowers and trying to read the messages of condolence, which was difficult as they'd been there a few days and the messages had been partially washed away by the rain, when the church door opened and I heard somebody walking out through the porch. As he came out into the yard I saw it was the vicar. He was wearing his dog collar and was in his full black regalia. At first he didn't speak, he just stood there looking at me. "Oh hello," I said, "I've just come to read the cards."

"Good afternoon," he replied, "Yes, I can see that. Some kind souls put them here the other day to mark the six months that have passed since we lost poor Mrs. Travis-Moore."

"Six months?" I replied, "It certainly doesn't seem that long, since we had the first... murder."

"No, indeed," he said. "Now look, it's very nice of you to take an interest in the cards, but you I'm afraid I have to inform you that no dogs are allowed in the churchyard."

"I'm so sorry," I said, "I'll go back out onto the road straight away."

"No, no, there's no need to dash off immediately," he said, "I'm sure your dog is perfectly well behaved, but we have had several instances of dogs fouling the churchyard."

"Well, that's an awful thing to happen," I said.

"Indeed," he said, "but there's one thing you can help me with."

"Well... yes," I said, "If I can. What exactly do you have in mind?"

"I've been such a clumsy fool," he said "and knocked over a vase of flowers. I've tried to put them back in some sort of order, but I'm afraid I've made a terrible mess of it. I'm partially colour-blind you see, that's my excuse, but I'm also completely useless when it comes to arranging flowers. I don't suppose you have any experience in such matters?"

"Well," I told him, "I have been to a couple of classes, I suppose, but I'm certainly no expert."

"Well, I bet your efforts are much better than mine, so if you'll just come into the church I'll show you," he said. "I hate to ask really, but we've got a service this evening at seven, and I do like to have things looking just right."

"Would you like me to tie my dog up outside? She'll be perfectly happy for a few minutes while I go inside."

"No, no, you can bring your dog, she looks perfectly clean and well behaved. We have an owners' and pets' service you know, every September, the Sunday after harvest festival."

"That's nice," I said.

"By the way," he said, "I'm the Reverend Alan Clitheroe."

I told him my name, said I was just in the village for a walk.

"Are you, by any chance, a churchgoer?" he asked me.

"No, not really," I told him, "But I sometimes go for a Christmas Eve carol service."

"And where would that be?" he asked.

"I'm from Middleton," I said. "We have a lovely church there."

"Yes indeed," he said, "Holy Trinity Church, I know it well and of course I know the minister too, the Reverend Linda Davies, but I understand she doesn't live in the village."

"No, she lives in Eastbridge," I said, "and I think she's the parish priest for five churches."

"Some of us have even more parishes than that to cover," he said.

By this time we'd walked through the porch and along the aisle towards the vestry at the east end of the church.

"So where are these troublesome flowers?" I asked.

"Here," said the vicar, pointing to a motley bunch of flowers stuffed into a vase on a side table. The greenery and flowers of all colours were arranged higgledy-piggledy as if a child had done them, but of course I didn't tell him that.

"I'm surprised the vase didn't break when it hit the floor," I said.

"Luckily, it landed on that bit of red carpet," he said, "Otherwise there'd have been an even bigger mess. You can see the carpet and the floor is still wet where I mopped up the water. I put more water in the vase, of course, but I'm afraid my efforts at flower arranging are enough to make the heavens weep."

He gave me a wan little smile, at this rather lame attempt at humour.

That was when I first smelled the horrible aroma of alcohol on his breath. He smelled as if he had been at the spirits, whisky or brandy or something like that. I'd thought he was walking rather strangely too, but now I saw it wasn't his natural way of walking, but the result of him having consumed a bit too much earlier in the day.

I looped the dog lead round the end of a pew, and approached the table. It was quite low, only about two feet high, long and narrow with a cloth along the top to protect the varnish from the vase. I set to work rearranging the flowers, firstly by taking the whole bunch out of the vase, being careful not to get drips all over the top of the table. Then I put in the greenery which was mainly small ferns, followed by some focal flowers, for which I used three large pink peonies. There were also small red carnations and a number of tiny white blooms which I didn't recognize, so I put together my combination as best I could and rotated the vase to make sure it looked good from all sides, though I supposed the congregation would only have seen it from one angle. When I'd finished, I turned to the vicar and said:

"There, that's about the best I can do."

"They look absolutely delightful," he said, "and not so different from Mrs. Chamber's original arrangement, as far as I can remember. She'll probably be most annoyed that her handiwork has been moved around, but I couldn't really ask her to come all the way from Hinton this afternoon just to redo one of her arrangements."

"No, I suppose not," I said. "Right, now I'd better be going, my son will be home from work soon, and it's my turn to cook supper tonight."

I'd just turned to collect the dog from the end of the pew when I felt quite a firm hand on my shoulder. I turned in surprise to find him smiling – but it was more of a horrible leer then a normal smile.

"Has anybody ever told you that you're a very, very good flower arranger?" he said.

"Not lately," I said, grabbing hold of the dog lead.

At that point I saw that he had something in his hand. I glanced down and to my horror saw that from somewhere he'd produced a very large pair of scissors.

Suddenly, all I could think of was that poor woman who'd been murdered outside the church, and I began to panic. I walked swiftly towards the the door, dragging the dog behind me.

"Don't run away from me!" said the Vicar in a very strange voice, and he came after me, still with the scissors in his hand. His eyes had a strange look about them, seeming to look straight through me. Maybe it was just my imagination, but *he looked like a man possessed!* Well, that was it! I took to my heels and ran straight down the aisle.

"Wait, wait!" he said, and came running after me. By this time I had put a good distance between us, and had the dog running behind me on the lead. I was out of the door, through the porch and across the churchyard before you could say Jack Robinson. I could hear his footsteps behind me and he was saying *"Wait, wait, you've got the wrong end of the stick, Mrs. Salter!"*

But I didn't wait to see what he was doing behind me, and I was in no mood for an apology. I ran straight back to the car let the dog jump over the driver's seat and into the passenger side and did a three point turn as fast as I could, and then I was away into the countryside. I've never felt so relieved in my life! I must confess I've often found vicars a little bit creepy, but the Reverend Alan Clitheroe takes the biscuit. What the hell would have happened if I'd stayed in his church I don't know, but I'll tell you one thing: I won't be going back to Walberswick for a while.'"

'Wow,' I said, 'That's quite a story. I'm surprised you didn't phone your friends at police HQ as soon as you were safely back in the car.'

'I did think of doing that,' she said, 'but after a few seconds of driving down the road I began to doubt myself and wondered if he hadn't just been drunk and not meant me any harm after all. But he had those huge scissors in his hand, that was what made me panic, and I couldn't take any chances. He wasn't holding them like you would normally hold a pair of scissors, he seemed to have them clenched in his hand like you would hold a dagger ready to stab someone.'

'Mum, I think we really should call the police,' I said, reaching inside my pocket for my phone.

'No,' she said, taking hold of my hand, 'We won't do that. There's not enough evidence that he really did want to do me harm. Maybe I was just acting out of pure blind panic because of the proximity of that murder back in January.'

She released my hand, and picked up her cup, took a few sips of the strong Earl Grey tea.

'Also,' she said, 'You have to remember I'd got into a real panicky state, so maybe I wasn't seeing things as they really are...'

She sipped her tea thoughtfully.

'Or, maybe,' I said, 'The Reverend Alan Clitheroe is really the East Coast Killer – stranger things have happened, you know.'

'Oh, don't say that,' she said with a shudder. 'That Hadiscoe man has confessed, and the evidence for his trial is piling up. I have to read about it, and type stuff up about it every day. That's probably why I got so stressed out this afternoon, imagining a perfectly innocent vicar was about to attack me.'

'Well it does sound a little far-fetched,' I said, 'That the Reverend Alan Clitheroe would lure you into his church to murder you. Have you not considered the possibility that he was merely about to hand you the scissors to trim the flowers in the arrangement?'

She looked at me and blinked a few times.

'That was the funny thing,' she said, 'He was holding those scissors as if he really was going to do me some harm.'

She continued to sip her tea.

'But on the other hand,' she said, 'I have had these horrible, panicky feelings from time to time lately. And I think I'm beginning to imagine murderers and danger and get all jittery at the slightest provocation.'

'Seeing a creepy, drunken man looming over you with a giant pair of scissors is more than a slight provocation.'

'Yes,' she said; 'But now that I'm home, the more I think about it, the more I think I just had some kind of panic attack...'

She sipped her tea again, looked up at me apologetically.

Then, a strange mood seemed to come over her, and she began to smile, then giggle, and finally she burst into hysterical laughter.

Soon I was joining in, and, as we leaned across the table to hug, spilled tea all over the clean cloth. When we finally stopped laughing and hugging, we discovered the dog in its basket was staring at us with its head on one side in utter bewilderment and confusion.

Mum went over and patted Tilly on the head, saying:

'You poor old thing, not knowing what the heck is going on – and I know how you feel. I think that living and breathing this East Coast Killer murder case has made me into a nervous wreck these past few months.'

'Yeah, mum,' I said, 'I know *exactly* how you feel...'

Chapter Twelve:
The Catastrophe

Saturday August 23rd 9.15 p.m.

My orange Ford Fiesta carried the three of us safely through the warm August evening sunshine onto the driveway of Rowan Tree Farm. It was just after nine o'clock in the evening, and the sun in the west was tinged with pink, casting the kind of light over the woods and meadows that would have had Gainsborough and Constable scrabbling for their paint boxes.

There were balloons tied to the farm's sign at the end of the driveway, and a traffic jam of cars had built up on the big tennis court sized concrete pad before the giant barn. About fifty teenage kids were milling around the huge barn doors which were opened wide. We could see more people inside, illuminated by the flashing multi-coloured lights. The pulsating trance music was already quite loud, though it was barely eight o'clock, and the party, if Fleur was to be believed, would only be fully in swing much later in the evening.

'It looks more like the scene outside a nightclub in London,' said Baz, 'than a barn in the middle of nowhere.'

'How would you know?' said Freddy, 'You've never been to a London nightclub.'

Well, I know Fleur asked me to bring some good-looking friends, but all I could drum up at fairly short notice were my two old sixth form chums from Thomas

Mills High School. Baz Barford was a gangly six-foot-two human version of Disney's goofy, while Freddy Kingsley was a five-foot-six Ed Sheeran lookalike, complete with red tussled hair and a slightly overweight belly. Alas, though Freddy had attended the same school and sixth form as the pop icon, he sadly lacked any musical ability, or charisma of any kind, his talents being strictly limited to attaining straight A's in 'A' levels of Maths, Physics Biology and Chemistry. He was off to Oxford in a few weeks' time, destined, no doubt for great academic things, perhaps even to find his very first girlfriend. Baz, on the other hand, real name Brian Barford, had passed his exams with more modest results, and was already working in his father's classic car restoration garage in Framlingham. He had been going out with a large-boned hockey-playing girl called Sophie who'd ditched him at the end of term in favour of a strapping farmer's son from Dennington, leaving Baz broken-hearted and in desperate need of cheering up. To make things worse, Baz and Freddy's plan of backpacking in Indonesia had been indefinitely postponed due to their lack of funds and the insistence of Freddy's parents that he started the course offered him.

'I can see a lot of good-looking girls,' said Freddie, who was riding shotgun, 'mostly ones I haven't seen before – but look, bloody hell, there's Esme and Catriona from *our* sixth form - I wonder how they got invited.'

'That's easy enough to work out,' I said; 'Catriona's younger sister goes to Alde Valley Academy, where most of this lot go – or went – to school.'

'How the hell do you know that?' asked Freddy.

'Catriona was in my ex-girlfriend Georgia's circle of friends,' I said; 'I got to hear all sorts of boring details about their families.'

'Do you think Georgia's here too?' asked Freddy.

'I bloody-well hope not,' I said.

'I wonder if my Sophie is here,' said Baz, who was sitting in the back.

'Forget Sophie,' I said, 'She's not *your* Sophie any more. There's loads of other beautiful girls here to choose from.'

'I suppose you're right,' said Baz rather gloomily. Then he seemed to perk up a little.

'Hey, Ivan, where in the hell are we supposed to park? This place is heaving with cars already.'

A girl in tight jeans and a crop-top waved us towards an open gateway on the opposite side of the concrete forecourt. It turned out to be the entrance to a meadow. It had a card pinned to its open five-bar gate with *'car park'* written on it in blue felt tip.

We drove in and parked in a line of cars. Already, there were about thirty vehicles in the field, with more arriving all the time. Some parents were dropping off their sons and daughters, then attempting to get back along the driveway. This was only possible if the cars which were entering and leaving made use of the wide grass verges.

'Tell me again,' said Freddy, as we got out, 'How the hell did we manage to get invited to a cool party like this?'

'I told you before,' I said, 'I know a girl from Fordley who's best mates with the girl whose party it is.'

'Wow, so for once we're not gatecrashers, we've actually been invited?' asked Baz.

'Absolutely,' I said.

'Do you think we'll be able to buy some E's?' asked Freddy; 'I've always wanted to do some 'E's' at a party.'

'We're in Minsmere, not Camden,' I said. 'Anyway, even if someone were to offer you some, you wouldn't know an 'E' from an aspirin.'

'Yes, I would,' said Freddy. 'E's are usually yellow with a butterfly on them.'

'Rubbish,' said Baz; 'They're blue with a smiley face on the top.'

'I should have brought some aspirin I said; 'I could have sold you one each for a tenner apiece.'

'Ha, bloody ha,' said Baz. 'Anyway, Freddy, from what I hear, when you get to Oxford you'll soon be offered plenty of ecstasy pills, and every other kind of drug known to man, too.'

'Now, no more drug talk,' I said as we approached the group of people milling about by the doors. Some of them were smoking, some vaping, and most had a plastic cup of drink in one hand.

The girl in the crop top who'd ushered us into the car park came to greet us. She had mousey hair over her shoulders, strawberry-red lipstick and wore high-heeled cowboy boots with pointed toes. She strode boldly up to us, smiling and friendly, but, I thought, a little suspicious at the same time.

'Hi', she said; 'And who might you be?'

Before I could answer, Fleur appeared at my left shoulder, blowing menthol-scented vapour into the air. She was wearing a stunning and rather short black halter-top dress and black high-heeled shoes. Her stunning eye make-up must have been modelled on pictures of Queen Cleopatra, but unlike the queen of Egypt, Fleur's long brown hair was piled up high in a 'beehive' style.

'This is Ivan,' she said to the crop-top girl, 'and these must be his Thomas Mills pals.'

'We are indeed,' smiled Freddy, 'This is Baz Barford, and I'm Freddy Kingsley.'

'I thought you were going to say Freddy *Kruger*,' said Fleur, with a deadpan face.

'Fleur!' scolded Beatrice, 'That's a bit rude.'

'Oh, don't take any notice of me, people say I'm rude to everyone,' said Fleur. 'So, boys, what kind of booze did you bring?'

Baz, who was carrying the box from the back seat said:

'We've got some really good stuff in here.'

Beatrice took a step forward and peeked into the box.

'Wow,' she said, 'Four litres of extra strong cider, and eight cans of Oranjeboom super strength lager!'

'Bloody hell,' said Fleur, 'You Thomas Mills boys certainly are a hard-drinking bunch.'

'That's us,' said Baz, with a silly grin.

Fleur gave him a dismissive glance and wandered over to another group of four boys who'd just arrived.

'You can put the booze on the table at the back of the barn,' said Beatrice, moving off to join her friend. Freddy, Baz and I watched as they gave these lucky lads warm embraces and kisses on both cheeks.

'We didn't even get a kiss,' said Freddy rather wistfully, watching the group hug and laugh together.

'That's 'cos we don't know them,' shrugged Baz.

'Fleur is really something,' said Freddy. 'I wonder if she's going out with anyone.'

'Bound to be, with our luck,' said Baz.

'Ah well,' I said, 'Let's go take a look inside and get a drink.'

Inside the barn the lighting was dim, with the windows covered with black paper, and only some spotlights shining on the makeshift stage to our right. The stage was made up of a layer of straw bales with flat sheets of plywood on top. There were some big amps, a set of drums and three guitars on stands, along with microphones and a backcloth pinned to the wall behind the playing area that announced 'The Catastrophe' in gothic letters.

On one side of the stage was the DJ's equipment on a small desk. The girl at the desk was wearing earphones, and she was jigging around to her atrocious trance music, but fortunately she'd kept the volume relatively low for the moment.

As we were moving towards the drinks tables, a girl in a leather biker's jacket literally bumped into Freddy and spilled a little of her cup of drink on the floor.

'Sorry,' said Freddy, though it wasn't his fault.

The girl rolled her eyes up to heaven and swore, before giving Freddy a dismissive push to the chest as she passed him. Baz put his box down on the floor and placed the cans and bottles on the congested table, saying to Freddy:

'What was all that about? What a bitch.'

'Yeah,' said Freddy, 'I don't think she liked my T-shirt.'

Freddy's T-shirt had *Led Zeppelin* on the front. His 'retro' look included his wearing a pair of his dad's 1970's Levi 501's, with red baseball boots. But his hair looked as if he'd left it un-brushed for a week, and he had a bit of a belly, even though he didn't yet drink much beer. Alas, his days of acne were not quite over yet, and, all in all, his best bet for getting a girl tonight might be to hang around in the darkest corners and hope that they kept the lighting down all night.

Baz, on the other hand, was slightly more trendy, with his spiky neo-punk hair, tartan trousers and black T-shirt. He was six feet two, and despite his prominent front teeth, had been out with a string of attractive girlfriends, the last of whom, Sophie Meade, had ignominiously dumped him just before our sixth form prom back in June. Since then, Baz had been moping and wallowing in self-pity, completely failing and refusing to move on with his love-life.

Our attention was taken by the sudden cessation of the trance music, replaced by the sound of guitars tuning up at the far end of the room on the stage. Four lads with retro eighties' hairstyles, black cargo pants and white sleeveless T-shirts with 'The Catastrophe' emblazoned on the front were preparing their instruments. As the band members limbered up for a sound check, my two companions grabbed a plastic cup of cider each, while I, the unfortunate driver, chose orange juice. As we edged towards the stage, sipping our drinks as we went, a gaggle of girls elbowed their way past us. Just then, the drummer tapped out a rhythm, and the guitars and bass struck up a familiar song. It turned out to be a very respectable cover of *'This Charming Man'* by the Smiths, complete with the difficult jangly guitar riff made famous by Indy dinosaur Johnny Marr.

They then launched into one of their own songs, which appeared to be called *'We are Catastrophe'*, with its own catchy riff.

'They're bloody good,' said Freddy in my ear.

Baz gave me a thumbs-up sign, indicating his approval. The girls at the front were giving the band adoring looks and starting to waggle their bums, ready to break into a full-blown dance, but as suddenly as the warm-up had started, the song abruptly stopped with perfect, well-rehearsed co-ordination.

'More!' called out the groupie girls next the stage, but the four lads only laughed.

'We'll be back at ten,' said the lead singer into his mike, putting his guitar back on its stand.

I sipped my juice, and surveyed the room, as the thirty or so revellers around the stage dispersed outside again, or made their way towards the drinks.

'I was expecting a really crap band,' said Baz, 'but those lucky sods can really play.'

'Yeah,' said Freddy, 'Did you see the way those girls were staring at them?'

'Makes you sick, doesn't it,' said Baz.

To illustrate the point, one of the band members slid past us, and put his arm around a pretty girl. She looked up at him with dreamy eyes and planted a kiss on his lips.

'Come on,' I said to the others, 'Let's go take a peek at what's going on outside.'

We positioned ourselves outside to one side of the doorway so that we could see the guests arriving. There was a steady stream of kids arriving by car, most of them dropped off by their parents, but a good many also coming in their own cars like me. The boys and girls were milling around in groups, drinking, laughing, joking, vaping, smoking, all seeming to know each other.

There was one arrival that really surprised me. A black kid arrived in a shiny new hatchback driven by none other than the Reverend Alan Clitheroe.

'Thanks, Dad,' said the boy as he got out, 'See you at midnight.'

'Be out here ready,' said Clitheroe, 'Nigel and I had to wait out here half an hour last time...'

There was no reply, as the boy was rapidly absorbed into a crowd of his friends, leaving the vicar to turn his car around and go back the way he had come.

Baz and Freddy went back inside for more drinks, coming back with cans of the super-strength

Oranjeboom lager. I knew they were loading themselves with Dutch courage so as to aid them in their attempted chatting-up of girls. Alas, no such easing of nerves was available to me, as I had resolved to drive home some time after midnight, rather than sleep all night on the straw bales as Fleur had said she and her friends liked to do. Fleur caught me looking her way as she hugged two newly arrived girlfriends, and smiled ever so briefly before looking away.

I felt a nudge on my arm, and turned. It was Esme Harmon from our own sixth form, smiling broadly, having recognised me. She was a short little thing, with silver-rimmed glasses over her large blue eyes. Her hair was long, almost down to her waist, of a distinctive and very beautiful chestnut brown colour. Her mouth had a very fetching colour of dark crimson lipstick. She had a vape in her left hand and a glass of wine in her right.

'Ivan!' she said, 'What are you doing here? This is an Alde Valley party... Catriona and I thought we were the only ones from our school here.'

She gave me a little kiss on the cheek, and I caught the extremely pleasant smell of melon flavoured vape mingled with red wine on her breath.

'Here's Baz and Freddy too,' I said.

Esme nodded and smiled in recognition at my two companions.

'So how come you got invited here?' asked Esme.

'I know Fleur, who's best friends with the hostess Beatrice. And I'm guessing you were invited because Catriona's sister goes to Alde Valley?'

'Correct,' said Esme. 'Alice was in the lower sixth form last school year and knows Beatrice pretty well. Apparently, Beatrice and Fleur have invited almost their entire sixth form to this bash, so it's going to get pretty crowded later.'

'It's a wonder that Beatrice's parents agree to all this going on,' I said, marvelling at the scene of revelry which was rapidly descending into a debauch of drinking, smoking, vaping and, latterly, as the darkness closed in around the barn, couples pairing off and indulging in long, lingering kisses.

'Oh, I hear they're very indulgent of their daughter,' said Esme. 'They've let her have parties here before. They're even giving her money to go travelling in Australia.'

'So I hear,' I said. 'So what are you doing this autumn?'

'Oh, I'm off to Homerton,' she said, taking a big lungful of melon vape. 'My course starts in October.'

'Homerton?' I asked stupidly.' Where's that?'

She laughed.

'That, my dear, is a part of Cambridge University. I'm doing a BA in Education... and I happen to know you're doing a BA in English and Drama down the road from me in Anglia Ruskin.'

'How on earth do you know that?' I asked.

'I know because I read the school website where all the results and courses our classmates have chosen are listed. Don't tell me you didn't bother to read it, and see where all your old friends were heading?'

'I did look at it,' I said, 'though I've already forgotten where most of our lot are studying. Hey, what happened to Catriona?'

'Are you trying to get rid of me?' she said, with a flash of her big blue eyes.

'Not at all,' I said, 'As a matter of fact I quite like your company.'

She smiled, and finished her drink.

'Good,' she said, 'You can come with me to get some more booze. By the way, Catriona's run off with the first boy who talked to her, leaving me all alone, so I'm depending on you to talk with me till she comes back. I'm like you, I hardly know a soul around here. By the way, I keep seeing you glance at Fleur over there. Sorry to disappoint you, but you're wasting your time ogling her.'

'I don't really fancy her,' I lied, 'But why do you say that?'

'Because,' laughed Esme, 'Fleur is already going out with somebody. Just look.'

She pointed through the crowd, and, sure enough, there was Fleur intertwined with someone else, indulging in a passionate kiss. And the person she was kissing... was Beatrice.'

'Don't look so shocked,' said Esme, poking me in the ribs. 'Surely you've seen two girls kissing before.'

'Oh yes, of course,' I said. 'Let's get that drink.'

I noticed Baz and Freddy discretely nudging each other as they spotted Fleur and Beatrice. Then they walked off, and disappeared into the crowd of revellers at the far side of the room.

As darkness slowly descended, the crowd of people filtered inside the barn, their faces illuminated by the flashing colours of the strobes and spotlights, with the awful dance music buzzing and throbbing in the background.

'I have to drink juice,' I said apologetically to Esme, as she filled her glass to the brim with more red wine, 'as I came here in my car.'

'Nonsense,' she said. 'If you're driving you're allowed two glasses of wine, so here you are.'

She put a small measure in my glass, and I took a sip.

'And I know you vape as well,' she said, putting the melon-scented vape between my lips. I've seen you many a time behind the gymnasium wall, vaping with that Georgia girl you used to go with. Now relax, Ivan, this is a party. And in case you haven't realised, it's the last one you'll go to in dear old Suffolk for quite a while, so bloody-well enjoy yourself.'

I drew in the vapour, and my head swam for a few seconds. Then she took the vape and inhaled deeply, blew the sweet-scented fog in the air, then took an enormous swig of wine.'

'It's funny, we barely talked while we were in sixth form,' she said. 'But then, you were going out with Georgia, and I was going out with James.'

'No more James, I suppose?' I asked.

'He dumped me in June, after the exams, she said. 'He said there was no point, as he was going to Exeter.'

'Sorry to hear that,' I said.

'And I was sorry to hear that you and Georgia split,' she said. 'You were together quite a while, weren't you?'

'Eighteen months,' I said, 'before she decided I wasn't quite right for her, as she put it. She's off to Liverpool now. She's going to be a vet, apparently.'

'Eighteen months is a long time,' she said, putting the vape in my mouth again. 'Sixth form romances never last, my mother told me that, miserable cow, but I wouldn't believe her.'

'Ah well,' I said, touching my plastic glass against hers, 'Here's to new beginnings. When we get to Cambridge I'll invite you out for tea.'

'That's very sweet of you,' she grinned.

She drank deeply again and put an arm around me. 'Don't keep looking at those other girls,' she said. 'I'm hoping you'll be a perfect gentleman, and look after me tonight.'

'All right,' I said, 'As long as I don't catch you kissing one of those other girls.'

'I haven't seen one I fancy, yet,' she said. 'Hey look, the band is getting ready to play.'

Sure enough, the dance music stopped as the four boys with cute eighties' hair stepped onto the stage.

Now the barn was full, with almost everyone from outside crowding in for the highlight of the evening.

A cool-looking kid at the front of the stage picked up his microphone from its stand, tapped it to check it was working and wedged it back in position. He strummed his guitar to make sure its strings were tuned, and the other guitarist and bass player fiddled around a bit with their own tuning. The drummer hit a couple of beats to flex his muscles, then looked up.

'Hi, we're the Catastrophe,' said the lead singer, to wild cheering, *"One, two, three, four!"* and they were away, starting with their signature tune we'd heard earlier. It went something like this:

> *The Catastrophe is coming,*
> *To a place near you*
> *You can't escape Catastrophe*
> *Whatever you do*
> *You've never seen anything like it*
> *Panic everywhere*
> *Lock up your sons and daughters*
> *The Catastrophe is here!*

The kids at the front, knowing the song, all joined in and sang along, jiggling away in time with the music. Esme and I exchanged glances, and she said:

'Wow, they can actually play!'

She took a big gulp of wine in celebration. We were standing side by side, watching the band, and began to get jostled by kids dancing around us, so I put a protective arm around her and I felt her own arm, still holding her vape, slide around my waist. I pulled her a little closer and she looked up at me and smiled briefly, before draining the last of her wine. I sipped my own wine, clutched in my free hand, and had a sudden revelatory moment, when I realised that, for the first time in a long while, I was actually feeling relaxed and happy.

The band played several numbers, during one of which Esme dragged me through the dancing throng over to the drinks table.

'The booze always runs out early at these parties,' she grinned, taking yet another gulp. I realized she was getting quite drunk, and determined I might try to dissuade her from going way over the top and getting ill, as I had done a few times before at friends' parties, and made a perfect fool of myself.

We turned and watched the band from the back of the room, which was pleasant, as the noise was not quite so deafening. There was one very memorable song they played, quite funny, with the Catastrophe's usual deadpan black humour. It was, I thought, in pretty poor taste, considering the fact that there'd been five murders in the area. Still, rock musicians have never really shown a great deal of respect for public decency and taste.

So they sang, to a raunchy guitar riff:

It's sheer bloody murder, baby
Out there on the streets
There's a man with a machete, baby
Kills everyone he meets
It's sheer suicide, now baby
Going out alone
That man with a machete, baby
Will kill you for your phone
He'll kill you for your sneakers, baby
He'll kill you for a lark

It's sheer bloody murder, baby
Out there in the dark...

And so on. The next song was a repeat of the Smiths song we'd heard earlier, and it sounded better than ever. A little way off I caught sight of Beatrice and Fleur, dancing next to each other, and over by the door were Freddy and Baz, also dancing around but not quite so elegantly. Catching sight of them, Esme poked me in the ribs and pointed them out to me, smiling broadly, but not unkindly, to see the two boys' slightly clownish behaviour.

But then, a strange thing happened. A rather familiar adult man and a woman pushed through the revellers blocking the door, and began shoving their way through the crowd. The man and woman kept stopping and looking around as if looking for someone. The party-goers were staring at the intruders, wondering what two older people were doing in their midst.

Esme and I exchanged puzzled glances, just before the couple made a sudden push through the crowd and a loud scream rent the air, a cry which rose even above the sound of the music.

'Get off me!' shouted Fleur. Gabriel Miller seized her by the wrists, took a cannabis joint out of her hand, sniffed it suspiciously and threw it on the floor.

'Leave her alone!' shouted Beatrice.

Suddenly someone switched on the lights, and the band faltered and stopped playing. A circle of astonished onlookers had gathered around Fleur and Beatrice, *and there was Gabriel and Naomi Miller, one on either side of their daughter, holding her by the arms, attempting to drag her over to the door!*

Beatrice also had hold of Fleur, standing with her arms around her friend, physically resisting the parents' efforts to get their daughter out of the building.

'Get your bloody hands off me!' roared Fleur, 'I'm not going anywhere.'

'Let go of her!' screamed Beatrice, 'You can't just drag her away like this, if she doesn't want to go...'

'She's only seventeen,' shrieked Naomi, 'and she's not staying here to take drugs and get up to God-knows-what.'

Some of the crowd of spectators began to heckle and make comments at these over-protective, not to mention half-crazy parents.'

'Leave her be!' they shouted, 'Let go of her!'

'Stop pulling her, you're hurting her,' shouted Beatrice, her eyes full of fire and fury.

As for poor Fleur, she planted her feet firmly on the concrete floor and resisted with all her might.

'We're not leaving without you,' said Gabriel Miller. 'I'll not see you stay here and take more drugs!'

'It was only a bit of grass,' shouted Fleur, 'It's less harmful than those bloody fags you smoke.'

'What's going on here?' said a loud voice away to our right. We all turned.

And as we did, we caught sight of the two uniformed police officers, a man and a woman, standing ominously in the doorway.

CHAPTER THIRTEEN:
THE LONG ARM OF THE LAW

Saturday 23rd August 11.30 p.m.

Not a soul spoke in reply. Nobody stirred, except Gabriel and Naomi, who released their grip on their daughter's arms. Fleur stepped away from them. The police officers approached.

'We're here to investigate a complaint of excessive noise,' said the male officer, 'but we can see there's also been a bit of a disturbance.' He looked directly at Gabriel. 'So you'd better tell us exactly what's going on.'

The officer was a bit overweight and pink in the face, but he cut a big, imposing figure in his black uniform, a black flashlight, unlit, in his right hand. The other PC was only a bit shorter, with red hair tied back behind her hat, and had a bemused look on her face.

'Could it be,' she said to Naomi and Gabriel, 'that you've come to take your daughter home, and she, perhaps, doesn't want to go?'

'Too bloody right,' said Naomi, 'but she's coming back with us right now.'

'I'm not bloody going,' said Fleur.

The officers exchanged knowing glances and took a few steps forward.

'And how old are you, young lady?' asked the female officer.

'I'm eighteen,' said Fleur.

'She's not eighteen till next week,' said Gabriel. 'That

gives us the legal right to take her home.'

'But not by force,' said the male officer, removing his cap. 'In these little domestic disputes, we like to settle things amicably. If anybody starts getting dragged about, that opens a whole new can of worms, and we wouldn't want that, would we?'

'Well, no,' said Gabriel. 'But she's been smoking...'

His voice trailed off, as the implications of his words suddenly dawned on him.

I saw Beatrice move her right boot, to cover the stub of the joint, which was still smouldering on the concrete floor.

'They're upset that I vape and smoke tobacco,' said Fleur, and to illustrate her point she took out a little green plastic pouch from her pocket and showed it to the officers. 'It's just golden Virginia,' said Fleur, 'and I'm over sixteen, so it's up to me.'

'Well,' said the male officer, scratching his head, 'You're perfectly within your rights to smoke if you really want to, but if we were to search everyone in the room and find, for example, some grass or cannabis resin in your pockets, that would be a much more serious matter.'

'We've been sent here,' said the woman police officer, 'to ask you to turn down the volume of the music. Now, if you were to do that, and promise not to switch it up again after we've left like you did last time – yes, we did get to hear about that – then we can get on with our shift and say "mission accomplished." But what we don't want is a messy domestic incident with parents trying to take away a girl of *almost* eighteen against her will.'

'Now, young lady,' said the policeman, 'I'll take a wild guess you're not quite ready to go home yet.'

'Too bloody right,' said Fleur, with anger in her eyes.

'And what time would you consider is a reasonable time for your very kind parents here to come and get you?'

'Tomorrow morning at ten would be fine – I'm sleeping over with Beatrice. It's her party, and her parents know all about me staying over.'

'Did you not think of clearing this with *your own* parents first?' said the woman officer.

'I told them all right,' said Fleur.

'And we told her we didn't want her to go,' said Naomi, 'but she scrounged a lift with one of her buddies and came anyway.'

'I see,' said the male officer. 'So what are the three of you going to do? I'm sure all these young people would love to get on with their party – with a much lower volume of music of course – and my colleague and I have to get back to Saxmundham, where the pubs will soon be closing and we'll doubtless find a few boisterous souls who might need a little shepherding on their way home, if you see what I mean. So, how about a good old-fashioned compromise? Why don't you two agree to fetch your lovely daughter at, shall we say, nine o'clock sharp tomorrow morning, and then my colleague and I can be on our way?'

'But I want her to come with us *now*,' said Gabriel through gritted teeth.

'Not a chance,' said Fleur, with her hands on her hips, 'I'll be ready at ten tomorrow.'

Gabriel and Naomi stood fuming for a few seconds.

The male policeman looked at his watch theatrically and tutted loudly.

'What about *nine* tomorrow morning?' said the woman officer.

Somebody in the crowd – it sounded like Baz – shouted:

'Go away and leave her alone!'

The two officers shot him an annoyed look, but said nothing.

Finally, after a few more strained moments of waiting, Naomi pulled Gabriel away.

'Come on,' she said, 'If she wants to smoke herself to death and sleep like an animal in the straw we'd better just leave her with her druggy little friends.'

Gabriel, reluctantly, allowed his wife to pull him by the arm, back towards the barn door. At the threshold the pair paused, glanced back angrily at their daughter.

'Thanks for making a fool of me in front of all my friends – I'll never forgive you for this!' said Fleur.

'We'll talk later,' growled Gabriel, as Naomi pulled him out into the dark.

The crowd of partygoers erupted in an enormous cheer, and the policeman, in the lull that followed, called out:

'Remember, everyone, keep the noise down – you're right next to the RSPB Reserve, and if I get another complaint this evening and have to come back I'll close you down for good. Now, who's in charge of this party?'

'Me, I suppose,' said Beatrice, stepping forward.

'Consider yourself warned,' said the male police officer. He turned to go, then checked, and turned back towards Beatrice and Fleur.

'One more thing,' he said with an air of confidentiality, 'If I were you, I'd keep off the wacky-baccy. I've seen a lot of good kids start off on grass and end up lying dead on the floor with a needle full of smack still stuck in their arm. One thing leads to another, believe me, I've seen it all.'

The two officers put their hats back on and made for the door. Only when they'd got into their patrol car and exited down the driveway did everyone breathe a sigh of relief. One boy took out a joint and lit it, others milled around the drinks table. The four members of the band fiddled with the amps. Then the three guitarists re-tuned their instruments and looked up. With a cry of *"One, two, three, four!"* they struck up the old 'Clash' classic, at a slightly reduced volume:

> *Breakin' rocks in the hot sun*
> *I fought the law, and the law won*
> *I fought the law, and the law won!*
> *I needed money 'cause I had none*
> *I fought the law, and the law won*
> *I fought the law, and the law won!*
> *I left my baby and it feels so bad*
> *Guess my race is run*
> *She's the best girl that I ever had*

> *I fought the law, and the law won*
> *I fought the law, and the law won!*

'Well, Esme,' I said, borrowing her vape again, 'What did you think of that little drama? Do you think *your* dad will come storming through the door next?'

'I shouldn't think so,' she said, 'My parents are in Tuscany at the moment.'

'So who's looking after you?' I asked, instantly regretting my stupid question.

'Only you at the moment,' she said, moving closer and closing her eyes for a kiss.

At about two in the morning the acting DJ turned off the dance music. The booze had long since run out, and the number of partygoers had reduced by about three-quarters. Beatrice and Fleur, along with many other couples, were rolling around on the hay bales that provided seating and bedding all the way around the wall of the interior with the exception of the stage, drinks and door areas. Esme and I lay snuggled up in a dark corner, her warm and fragrant body pressed up against mine, her vape still clutched in one hand, her arms wrapped deliciously around me.

'Do you want a lift home?' I asked; 'I only had the one glass of wine, so I'm fit to drive.'

'Yes please,' she whispered; 'Catriona and her sister have left already in their mother's car, so without your help I'd be stranded. But let's stay a bit longer, I'm sure your friends would appreciate a bit more sleep.'

A few feet away was the body of Freddy, snoring away on his cushion of bales. Baz was a little further away, lying beside a girl with hair even spikier than his. All was hushed and relatively still within the barn. Somebody had closed the big wooden doors. From time to time a reveller got up and went outside to visit the farm workers' toilet and washroom a short distance further along the driveway in the main yard. The queue for this valuable facility had finally diminished. Beer cans and plastic bottles littered the concrete pad outside the barn and the route to the loo – so much for the environmentally conscious younger generation.

I hugged Esme even closer, as she took her final puffs of watermelon flavoured vape and closed her eyes. Soon we were both sound asleep, the most glorious and sensual sleep I had enjoyed for a long, long time, and when we woke up it was broad daylight. I glanced at my watch, and found that it was just after seven o'clock.

'That's the first time I ever slept with a boy,' grinned Esme, as she opened her eyes. 'What about you, was it your first time too?'

'First time this week,' I whispered, and she punched me playfully in the ribs.

Just then, somebody opened the door and went outside. A few seconds passed, and then from some distance away a loud scream rent the air. Everybody lying around in the barn suddenly sat up, rubbed their eyes and looked at each other, wondering who on earth was making that unearthly noise, and, more importantly, what had happened to make them do so.

A girl with brown, tussled hair and a haunted face came running back into the barn, her face in a panic.

'Quick, quick,' she said, 'I've just seen Beatrice's mother lying out there on the driveway – and I think she's *dead!*'

CHAPTER FOURTEEN:
A KILLER ON THE LOOSE

Sunday 24th August 7.20 a.m.

It was the most horrible thing I've ever seen in my life. A woman lay on the driveway about thirty feet away from the front door of Rowan Tree Farm's main house. Her dead glassy eyes were staring straight up at the sky. On one side of her stood Beatrice, wailing pitifully, with her hands over her mouth, with a tearful Fleur hugging her and trying to pull her away. On the other side of the body knelt the woman's weeping husband, his hands gently shaking her shoulders as if trying to wake her. But, it was plain to everybody except him that no amount of shaking, nor even medical help of any kind was going to revive her. There was a deep gash on the side of her head from which blood had poured and gathered in a sticky mass around her crown like a glistening crimson halo.

Standing in shock among the circle of about twenty-five dazed and hung-over party-goers, Esme and I held each other tight and stared at the body, our feet rooted to the spot, our hearts frozen by the surreal sight before us.

Freddy and Baz were on the other side of the circle, their arms around each other's shoulders, with the same stunned looks as the others.

I don't remember how long we stood there, helpless and gaping, but only that the spell was broken by an ambulance thundering up the driveway, sirens blaring and blue lights flashing, though god knows there was nothing in the way of traffic to obstruct it in that remote and lonely corner of the countryside, surrounded as it was on three sides by the woodlands and scrub of the Minsmere Bird Reserve.

The green uniformed paramedics, both women, pushed their way through the little crowd with their bags of equipment and knelt down beside the body. One of them took the dead woman's wrist and checked her pulse. Then with a knowing exchange of glances, they stood up and took charge of the scene. After a few brief questions to the grieving man, who identified himself as Daniel Chalmers, he was told to take Beatrice into the house. The dazed party-goers were ushered back to the barn, and told to wait there till the police arrived. From the paramedics' questioning, those of us who didn't already know learned that the woman was Anne-Marie Chalmers, Beatrice's mother.

Back in the barn Esme and I sat on a hay bale and held hands, for the moment lost for words. She began to cry, and I put my arms round her.

'I'm not crying for me,' she said after a while, 'I'm crying for poor Beatrice. And did you see that wound in her mother's head? Somebody had... *murdered* her! Whoever would want to do a thing like that?'

'I think it's the East Coast Killer,' I said. 'From what I've read, that's his way of... doing it'

'But surely that man's already in prison, waiting for his trial?'

'Maybe he wasn't the killer after all,' I said, 'and the real criminal is still out there.'

She shuddered, and took out her vape, switched it on and stuck it in her mouth. I went over to the drinks table and managed to find a stack of clean plastic beakers. Under the table was an open carton of two-litre bottles of mineral water. I took one bottle and two cups over to Esme, poured out some water and gave it her. I poured some for myself, and we sat there, hunched over, sipping, deep in shock, nervous as hell.

'What do you think will happen now?' she said softly.

By way of an answer, a police car siren became audible, the wail of its approach getting louder and louder. It roared up the farm drive, kicking up small stones as it went, and screeched to a halt up near the farmhouse.

'They didn't take long to get here,' said Esme, 'considering we're in the middle of nowhere.'

'Yes,' I said, 'and I think they're going to keep us here a long time. They'll need to seal off the scene of crime, get some people to help Beatrice and her dad, and interview absolutely everyone who stayed the night here. Pretty soon they'll be dozens of plain clothes officers descending on this place, and we're stuck right in the middle of it.'

Esme looked at me curiously.

'How do you know all those things,' she asked.

'Oh, just by watching a few films and programmes about the police,' I said, 'Plus the fact that my mother works for them – not as a cop, but as a kind of personal assistant.'

'Really? Who to?'

'The Chief Constable of Suffolk Constabulary.'

'Wow – maybe you can get her to ring him, and they'll let us go home.'

'No chance,' I said; 'That decision will come from the detective in charge, the Scene of Crime Officer.'

'You really do know your stuff,' she said. She took a big lungful of vape, then turned to me. 'You want some of this?'

'Too early in the morning for me,' I said. 'I'll stick to water.'

Freddy and Baz came over, and sat with us.

'What happened to your girlfriend, Baz?' I asked.

'I think she was afraid her carriage was about to turn into a pumpkin, so she ran off.'

'Any glass slipper left behind?'

'Not even a phone number,' he shrugged. 'Ah, well, too bad.'

'Never mind all that,' said Freddy, 'What do you make of that terrible scene outside. I mean... Beatrice's mum... got killed.'

'We think it was the East Coast Killer,' said Esme.

'Can't be,' said Freddy, 'He's in jail.'

'Maybe he escaped or something,' said Baz.

'Or they locked up the wrong man,' I said, 'and the killer's still out there doing his thing.'

'He must be,' said Esme, 'Otherwise Mrs. Chalmers would still be alive.'

'My head hurts,' said Freddy, 'Where'd you get that

water?'

'Under the table over there,' I said. 'There's plenty more, in big bottles.'

Freddy went to get one.

'Bring some for me, too,' said Baz. 'Anyone got any aspirin, or paracetamol?'

'Only those medics,' I reckon,' I said.

At that moment two more cars sped up the driveway.

'More cops,' said Freddy. 'Hey, I just thought of something. What if the killer is someone who slept in the barn with us? Then went out in the morning, and... you know, whacked her on the head.'

'That's a horrible thing to say,' said Esme, 'not least because that would mean the murderer is... one of *us*.'

'Let's not get paranoid,' said Baz. 'In these kind of murders, it's usually a member of their own family who did it.'

'Good point,' said Freddy, 'though slightly creepy.'

All the time this conversation was going on, the thought grew stronger and stronger in my head. *I know who the killer is –and I even know why he did it!* Surely, Gabriel Miller had returned in the night, or early morning, and wreaked his revenge on Mrs. Chalmers for allowing her daughter to have a wild party which Fleur had attended in direct defiance of her parents. To make matters worse, not only had Fleur disobeyed her father and mother, she had smoked grass and spent the night with her lesbian lover. These things, I was sure, proved too much for the homophobic and twisted Gabriel Miller to stand, and he had responded in the only way he knew how. Somehow, he had returned, unnoticed, and exacted his revenge on Beatrice's mother.

Now I was faced with a dilemma. While I desperately wanted to secure that fifty thousand pounds of reward money as soon as possible, I was torn between going straight to the police and telling them Gabriel Miller was guilty as hell, or waiting until after he was interviewed and wheedled his way out of trouble yet again, and then pouncing with my evidence to secure his conviction.

As I was thinking this over, who should come driving along in his white van, but Gabriel Miller himself!

'Talk – or think – of the devil!' I said under my breath.

I watched his vehicle drive very slowly, and as I thought, very slyly by, and I walked outside the barn, thinking of going there and then to turn him in and tell the police what I knew.

Gabriel pulled over onto the far end of the concrete pad area and got out. Seeing the ambulance, police cars and people gathered around the body, he looked confused, staring straight ahead along the driveway towards the farmhouse.

I was mortified to see a plain clothes police officer walk up to him and address him by his name as if he were expecting him:

'Mr. Gabriel Miller?' said the detective, 'Come with me sir, we'd like to speak with you for a minute or two.'

Wordlessly, the two of them walked off towards the scene of crime. By this time there were about six marked police cars parked along the verge of the driveway between the party barn and the house. The body was still there, but already surrounded by a fence of coloured tape. There was no sign of Beatrice, Fleur, or Mr. Chalmers.

'Could you go back inside the building, please?' said a woman officer who'd appeared from around the corner of the barn. 'An officer will be with you shortly who'll tell you what he'll need you to do next.'

I opened my mouth to tell her about Gabriel Miller... then closed it again, as I realised the moment had passed. It looked as if Gabriel had been rumbled, perhaps having been seen returning to the farm, or even spotted, for all I knew, in the act of killing his victim. Quite possibly, rage had got the better of him, and his crime had been detected...

I am ashamed to say that, rather than feel sorry that Mrs. Chalmers had been murdered, I was more upset by the fact that I wouldn't now get my fifty thousand pounds. How stupid I had been not to go to the police and newspapers before. But I had lacked that one crucial piece of damning evidence, and without that the money, the fame, the glory, remained tantalisingly out of reach.

'I've told you already,' said the police officer, now a little annoyed, 'Please go back inside the barn. An officer will be with you shortly.'

A small hand placed itself in mine, and I caught the now familiar and well-loved scent of watermelon, as Esme led me back into the barn.

'Come on,' she said, 'Don't worry, you've got me as an alibi.'

'Thanks,' I said; 'And you've got me.'

'Aw, how sweet,' said Baz. 'But she's got a point, you know, every one of us is a suspect. We all of us went up the driveway to that washroom, several times in fact. Those cops will be very interested in that.'

'I've been thinking,' said Freddy, 'They'll hardly think that one of us at the party did it. All things considered, what possible motive would we have?'

'Good point,' said Baz.

More cars arrived, and a few minutes later a solemn-looking man of about forty in a crumpled navy blue suit and a burgundy tie walked into the barn, accompanied by an older woman in a dark green skirt and light green blouse. She had bags under her eyes and looked tired and fed-up, as if she'd been roused from her bed and told to attend a murder scene-of-crime on her day off. Together they strode into the barn, and looked around.

'Morning everybody,' said the man. 'I'm Detective Inspector Keith Gray, and this is Detective Sergeant Colleen Turner. We've been sent to do initial interviews with you lucky lot, and our questions will first be directed at what went on last night, everything you can remember happening before you turned in for the night, passed out, or whatever. Then we'll be focusing on whether any of you left this building, perhaps to go to the loo, or whatever, in the night or early this morning. So take a few moments, think hard, and then I'll make a note of your names, and we'll work down the list so that eventually we can start to let you go home. But I warn you, that won't be for quite a time. There's been a murder, and you can appreciate that we're keen to get as much information out of you as possible. Now, if you haven't done so already, I'd like you all to give your parents a quick call to say you're all right, and ask them not to pick you up until we give you the all-clear. Those of you with cars parked in that meadow, I'd like a word with you first, as we'll have to take a look inside them. More officers are coming along to help shortly, so bear with us, be patient and we'll have you on your way home as soon as humanly possible.'

As it turned out, not one of us from the barn were released until two o'clock in the afternoon, when parents and friends arrived to give lifts home, or the lucky ones with cars like me were given permission to reclaim our vehicles. With Esme only finishing her session with the officers at 2.45 p.m. it was not until after three o'clock in the afternoon that we finally set off from Rowan Tree Farm. Our interrogations had been staggered throughout the morning, beginning with me being questioned at about 10.30 a.m. by two plain clothes officers, then having my car searched. Baz and Freddy were questioned shortly after, but Esme was among the last to be interviewed by Detective Sergeant Turner. A detective with a camera took a photograph of every person in the barn, as well as several dozen pictures of all areas of the barn itself.

At about one o'clock, while the exhausted and bleary ex-partygoers were all still corralled inside, a uniformed officer had brought us a cardboard box full of service station sandwiches and cartons of orange juice by way of refreshment. Needless to say, it was just about the worst Sunday lunch we have ever had. We were finally allowed to use the washroom and toilet – presumably their forensics team had been over it by then, and we were escorted there and back by a uniformed officer. On the way to and from the loo it was possible to see the throng of police around the fenced-off area of grass near the house, but the poor woman's body was now out of sight under a sort of tent. One of the outbuildings had officers going in and out, having apparently been taken over as an incident room. The farm house door was wide open, also with officers, both uniformed and in plain clothes, coming and going and looking generally very serious and business-like.

At a quarter past three, I turned the ignition key and the car started first time. We sat for a moment, dazed and weary, staring straight in front of us

'That was a night and a day to remember,' said Baz. 'I had to give a DNA sample, and the officer was really rude as if he suspected me.'

'That's just their way,' said Freddy; 'They took a sample from all of us, *"to eliminate us from their enquiries"* as they put it. I don't think they really think one of us did it.'

'That sergeant was really nice to me,' said Esme. 'She gave me a number to ring in case I needed counselling.'

'I think they gave that number to everyone,' said

Freddy, 'along with that second one to ring in case we remember "*something significant*" later on.'

'I'm surprised they didn't seize our passports,' said Baz, 'and tell us not to leave town.'

'Ah well,' said Esme, opening her window and switching on her vape, 'it's all over for now. Let's get the hell out of here.'

I turned the car around and headed for the gateway. Just as I got there, I saw the most unexpected sight: I had to wait a few seconds while Gabriel Miller drove past us in his van, with Fleur in the passenger seat. I was absolutely *stunned* to see him released so early – surely the police must have cottoned on to the fact that he'd killed Mrs. Chalmers by now? And yet, though I was shocked to see that killer going free, I was secretly *thrilled* – for I still had that chance to claim my reward money. Soon, very soon, my time would come.

Gabriel drove slowly by, turned his head towards us, but did not wave or show that he'd recognised me. I hadn't, so far, told my friends I actually worked for a crackpot like Gabriel, but I knew it wouldn't be too long before they asked about my acquaintance with the Miller family.

'Isn't that Fleur and her father in that van?' asked Esme. 'What a crazy man – I'm glad I don't have a father like that.'

'I wonder if he's the murderer,' said Freddy.

'What makes you say that?' I asked.

'Well, that scene he and his wife made last night, for a start,' said Freddy. 'He looked mad enough to do just about *anything*.'

'It's never the obvious one that does the murders,' said Baz. 'He was just angry his daughter was smoking grass and staying over at parties against his will.'

'And he probably hates the fact Fleur and Beatrice are an item,' said Esme, 'that is, if he even knows yet.'

'He knows,' I said.

'What makes you so sure?' asked Esme; 'I mean, *you* didn't know she was gay till last night.'

'I know the family,' I said, 'and the crazy fellow once asked me if I'd noticed anything "*odd*" about his daughter. Now I know what he meant.'

'What a monster,' said Esme.

'I still say he's the prime suspect,' said Freddy. 'There's definitely something strange about that man.'

'For sure,' said Baz. 'We'll probably read in the papers tomorrow morning that he's been arrested.'

'I wouldn't be at all surprised,' said Freddy.

There was a pause in the conversation as I drove us slowly and carefully towards Sibton, where Freddy lived. Esme suddenly turned to me and said, quite suspiciously, I thought:

'How long have you known Fleur's family?'

'As a matter of fact,' I said shame-facedly, 'I've actually been working for Fleur's dad. His name is Gabriel Miller, and yes, he's a bit odd.'

'Oh my God,' said Esme, 'You kept that one a secret. And what exactly do you and this Gabriel Miller do?'

'He's a pest controller,' I said, growing red in the face, 'but he took me on to do timber preservation –

woodworm and dry rot treatment, that sort of thing.'

'*Pest control!*' said Esme, 'That's a horrible business to be a part of.'

'I told you,' I lied, 'It's mainly spraying old buildings for woodworm and death watch beetles. It was the only job I could get round here to help me pay for uni.'

'Spraying wood isn't quite so bad, I suppose,' said Esme. 'But you've had to put up with being with a disgusting man like that... for *how* long?'

'It'll be eight weeks when I finish next weekend. That is, if he's not arrested before then.'

'Wow,' said Freddy, 'You're working with that moron. How much does he pay you?'

'Four hundred a week,' I said, 'Plus some bonuses.'

'For burying bodies?' grinned Baz.

'Mainly getting covered in woodworm fluid and cobwebs in filthy farmhouse roofs,' I said.

'The things some people will do for money,' said Freddy. 'Hey, slow down, this is my road, remember?'

'I remember.'

I dropped Freddy off on his driveway, and we waved our farewells. Freddy's parents owned The Manor House, a seventeenth century building near to the ruins of Sibton Abbey. His father was an airline pilot, never at home, and his mother owned the biggest holiday letting company in the county. They were, reputedly, loaded, but Freddy told me he'd lived most of his childhood alone, sat in front of his computer, or lying on his bed studying like mad for a chance to go to Oxford, a new life all of his own making.

'Hey, Ivan,' said Baz, on the way to his village of Peasenhall, 'Do you have to catch *rats?* Is that what you'll be doing tomorrow, with the crazy man?'

'Can we not talk about the pest control?' I snapped. 'For your information, we're supposed to be spraying a barn at Cratfield.'

'Not killing rats and mice then,' grinned Baz, trying to goad me. 'Or burying any bodies?'

'Ha ha,' I said, trying to control my temper.

Esme's right hand reached out and took hold of my left hand, which had been resting on the edge of my seat.

'Poor thing,' she said, 'Having to work for a man like that. Still, four hundred pounds is a lot of money to earn in an area like this. I only get ten pounds an hour, waitressing part-time in a horrible café serving fat old ladies and rich tourists who're always complaining and never leave a tip.'

'My dad only pays me three hundred,' said Baz.

'That's 'cos your dad is a tight-fisted git,' I said.

'That's very true,' said Baz.

After dropping him off outside a house called Riverside Lodge it was time to take Esme back to Framlingham. We passed through Badingham, then Dennington and cut across country until the distant walls of the castle became visible over the houses and trees of that sleepy little country town.

Esme's house turned out to be a big detached building a short distance from the market square. 'Gainsborough House' looked very old, with wooden shutters latched next to its leaded glass windows.

'Everyone has a nicer house than mine,' I complained, in between kisses.

'I won't invite you in,' she said, a few minutes later, 'but listen, I *really* like you, so if you come back tomorrow after you finish burying all the bodies, I'll cook you a meal and we can watch a movie, or *something*.'

Then, to my great surprise, she handed me her most precious possession of all as a parting gift.

'That's for you', she said, putting her vape in my hand. 'It's still got a few puffs left in it.'

'But you'll need it,' I protested, 'You're the vape queen of Suffolk, and from what I've seen, you'll most probably shrivel up and die without it.'

'Don't worry,' she said, 'I've got another ten in my bedroom. See you tomorrow...'

Well, I vaped watermelon flavour all the way home, a poor substitute for her kisses, but at least this time I managed to get home safely without hitting a tree or driving straight off a bend and into a sugar beet field.

My mother hugged and kissed me, then held me at arms' length and said:

'Ivan! I've been so worried – since you phoned me this morning, all I could think of was you standing in that yard, having to see a dead body like that... you poor thing!'

'Actually, Mum,' I said, 'I'm all right, just a bit tired after sleeping on hay-bales all right. A bit of spaghetti and passata, and a good long shower, and I'll be right as rain. Seeing the body was horrible, but I guess I'll get over it. It's poor Beatrice Chalmers and her dad I feel sorry for.'

'Yes, said my mum, 'It's a horrible, horrible thing that's happened. I'll get you that spaghetti, and make you some strong tea... that'll make you feel a little bit better.'

'Thanks,' I said.

Ten minutes later, under the shower, I thought to myself, that it wouldn't be strong tea that would make me feel better, but getting that vital piece of evidence I needed to stop Gabriel Miller in his tracks. Time, I felt, was now running short, so I vowed to take whatever chances I had to, in order to get him to justice. Sooner or later, I knew, he would make a mistake and reveal to me how he managed to do those terrible things and evade the full scrutiny of the detectives. And, as it happened, the first breakthrough was to occur only a few hours later...

Chapter Fifteen:
Bed Bugs And Broken Legs

Monday 25th August

The seven a.m. news on radio, TV and online gave away no inkling that there had been another murder. More than likely, Suffolk Constabulary was checking its facts and evidence ready for the inevitable bombshell announcement and press conference that would occur, as usual, in the early evening.

At exactly eight a.m. that Monday morning, Gabriel Miller turned as usual up in his van to pick me up outside my gate. Nancy the terrier was absent that morning because, as I later discovered, we would be using some pungent chemicals whose smell would stink out every part of the van.

For the first two miles as we travelled my boss didn't say a word, but I decided it was going to be impossible to go all day without mentioning the obvious, and so I said:

'That was a horrible business yesterday, they made me take a DNA test and searched my car.'

Gabriel glanced at me briefly, but said nothing.

'I take it you knew I was at the party?' I said.

'Yes,' said Gabriel, 'I did see you there.'

We drove another mile in absolute silence. He began to roll himself a cigarette using only his left hand.

'I didn't give your daughter a lift, you know,' I said.

'Oh, I know that,' he said. 'She got one of her friends from Leiston to pick her up. I knew she would get there somehow. Where there's a will there's a way, I guess.'

'So what did the police say to *you?* I asked, trying to keep my speech as matter-of-fact as possible.

'Not much,' he said. 'They asked me why I was so angry the night before, and I told them. They searched my van and took my phone and examined it for four hours before they gave it back. I didn't get home with Fleur till nearly four o'clock. Later, they came round my house at about six in the evening and searched Naomi's car. They also asked if they could look around the house. I suppose they think we bloody well did it, but I told them straight they were barking up the wrong tree. I told them it's one thing being upset that your daughter is hanging around with a bunch of drugged up hippies at a party, but quite another thing entirely to whack a woman over the head with a hammer or whatever it was. People don't do that sort of thing just because they're angry do they? They do it because there's something wrong with them. I also told them they needed to pull their fingers out, because that killer was still on the loose, and they'd obviously got the wrong man when they arrested that man from Framlingham.'

He put the completed cigarette in his mouth and took a lighter out of his trouser pocket.

Sitting beside him, my first thought was what a brilliant actor he was. But he wasn't fooling me! Lying was obviously a way of life for him. Let's face it, his whole life was a lie, conning old people out of money, slaughtering squirrels after being paid to release them, poaching deer in an area of outstanding natural beauty, cheating on his wife, not to mention murdering people with a survival hatchet...'

'Do you think they've finished with us now?' I asked him.

'Absolutely not,' he said, lighting his cigarette. 'The police told me they'd be back in touch with me, and they also gave me a number to ring *"in case I had anything to share with them,"* as they put it.'

'They gave me a number to ring too,' I said, 'in case I suddenly remember something that can help them. Or perhaps they thought I'd phone them back and make a full confession.'

'It's all a load of baloney,' said Gabriel; 'They took away some tools from my van for the second time. I told them they'd all been tested before. I also told them I've got two vulnerable women in my household and if they'd done their job properly before, they wouldn't still be in danger.'

'More brilliant acting,' I thought.

'So where are we heading today Gabriel?' I asked 'This is the road to Halesworth isn't it?'

'That's right, we're off to do a very important job today. Not in Halesworth itself but in Walpole – that's about two miles outside the town. We've got a lady overrun with bed bugs. She's a lovely old girl, I've been doing jobs for her for years and years, mainly mice in the loft and kitchen. I don't usually do bed bugs, except for the holiday letting companies who pay very well, but hey-ho, another day, another dollar, we'll give it our best shot.'

'How do you think the bedbugs got in her house?' I asked.

'Apparently the poor old dear bought an antique chest of drawers a few weeks ago, and since then she's been bitten all over her body, and the problem has got worse and worse – at least that's what she's told me. So it's very likely the bed bugs were hiding in that chest, and hopped out when they got to their new home.'

'Is that the way bed bugs usually get into people's houses?' I asked.

Gabriel took a big puff on his roll-up, and exhaled smoke through his mouth and nostrils before launching into one of his little speeches:

'Bed bugs,' he said, 'are usually spread by people travelling from one place to another carrying luggage infested with the little devils. Holidays on the continent or further afield in hot countries often result in people bringing them back in the folds of their clothes or crevices in their luggage. Once they get into a house they're the most difficult thing in the world to shift – they'll get just under the buttons of mattresses, in chests of drawers full of clothes, inside light switches, behind books on bookshelves, through cracks in the floorboards, or they'll cling to the backs of pictures and mirrors, that's a favourite hiding place. They're the worst thing of all to try and find, unless you have the right technique and equipment.'

'Both of which I'm sure you have,' I said.

'Indeed I do, young sir. In the back here we have a

secret weapon. We shall have bed bug control at the press of a button. *None shall pass!* Now, who said that? Was it some film or other?'

'I think it was the black knight,' I said, 'in the film *Monty Python and the Holy Grail*. King Arthur tries to get past him and the black night says *'None shall pass!'* and the two of them end up having a big sword fight.'

'Oh yes, I think I remember something about that now. Don't they end up cutting each other's arms and legs off?'

'Something like that,' I said; 'I think it's King Arthur who chops off the black Knight's limbs. Are you a big Monty Python fan, then, Gabriel?'

'Not really,' he said, 'but I liked that one. Fleur was watching it on Netflix, and then Naomi and me sat down and watched it too – that's how I came to see it. Yes, I remember now, it was a very funny film.'

'How is Fleur?' I asked, trying to keep the conversation going.

Gabriel stiffened a little in his seat and threw his roll-up out of his open window.

'I don't really know,' he said; 'She's hardly been out of her room since yesterday evening, but I could hear her on her phone talking to her friends, so I guess she's all right. I told Naomi to keep an eye on her today. She's had a big shock. At least bloody Beatrice won't be trying to drag her off to Australia now. That's about the only good thing to come out of this, I think. Now, let's talk about something else. Who was that young lady I saw you with yesterday?'

'I met her at the party. She comes from Framlingham. She's nice.'

'Does she take any drugs?'

'I don't think so,' I laughed, 'but she does vape. You probably don't know, but more than half of all the kids in school are vapers. It's no big deal, it's just something we do.'

'Vaping? That's a terrible habit! I reckon it's worse for your lungs than smoking cigarettes – at least cigarettes are natural. But vapes use that oil stuff and turn it into aerosol. It looks like the fogging chemical we're about to use to kill bed bugs. I have a funny feeling that when all you young people grow old you'll develop all kinds of horrible lung diseases.'

'You're probably right. Judging by the way some of my friends are coughing now, I think they'll be lucky to make it into old age.'

'There you go,' he said; 'It's better to stick to old-fashioned cigarettes, if you have to smoke at all.'

Our somewhat strained conversation was cut short, as we arrived in Walpole and pulled off the main road into a big yard covered in pea-shingle. In front of us was a large sprawling bungalow with a Nissan Micra parked just outside the front door.'

'Excellent,' I said, 'No staircases to negotiate.'

'That's right,' said Gabriel 'but it's got three huge bedrooms and two large sitting rooms, plus the kitchen and bathrooms. But don't worry, as I said, we've got the secret weapon in the back. And I'm going to train you how to use it, so that if ever you go into the pest control industry, you'll have yet another string to your bow.'

'Maybe I'll go into business around here and see if I can steal some of your customers,' I said.

'You can try,' said Gabriel, half-smiling, 'but even though you've been working hard all summer you've only learned about one tenth of the things you need to know. Pest control may look like easy money to some people, but doing it properly is actually a lot harder than you think. That's why I often charge people a fair old whack. You see, they're paying for something they would never be able to do themselves. Lots of people buy chemicals and rat bait off the internet these days, and half of them are doing themselves a lot of harm, or poisoning their cats and dogs, and in some cases even their children. Some of the stories I've read on social media are enough to make you weep. So today, young sir, I'll be showing you how to do things the right way.'

'Good,' I said, trying to show some interest, 'I'm looking forward to it.'

A few seconds later, we were standing by the open front door.

'So, Mrs Block,' said Gabriel, 'What are you going to do while Ivan and I are fumigating your house? I told you it won't be ready for you to go back in until two o'clock.'

'Oh, don't you worry about me – I'm off to my sister's house in Halesworth, for coffee. Then we're going to have a look around the charity shops and get lunch at the Angel Hotel. I won't be back here until about three at the earliest, so, as I said on the phone, when you finish, leave the key under the blue flower pot at the front. That's the blue one with the geraniums, not the green one with the begonias.'

'Your key will be ready and waiting, madam,' he said.

'Now, how much do I owe you?' said the lady taking out her purse.

Gabriel's eyes lit up a little, as he said:

'Now let me see... there's five big rooms at fifty pounds per room which comes to two hundred and fifty, plus VAT makes, let's see, three hundred exactly. You said you'd pay cash, think?'

'Yes, that's right,' she said, 'You know I always pay you cash, and expect a really good job for my money.'

'Don't you worry about that,' said Gabriel, watching her counting the money, 'When we've finished there won't be a bed bug left anywhere in the house, I promise you.'

'Good,' she said, 'I've been bitten all over my body for the last three weeks. I've been putting it off and off, as I've read on the internet how difficult it is to get rid of bed bugs, but I'm trusting you boys to do a good job and not poison me with any dangerous pesticides.'

She handed over the cash and Gabriel stuffed it into his trouser pocket.

'Much obliged,' he said, with another of his little smiles.

The lady put her purse back inside her handbag and walked over to the Nissan Micra, got in and started the engine. With some very loud revving and a lot of manoeuvring she managed to turn it around, and drove it towards the gate. Even though she was still in her own driveway she signalled left before pulling out onto the road and disappearing down the road.

'Now then, young Ivan,' said Gabriel, 'It's time to do a bit of fogging. Not those puny little canisters we used before in Orford, but a proper man-sized machine that'll have those bed bugs on the run in two shakes of a lamb's tail. Now, take a good look at this little beauty.'

He opened the rear doors of the van, to reveal a strange looking gadget resembling a giant hairdryer. It had various pipes, tubes and an electric motor fixed on top of its circular plastic tank. It was about eighteen inches tall, and I guess the tank part of it held about a gallon of liquid.

'Very impressive,' I said. 'What is it?'

'That, young Ivan, is *an ultra low volume portable fogging applicator.* It is already fully loaded with the most powerful bed bug-busting chemical known to man, called Cyper-Regulin. It's a bit like the chemical we used on fleas in Orford, only a lot stronger, with an IGR that remains active for six weeks. And, of course you already know that IGR stands for...'

He raised his eyebrows at me.

'Insect Growth Regulator,' I chipped in.

'Ha! You remembered,' he said, with his first proper smile of the day. 'Now, we'll put on overalls, plastic hats and shoe-covers, and prepare our full-face respirators. And Ivan, remember, on no account when you start to fog, must you remove your gas-mask.'

'Just out of interest,' I said, 'What would happen if I

did?'

Gabriel laughed aloud.

'In that case,' he said, 'You'd be leaving here in an ambulance – you have been warned.'

'Jeez,' I said, 'In that case, do we *both* need to suit-up and go in?'

'Absolutely,' he said, 'for reasons of safety. Why do you think I employ you? This is a two man job. One of us fogs, the other opens and closes the doors and makes sure the electric cable doesn't get snagged. If one of us collapses or passes out, the other must drag him out into the fresh air. Do you think you can do that?'

'I think so,' I said. 'But if we're fogging, won't it saturate our clothing and necks and hair and so on with chemicals?'

'Of course,' said Gabriel, 'It's a fogging machine, isn't it? But as long as you keep your mask on, as I said, you'll be fine. You can have a good shower when you get home. And there's one good thing about using Cyper-Regulin, too...'

'What's that?' I said, rising to his bait.

'Well, if you happen to have any fleas or lice on you, you'll soon be one hundred per cent insect-free.'

He slapped me on the back, and had a little laugh to himself, as he connected one end of the electric flex into the ULV machine.

'Now, let's get suited-up and go take a look in the house. We'll rehearse our route through the rooms before we start. It only takes two minutes to fog each room, but we must make sure every trunk, chest of drawers and wardrobe is opened so as to receive the chemical. If Mrs. Block was listening when I talked to her on the phone, all the beds will already be stripped and ready, and she should have put away all foodstuffs, toothbrushes, pet food and suchlike. If not, that's her fault.'

'Just one more question,' I said, 'If these chemicals are so dangerous, couldn't they kill Mrs. Block too?'

'Probably,' he shrugged, 'Who knows? Wouldn't catch me using chemicals like these in my house, I'd rather have the bedbugs. Now let's get on with it, no more talking.'

Ten minutes later, and we were busy doing the fogging, Gabriel operating the ULV machine and me helping guide him as he started at one end of a room and walked backwards. I made sure the cable didn't trip him up, and closed each room's door after he had given it the required dose of poisonous fumes.

Gabriel was right about one thing, the stuff coming out of the machine did look like exhaled vape, but the quantity and thickness of it was extraordinary. After two minutes in a room, it was almost impossible to see, and our face masks soon misted over. We wiped them on our sleeves, and made our way around as best we could. Finally, we backed out along the hall toward the front door. Gabriel pointed at the ULV machine's plug in the electric socket, and made signs to tell me to pull it out. Finally, cable in hand, I backed out the door and Gabriel slammed it shut. The whole horrible procedure had taken us a mere twenty-five minutes.

We hauled off our masks, and actually did a high-five.

'I'm alive!' I said.

'Thank God that's over,' said Gabriel.

Then I noticed that fog was escaping from the front sitting room through a small window at the top of the frame which had been left open.

'Look,' I said, pointing it out to my boss.

'Bugger,' he said, 'I'll have to go back in and close it. It won't make much difference to the effectiveness of the fog, but Mrs. Block will blame us if someone gets in and burgles her before she gets back.'

Even in the open air, our clothes and overalls stank of chemicals. The areas of our upper bodies not covered by masks and plastic helmets, that is, our necks, ears, and the backs of our head, were wet and clammy with the noxious fog.

Our attention was taken by a black cat, which walked past us and leapt up onto a tall shrub which happened to be growing next to the front window. Before we realised what was happening, the cat leaned back, then sprang straight through the open window, into the swirling fog!

Gabriel swore, and rapidly put on his mask, but not his hard hat. Then he unlocked the door again and disappeared into the mist. I heard some muffled swearing, and then a loud crash. The cat sprinted out the front door, and I waited for Gabriel to re-emerge.

Seconds passed. Half a minute. One whole minute... and still he didn't come out.

'Gabriel,' I shouted through the front door, 'Are you all right?'

No reply.

I called again, but there was only silence. Wisps of fog wafted out of the front door. I realised something was wrong, and put my mask and hat back on, then ventured into the hallway. The door to the living room with the open window was ajar, just to my left. I entered the foggy room, and a grim sight met my eyes.

Gabriel was lying on the floor, next to a coffee table on its side and a broken porcelain vase. His head, with mask dislodged, was next to the tiled fireplace, which housed a black wood-burning stove. I realised that he had somehow tripped over and hit his head, and in so doing, had knocked off his mask.

I knelt beside him and replaced the mask over his face, adjusting it to fit as best I could. I could see that his eyes were glazed and rolling in a most disturbing way, but before I got him out of there, I checked him over for broken bones. Not detecting any fractures, I decided to drag him out through the hallway – carrying him was not an option, he was just too heavy. So I got my arms under his armpits and, by going backwards, I pulled him out of the sitting room, along the hallway, and out into the fresh air.

I laid him on the gravel, and yanked off his mask. His eyes were still rolling, but I could see the rise and fall of his chest, so I knew that at least he was still alive. But a cursory examination showed that he had an ugly lump on the side of his head where he had fallen and struck the wood burner.

'Gabriel, Gabriel!' I said, slapping him lightly on his

cheeks, 'Are you all right?'

His eyes rolled briefly back down to their proper positions, and he groaned aloud, just one word:

'Ambulance!' he said.

Then he seemed to pass out again.

I took out my phone and dialled 999, and went through the barrage of questions, beginning with *'Is the patient breathing? Is the patient conscious? What address are you calling from?'* and so on, for about five minutes. I was told an ambulance was on its way, and would take an estimated thirty to forty minutes, and that I must stay with the patient until help arrived.

I must admit, kneeling beside him there, the thought that he might die was foremost in my mind. His skin colour was deathly pale, and his breathing was shallow, but it was the rolling eyes I found most disturbing.

To my great surprise, after about ten minutes, he came round to something near consciousness. His eyes rolled back and he tried to focus on me. His breathing returned to something like normal, and his mouth began to move.

'Did you... lock up the house?' was the first thing he said.

'Don't worry about that,' I told him, 'I'll sort it all out in a minute. But first we'll get the ambulance crew to check you over.'

'My head hurts,' he said.

'You had a fall,' I said, 'and landed on the fireplace.'

'The cat,' he said, 'did you get the cat?'

'The stupid thing ran out again,' I told him.

'Ah,' he said, that's good. Now help me up...'

'I'm not so sure you can stand,' I said.

'Help me up...'

'No,' I said, 'You've got to be checked over.'

'Take my keys,' he said, trying to reach in his trouser side pocket, but his fingers only fumbled against his overalls.

'The keys,' he said, 'You'll have to drive.'

'You may have to go to hospital,' I said.

'Yes,' he said, 'but if I do, drive my van back home. You know the way, don't you?'

'Well, yes,' I said, 'I suppose so.'

'Then take the keys,' he said.

I reached inside his overalls, felt down to his trouser pocket and took out his big bunch of keys.

'My ankle,' he said, 'It hurts too. The left one... take a look, will you?'

I rolled up his overalls and trouser legs. Sure enough, his left ankle was about twice the size of the right one.

'Oh dear,' I said.

'Is it broken?' he asked; 'It's beginning to throb. I feel sick, too.'

Then he passed out.

Thirty minutes later, to my enormous relief, an ambulance came screeching down the road from the Halesworth direction, and pulled onto the gravel forecourt. In a few seconds the two paramedics, a man and a woman, were kneeling next to Gabriel, one on either side, and I stood back, keys in hand, to see what they would do.

I was relieved to see Gabriel regain some level of consciousness again, after they gave him some oxygen and moved him into the recovery position. After only five minutes of questions, feeling his various wounds and other examinations, the two attendants rolled Gabriel onto a stretcher and got him into the ambulance.

'Get the van back to my house in one piece,' was the last thing Gabriel said to me, his face a picture of agony.

'Don't worry,' I said. 'I'll be extra careful.'

Though he was now speaking more or less coherently, he didn't look at all well. His skin was still white and sickly, his features were contorted with pain and his ankle looked awful.

I asked the woman driver, as she closed the rear doors, what she made of Gabriel's injuries.

'We're not really sure' she said, 'but possible concussion, possible fracture of the ankle, and some kind of chemical exposure, from the smell of him. In case we get asked at the hospital, what kind of chemicals were you using?'

'Strong ones,' I said. 'I think they were maximum strength Cypermethrin with Insect Growth Regulator.'

She wrote this down on a little notebook.

'And what's the trade name,' she asked.

'It's called Cyper-Regulin,' I told her, 'and it's for bedbugs. He got a big lungful of it, I think.'

'Yes, I thought so,' she said, opening her door and getting in. She wound down her window.

'I wouldn't do your job,' she said, as the blue lights began to flash again, 'for all the tea in china.'

The ambulance did a three-point turn on the forecourt and sped off down the road. I watched it go, until it disappeared over the brow of a hill, and the siren grew fainter and fainter.

Then I looked down at the bunch of keys and saw the ones to the van, his house and the big barn where he kept his secret stuff – and straight away, I knew what I must do.

Chapter Sixteen:
Caught In The Act

Monday 25th August, 11 a.m.

Not wanting to suffer the same fate as Gabriel, I put on my mask and carefully made my way through the house. Once in the living room, I put the coffee table back in place and secured the window through which the cat had entered. After clearing up the bits of broken vase and leaving them on an old magazine on the sideboard, I locked up Mrs. Block's bungalow and put the key under the blue planter as she had instructed.

Next, I decided to phone Naomi to let her know what had happened to Gabriel. As I didn't have her mobile number, I called the Millers' landline, but nobody picked up the phone and I could only leave a message on the answering machine. I tried to be as optimistic as possible, giving a brief account of the accident, and saying that I was sure Gabriel would be OK after his fall, but had been taken to hospital as a precaution.

I took off my overalls and threw them in the back of the van, then made sure that everything in there was more or less secure, including the fogging machine which had been partly responsible for Gabriel's injuries. Then it was time to start up the Scudo and make my way back to Fordley. I was extremely nervous, as I had never driven a van that size before, and the controls felt stiff and unwieldy to me. Nevertheless, I made it back to the outskirts of Gabriel's village without a serious mishap, though I must confess I caused the van to have a few scratches by driving too close to a hedge when passing a car on a stretch of narrow country road.

Of course, when I reached Fordley, I had no intention of going directly to Gabriel's house, for, being now in control of his big collection of keys, my only thought was to have a look inside that barn, and, hopefully, find the evidence that would prove conclusively that he was the man the police were looking for. True, it was a pretty sneaky thing to do, taking advantage of my boss while he was sick in hospital, but I felt no loyalty to Gabriel at all, and if I could bring a serial killer to book, my actions were justified a thousand times over. Even so, as I parked on the concrete driveway in front of the big barn, I still felt a pang of guilt. What if I were wrong, and it turned out that Gabriel wasn't the serial killer after all? Could my gut instinct be incorrect, after all?

But then I thought of Gabriel losing his temper in front of all those people at the party, his anger towards Beatrice and most probably her entire family, and the way he'd slaughtered Mrs. Dove's cow without batting an eyelid, and then all doubt seemed to leave me. Yes, I would make a thorough search of the Millers' secret lock-up, and with a fair wind and a bit of luck, I might soon be able to go to the police, and the long and anxious ordeal of my summer job would be over.

I selected the correct key and first opened the padlock. Then I used a brass key to open the big mortise lock. I tugged at the big, heavy door, and it swung slowly towards me with a loud creek. I stepped inside, switched on the strip lights, and took a deep breath.

It was only then that I realised what an enormous task lay before me. There were stacks of boxes, trunks, tool chests, racks of shelving and various items of furniture all the way around the building, which was a good thirty feet long and fifteen wide. It would be impossible to make a thorough examination without moving a lot of that stuff, so I was going to have to be careful I got everything back in the same position when I'd finished so as not to be detected.

After depositing the ULV fogging machine in a corner, I started looking through the boxes and trunks to the left of the door, gradually working my way around the walls in a clockwise direction. The objects I came across were mainly antique and vintage items, the sort of thing that might be found in a collector's market, such as books clocks, engravings and oil paintings, porcelain and earthenware, dolls, teddy bears, gramophones, enamel signs, one or two old cameras, a rack of second-hand clothing, framed mirrors, a concertina and other musical instruments, and box after box of old tools and car parts. The first thing that really took my attention was a trunk of boots and shoes. I searched through them diligently looking for a pair of size twelve boots with smooth soles and that tell-tale defect on the left heel – to no avail. There were plenty of items of footwear, of various sizes up to men's elevens and women's nines, but none sufficiently large, or with the damaged heel as outlined in that summary sent by the case detectives to their Chief Constable.

Of course, the other item I was desperate to find was the hatchet or small axe which had been used as the murder weapon. While it was unlikely it would have been placed back with the other tools in the junk store, I still had to eliminate the possibility of it being there, or perhaps being hidden behind the boxes or high up on the top of one of the shelves. Though the store contained a couple of large tree felling axes, some butchers' knives, several claw hammers and a pickaxe, I was pretty sure that none of these would have inflicted the type of wounds that were present on the victims.

For nearly an hour I worked my way through all the boxes and obstacles, but to my great dismay I did not find that clinching piece of evidence that I needed. I'd been putting everything back in place more or less as I found it as I went round the room, and I was just about to leave, when I heard the sound of a vehicle pulling up outside.

I felt a nervous churning in my stomach as I went over to the door and looked out. Much to my surprise, I came face to face with Walter Tranmer.

'Hello, young man,' he said, 'I was just driving past when I saw your boss's van outside and I thought I'd have a quick word with him.'

'I'm afraid Gabriel's not here,' I said; 'He had a little accident and had to go to hospital, so I drove the van back for him.'

'I'm sorry to hear that,' said Tranmer, 'Nothing too serious I hope?'

'He fell over a coffee table and hit his head,' I said 'and his ankle doesn't look too good either. Also he inhaled a lot of bed bug chemical.'

'Good gracious! He really is in the wars by the sound of it,' said Tranmer. 'Well, I hope he's soon on the mend. Ask him to give me a ring when he's back in harness, will you? I've got a bit of an issue with the pig pens, where the rats are beginning to take over, so I'll need an extra visit on top of the quarterly one in the contract. Tell him I don't mind paying a bit extra but I need him over at the farm as soon as he can get there.'

'I'll tell him as soon as I next speak to him on the phone,' I said.

'You do that, young man,' said Tranmer, turning to go. 'By the way, how much longer will you be working for Gabriel? The summer is getting on now and I expect you'll be off soon?'

'Yes, this is my last week, I'm off to study in Cambridge soon.'

'Cambridge, eh? Well, that'll be a big change for you. I take it you decided not to make a career in pest control then?'

'Not just yet,' I said; 'It's been an interesting experience to say the least, but I can honestly say I'm not tempted to take it on as a career.'

'No, I didn't think you would. I expect you think the same way as my granddaughter Laura. She loves the countryside and she loves being on the farm, but she can't wait to get away to do her studies. I offered to send her to agricultural college and then train her to be my manager, and you know what she said?'

'I have no idea.'

'She said "Thank you very much Grandad, but I've already decided I want to go to the Royal College of Art in London". Well, I know her teachers said that she's a very talented girl, but she could have done her art as a hobby couldn't she? But now she's been accepted, and she's off in September, so I guess I won't be seeing very much of her in the future.'

He looked rather sad, his lips compressed as if he were trying to control his feelings.

'Oh, it's only a short-term, she'll be back for Christmas before you know it,' I said.

'Yes, I suppose you're right. Ah well, can't stand around here talking all day. Don't forget to give Gabriel my message when you see him.'

'I certainly won't,' I said.

As Tranmer pulled away in his old green Land Rover, black diesel fumes billowed into the yard before the barn, making me cough. I took one last look inside the barn, thought that everything looked more or less as it should, then closed the door. I turned the mortise lock, then put the big padlock back in place. I was just about to get back in the van and drive it down the road to Hawthorn Cottage, when a thought came into my mind.

I walked a short distance along the concrete drive to the old farmhouse and surveyed the scene of dereliction in front of me. The windows and doors were boarded up, and brambles and nettles grew right up to the front door. To the left of the building was an open cart shed, empty except for the rusting hulk of an old Morris Traveller, its tyres flat and its bodywork and windows covered in white streaks of birds' muck. To the right of the house was a huge open sided Dutch barn. The only things now sheltering under its rusting tin roof was an old seed drill and an ancient red Massey Harris combine harvester.

But then something caught my eye. Between the Dutch barn and the farmhouse was a tangled mass of brambles, but strangely, through the middle of the scrub was a path, leading round to the back of the house. It was only about a foot and a half wide, overhung by the thorny plants, nettles and dry grasses. It must have followed the line of the original path. I immediately wondered whether it led to the back door of the house, so I walked forward and made my way through the thorns and weeds to see where it might take me. Much to my surprise, the path led straight past the back door of the house, which, like the front door, was boarded and showed no sign that anyone had been there for a very long time. The path, however, went straight on, and in a few seconds I could see where it ended up. Ahead of me was a small outhouse, the original outside toilet of the farm. I walked up to the door and saw that somebody had put a metal clasp and padlock on it. I found this rather strange, for, what could they possibly be of value in a decrepit old building like that? I tried all the keys in the bunch, but found that none fitted the lock, which seemed to be in reasonable condition.

Back at the van, I was about to get in when I had another surprise. Who should come driving along in her red Renault, but Naomi Miller – the very person I least wanted to see that time. Now I had some explaining to do, and I had to think quickly.

She got out of her car, looked at me, nodded, then walked over to the driver side of the van, no doubt expecting Gabriel to be sitting there.

Finding the van empty, she turned to me once more.

'Where's Gabriel?' she asked, looking very surprised.

'I take it you didn't get the message I left?'

She took out her phone, and looked at it.

'There aren't any messages on here,' she said.

'No, I left it on the landline,' I explained. 'Gabriel had an accident, a bad fall, and hurt his head and ankle.'

'Oh my God!' she said, 'What on earth happened?'

I told her the whole sorry story, of the bed bugs, the fogging machine and the accident caused by tripping over a coffee table. I mentioned that he had breathed in a bit of the fog as well, and that the ambulance crew had decided that he needed to go to Ipswich hospital as a precaution.

'Oh my God!' she said again.

'I'm sure he's going to be all right,' I said hastily. But, judging by the horrified look on her face, she was far from reassured.

'I'll phone the hospital straight away, and see how he's doing,' she said. 'I'm going to have to go there as well. But Ivan, what exactly are you doing here? And why are you driving Gabriel's van?'

I felt my face growing red, but tried my best to be as matter-of-fact as possible.

'Oh, he told me I have to get the van back to your house, and I, er, decided to put the fogger back in the barn.'

'Did Gabriel tell you to come here?'

'No, that was my decision. It absolutely reeked of the chemical we used, so I thought it best to put it back in the barn as soon as possible.'

She stared at me blankly for a few seconds.

'You decided that on your own?'

'Yes,' I said; 'The smell was terrible. On the way back...'

'Was it?' she said. 'Just give me the keys, and I'll quickly open up the barn. You shouldn't have come here on your own, but I guess it's all right, just this one time.'

I handed her the keys, and followed her over to the barn. She opened the two locks and pulled open the door. Once inside, she switched on the lights and cast her eyes around.

Having followed her in, I pointed out where I'd put the fogger, on the floor in the corner.

'I hope it's OK over there,' I said.

This she ignored. She took several more seconds scanning the barn, before looking at me for a second.

'All right, let's go,' she said.

We walked back outside and she locked up again.

'Wait a minute,' she said, 'I've just thought of something. If you leave the van back at the house how are you going to get home? I'm going straight up to

Ipswich hospital, and I haven't got time to take you back to Middleton. If Gabriel said it was OK for you to drive the van this far, I think it'll be all right if you take it back to your house. As soon as Gabriel's back home, I'll give you a ring and you can bring the van over, and I'll run you back to your house.'

'That sounds sensible,' I said.

'It's settled then,' she said, taking out her phone. 'You go home now, and take the van. And Ivan–'

She gave me a long, penetrating look.

'Yes?' I said, trying not to betray the sick, nervous feeling in my stomach.

'Please don't come to the barn again on your own, you understand me?'

'Yes, of course,' I said.

Despite my best efforts at self-control, I could feel that my face was still flushed, and likely to be giving me away.

I got into the Scudo, manoeuvred it back far enough so that I could turn around, and set off towards Middleton. I felt both uneasy and relieved at the same time, sensing that I had aroused Naomi's suspicion, perhaps thinking that I was there to steal goods from their lock-up, but satisfied that I had offered a reasonable explanation for my actions.

Having the rest of the day off, the first week-day I hadn't worked for the whole summer, was a novel and pleasant experience. Once home, I checked on the BBC's news website for anything connected to the Minsmere murder, but nothing had been posted. I listened to the latest radio news on BBC Radio 5 Live, but again, there was no breaking news of a murder in Suffolk. That was very typical of the local police in this series of murders, withholding information from the media, or asking journalists not to break the story until they were ready for a news release delivered on their own terms. I wondered how they would excuse themselves, for charging the wrong man and letting the real killer carry out another sixth murder.

Relieved that the media storm had not yet broken, I cooked a pleasant lunch of my speciality, spaghetti and passata, and took a long shower. Once dressed again, I phoned Esme, and asked if I could come to her house a little earlier, and she seemed very pleased with the idea. Then, leaving a note for my mother, I set out in my own car for Framlingham. I stopped on the way at Peasenhall village shop and bought a bottle of red wine, a rather tasteful bouquet of small flowers and two watermelon flavoured disposable vapes.

I reached Gainsborough House at five minutes to five, and before I went in I phoned Gabriel's number, but the call went straight to his answering service. I left a message for him to phone me as soon as he was able. Not having Naomi's number, I couldn't ask her for an update on Gabriel's condition, so it would be up to her to get in touch with me with any important news. Then I put my phone away, and tried to put all thoughts of the Millers out of my mind – which was easier said than done.

Esme was wearing a long Indian cotton dress, and her chestnut hair was tied back in a pony tail. She was not wearing her glasses, and her eyes had been made up with skilfully applied eye liner and mascara.

'Hello, you,' she said, as she opened the door. 'Long time no see. How did the woodworm spraying go today?'

When I told her my boss had inhaled chemicals, cracked his head and probably broken his ankle she burst out laughing, then put her hand over her mouth.

'Sorry,' she said, 'I'm sure the poor old man is in excruciating pain, but I can't help thinking it's a case of karma – he seemed an absolutely awful human being, and if ever anyone brought misfortune on himself, it must be him. I didn't like the look of his wife, either. I only feel a bit sorry for their daughter.'

'Yes,' I said, 'It's a pity children can't choose their parents.'

'Yes – but let's not get started on that one. And I don't want to talk or think about our horrible Sunday, either. Let's talk about something else. Do you realise you have rather a nice a bunch of flowers in your hand?'

'So I do,' I said; 'Would you like them?'

I gave her the bouquet. That earned me my first kiss. I was still holding the bottle of red wine.

'If I asked you to open that bottle right now,' she whispered, 'would you think I was an alcoholic?'

'Probably,' I said, 'but I'll open it anyway. I brought you a couple of watermelon flavoured vapes too.'

'How well you know me,' she said, with her arms still

wrapped around me. I received my second kiss, then she took me into an enormous sitting room. It was full of antiques, with a big oil painting of deer drinking water at a highland stream hanging on one wall.

'Is your father a bank robber?' I asked, staring at the picture. She punched me playfully in the ribs.

'No, he builds houses.'

'What – he's a builder?'

'Well, he doesn't personally put the bricks on top of each other, but have you noticed how all the fields around here are getting built on and concreted over?'

I said that I had noticed such things.

'Well,' she said, 'most of that is my father's doing. I think his ambition is to turn the whole of Suffolk into one enormous town.'

'I see,' I said.

'And what does *your* father do,' she asked.

'He runs off with secretaries and disappears, mostly, I said, 'but I did once get a Christmas card.'

'Any money in it?'

'Not a penny.'

'Poor you.'

'Yes poor me. Now, shall we drink some of this wine, or shall we wait till six o'clock?'

'Oh, I think it's close enough to six for us to have a little glass right now,' she said. 'Now, let me see the vapes you have in your hand.'

I gave them to her, and she smiled broadly.

'*Lone Tiger* brand,' she said, switching one of them on. 'You do realise these are the ones unscrupulous shopkeepers sell to small children?'

'Is that bad?'

'It's terrible,' she said, taking a long draw. She exhaled luxuriously. 'Still, they seem to work all right. Here, take a pull.'

Not wishing to disappoint her, I sucked on the vape.

My head swam for a second or two, and I gave it back to her.

They seem to be very strong,' I said.

She nodded sagely.

'That's so children get addicted quickly and come back for more.'

'It certainly worked on you,' I said.

'It certainly did,' she said, taking another puff. 'Now, are you hungry?'

'I'm always hungry,' I said. 'What have you got?'

'I've got pasta, or... pasta.'

'Pasta would be nice.'

'With pesto or passata?'

'Do you know,' I said, 'that I'm going to have pesto, just for a change.'

'Red or green pesto?'

'Red.'

'I was hoping you wouldn't say that, I've only got green, but I did make it myself from pine kernels, fresh basil, parmesan cheese and olive oil. By the way, you haven't opened my wine yet.'

'You mean *our* wine.'

'A Freudian slip,' she said; 'You caught me. Now, let's put on a movie, and then we can ignore it and stare in each other's eyes instead of watching it.'

'What film do you have in mind?'

'Oh, I think it should be something really cheesy... how about *Breakfast at Tiffany's,* or *Four Weddings and a Funeral?'* I know, better still, we'll watch *Jules et Jim,* by Francois Truffaut – that'll help the red wine go down.'

'Is it romantic?'

'I'd say more tragic than romantic. It's about a woman who gets involved with two men who are best friends, and can't really decide which one to live with and marry, so she gets off with both of them, and keeps swapping her affections from one to the other.'

'What a bitch,' I said, before I could stop myself.

'I'd say she was more a child of her passions, rather than a truly bad person. Her problem is that she just can't bear to part with either man.'

'How very French of her,' I said. 'We'd better watch that one, then. Do you have something I can use to open this bottle?'

We were still hugging, and I still had the bottle in one hand. She showed no inclination to let me go as she said:

'The corkscrew's in the drawer of the chiffonier. Try not to spill red wine on the white carpet.'

'I'll be very careful,' I said. 'By the way, will you marry me?'

'Pardon?' she said, pushing me out at arms' length.

'I want to be the first one to propose to you, so I'm asking you to marry me.'

'That's very sweet of you,' she smiled, 'but what happens if you decide you don't like all my bad habits?'

'I'm prepared to take a chance,' I said.

'Wait here,' she said, and left the room. She came back with something small and shiny in her hand.

'What's that?' I asked pointing to her hand.

'That,' she said, 'is my grandmother's engagement ring. I'd like you to put it on my ring finger and then we'll see how we get on.'

'Good idea,' I said, 'Plus, you've just saved me a lot of money.'

She punched me quite hard in the ribs and gave me the ring. She held out the ring finger of her left hand.

'Now,' she said, 'Do you have something nice you'd like to say to me?'

'Yes,' I said, 'I do. Every time I look in your eyes I feel all funny inside.'

'You mean I make you feel sick?'

'Not exactly,' I said. 'It's more a kind of warm feeling, and it makes me want to hug you.'

'You do realise this means I could treat you horribly and exploit you and you'd just come back for more?'

'Like those two poor men in Jules et Jim, you mean?'

'Something like that. Now stop talking and put on the ring.'

I slipped the ring on her finger.

'Now *I* feel all funny inside,' she said. 'Do you think you could possibly stay here all night and stop me from feeling so lonely?'

'I'll text my mother,' I said.

'Do you need her permission, then?'

'No, but she'll worry if I'm out all night.'

'That's good,' she said. 'It shows you don't usually stay out all night with wild women.'

'I did on Saturday night,' I said.

'Was she really that wild?'

'Actually not so wild,' I said, 'apart from her heavy drinking.'

That earned me another dig in the ribs.

'I love the way you throw a punch,' I said.

'Thanks,' she said, 'Now get the corkscrew and open that bottle.'

I found the corkscrew in the chiffonier drawer. There were also a set of well-used cards. For some reason I picked them up and saw, from the picture card on top, that they were tarot cards. Esme saw me looking, and came over to take them off me and put them back in the drawer.

'Yours?' I asked. 'Do you read the tarot?'

'Sometimes,' she said with a twinkle in her eye, as she closed the drawer. 'I'll just get us some glasses.'

'Talking of glasses,' I said, 'why aren't you wearing yours tonight?'

'I put in some contact lenses,' she said, 'especially for you. How do you like me with my lenses in?'

'You look good,' I said, 'but I must confess I like you equally well with or without the glasses.'

She moved in closer for a kiss.

'You really are so sweet,' she said, closing her eyes. 'Now stop talking and hold me for a while, and we'll make each other feel all funny again.'

The pasta was so good that next morning I ate the leftovers that were still in the pan for breakfast. I have to admit, Esme's delicious home-made pesto was much better than my own passata sauce. The dessert was home-made chocolate mousse, which was pretty wonderful too. In fact, the way I see things now, everything about Esme is pretty wonderful.

'Do you really have to go now?' she said, as she gave me a farewell hug at her front door at seven a.m.

'I'm afraid so,' I said. 'I got a text last night telling me to take back my boss's van back first thing this morning. It looks like he's going to be discharged from hospital, so I might have to work today after all. But I'll be back at seven this evening – if you like...'

'My folks aren't back till Saturday,' she said, 'and as far as I'm concerned, you can stay round here till then.'

'In that case,' I said, 'I'll try my hardest to get myself fired today. Anyway, if it turns out that Gabriel Miller is wearing a plaster cast, or is still somehow incapacitated, that will pretty much wrap up my summer job, and I'll be back here as soon as I can.'

'All right,' she said, as I walked over to my car, 'See you later... and thanks for the ring. It was a very nice gesture, even if you didn't mean it.'

'When I said those things last night,' I said, 'I must admit I was only half-serious, and being a bit whimsical because I was sure you'd say no.'

'But I didn't say no,' she said.

'And you didn't say yes, either.'

'Let's keep it that way,' she smiled, 'and as I've already told you, let's see how we get on.'

'All right,' I said, opening my car door.

'But tell me one thing, before you go... if I'd said yes, what would you have done then?'

'In that case,' I said, 'You wouldn't have needed your grandmother's ring.'

'What do you mean?'

I took out from my pocket the diamond ring I'd inherited from my own grandmother, and held it up for her to see. The early morning sunlight lit up the several diamonds, and glinted off the ancient yellow metal.

She stopped smiling, but her eyes were still wide and loving, only filling with tears, beautiful tears.

'You're such a fool,' she said, blowing me a kiss, and then slowly closing the door.

CHAPTER SEVENTEEN:
A HARD TASK MASTER

Tuesday 26th August

By the time I'd driven home, then taken the Scudo van to Gabriel's house it was just after eight-thirty in the morning. I had hoped that Naomi would be in, and able to ferry me back home to Middleton in her car, but as I parked on the edge of the road outside Hawthorn Cottage I could see that, much to my disappointment, Naomi's car was not in their driveway. I didn't have her mobile number, so, still sitting in the driver's seat, I decided to phone Gabriel's mobile and see if Naomi was with him at the hospital, and ask if he were likely to come home that day. I had just selected his number and was just about to press the green 'call' button, when I saw a news update notification appear on my phone, with the *title*
'Suffolk Murder: Woman found dead on driveway, not linked to East Coast Killings, say police.'
I read through the BBC News article, and was utterly astounded to learn that while Esme and I had been cooking pasta and drinking red wine, Suffolk Constabulary had delivered their news conference, and taken the line that Anne-Marie Chalmers may have died as a result of a domestic dispute! What idiots Suffolk Constabulary were, I thought.

My focus on this astonishing piece of news was suddenly broken by the sound of a car coming along the road behind me. A quick glance in the wing mirror revealed that it was Naomi's Renault Clio, and as she drew closer I could see she had Gabriel sitting beside her. My heart sank a little, as I'd hoped my boss might be detained in hospital for a while, thus giving me a day or two off, in which case I was going straight back to Esme in Framlingham.

Naomi pulled into her driveway, and both front doors of the Renault swung open. Much to my surprise, Gabriel got out unassisted from the passenger side, and hobbled back up the drive to talk with me. Naomi followed just behind him, and I got out of the van, taking the keys with me, to see what they had to say.

Gabriel spotted the slight scratches on the passenger side wing of the Scudo, and tutted loudly.

'Ah, well,' he said, 'could've been worse.'

'Sorry,' I said, 'A car forced me into the hedge. But never mind that, how are you?'

Gabriel half smiled, and touched his head.

'I've still got a big lump right here,' he said, 'but the doctors told me I've got off lightly – no broken bones, and the effects of that fogging chemical wore off pretty quickly. The trouble is, I've got a swollen ankle, so I won't be able to drive for a couple of days.'

'That's a pity,' I said.

'Yes, it is, but with your new-found van driving skills, we can still get around and try to catch up with the jobs we've missed.'

'Surely you don't mean to try working today, on that dodgy ankle of yours?'

'That's what *I* told him,' said Naomi, 'but he's determined to get on with things.'

'Too bloody right I am,' said Gabriel, 'I've a list of six jobs we have to get through today. They're mainly wasps and hornets, so you'll easily to able to cope, and in any case I'll be right behind you to make sure you don't mess up.'

My heart sank even deeper, but I tried to put on a cheerful face.

'All right,' I said, 'I'm game. Where do we go first?'

'Oh, there's no rush,' said Gabriel, 'First we'll get you some coffee while I take a shower and get some clean clothes. Then we'll decide which route to take, and I'll fill you in with details of the jobs. And if you cope OK, I'll up your wages a little bit, as you'll be doing more than usual. How does that sound, young fellow?'

'Great,' I said; 'Though I'm a bit nervous about driving all day. By the way, have you seen the news?'

'Yes, and it's terrible to have another tragedy like that making this area look so bad. But I look on it this way, there's nothing we can do about it, and we'll just have to put up with police and lots of nosy reporters buzzing about looking for murderers all over again. Naomi and I discussed it on our way back home, and we've just decided to put it out of our minds and get on with our work. But forget all about that, I'm more concerned with your driving. Let's not put any more scratches on the van, so be extra careful and don't let any more cars force you off the road.'

'All right,' I shrugged, 'I'll try my best.'

'Good man,' said Gabriel. 'Now let's get that coffee, and maybe a bacon roll – or toasted cheese in your case, I think.'

An hour later, and we were standing outside a house in Saxmundham, ready to dust a wasps' nest located in a crack in the brickwork over our heads. I had to attach two six-foot hollow aluminium tubes together, and screw in a hollow spike at the business end. The other end was connected to the dust-pot apparatus, which was a small cylinder with a pumping plunger sticking out the top. By charging the dust-pot with compressed air the dust-pot could blow permethrin dust through the tubes and spike into the hole. I had to wear a beekeeper's suit and veil to keep me safe from the angry wasps, while Gabriel kept a respectful distance and looked on approvingly.

'Good job, Ivan,' he said, at the end of the procedure, with the sixty-five pounds safely in his pocket. 'Now we do the same thing again in the next street. Then we've got another one in a hole in the ground at Thorpe Ness golf course, and one in the roof of a thatched house at Knodishall.'

'I can't wait,' I said, as I removed the bee suit. My shirt and jeans were soaked with sweat, the temperature being close to thirty degrees centigrade.

'That's the spirit,' laughed Gabriel, slapping me on the back; 'You're beginning to get the hang of these dusting jobs.'

'But I'm boiling in that damned suit,' I complained.

Gabriel shrugged.

'Maybe you won't need it at the next job. Anyway, we'll stop at the convenience shop and get you a cold drink in a minute.'

One cold can of cola later, and then we tackled the one a few hundred yards away in an adjacent street. Soon we were on our way to Thorpe Ness, which was about nine miles away. We were travelling in silence, when Gabriel suddenly said:

'Naomi says you went into our barn yesterday afternoon. Why was that, Ivan?'

'Oh,' I said, 'That fogging machine really stank, it was making me feel sick, so I decided to put it in the barn.'

'You could have opened the van windows, though.'

'I tried it, but I could still smell it.'

'Even though it was sealed in the back?'

'Well... yes, I could. That chemical smell really got to me.'

'Yes,' said Gabriel, 'I can understand that. It really got to me, too.'

He let the matter drop, and contented himself with rolling a cigarette. I glanced sideways for a split second, and had an impression of Gabriel wearing a sly, knowing expression. I had no doubt that both he and Naomi were suspicious of my reasons for going in the barn. My guess was that they believed I might steal something from their vast horde of goods, and if this was so, I was happy for them to believe it. I just wondered what he would say if he knew I was thinking of going back and somehow getting into that locked outhouse. The more I thought about that trail leading through the bushes, and the fact that the padlock on the door was in such good condition, the more I was convinced I might find something conclusive. I had an even greater sense now, that time was running out if I were to claim my bounty money, with only this week to go before my employment with Gabriel ended. Adding to my sense of urgency was the fear the police might any day now beat me to it, and come up with some forensic or other evidence linking Gabriel to the murder of Anne-Marie Chalmers. The wonder was that a whole army of detectives had so far failed to connect him to this, or any, of the six shocking murders.

The wasp nest at Thorpe Ness turned out to be an easy one, and I didn't even have to wear the beekeeper's suit. Then we were on the road again, a short four mile hop to the next job.

'Stop over there by the pink house,' said Gabriel, as we slowed down by the wasp-infested thatched cottage at Knodishall. A little old lady came out to greet us.

'They're in my thatch,' she said, 'Thousands of them, just above the dormer window.'

'Oh, yes,' smiled Gabriel, 'That's another one we can do from the ground. And they're so high up, you won't need the bee-suit.'

'Thank God for that,' I said.

I had just opened the rear doors to get out the dust-pot when a car pulled up behind our van. It was a big Land Rover Discovery, a new diesel model in shiny silver paint. Two men got out and walked up to Gabriel.

'Gabriel Miller?' said one of them, holding out his

warrant card. 'I'm Detective Chief Inspector Derek Smethurst, Suffolk Criminal Investigation Department. Can I have a word with you?'

'I suppose so,' said Gabriel, 'But how did you know I was working here?'

The two policeman exchanged glances.

'Never mind that for now,' said DCI Smethurst, 'We'll talk over here in my car. If you'd like to get in the back, I'll keep the air conditioning on, and that way we'll stay cool.'

The three of them got into the Discovery, their doors closing behind them, and their windows staying firmly shut. Being rather surprised by the police's sudden and unexpected arrival, my thoughts were racing to the conclusion that Gabriel Miller had finally been rumbled, and my reward money was lost. Despite my huge disappointment, and trepidation over what might happen next, I decided to busy myself with the wasp nest, just to give myself something to do as I mulled over this latest development.

I opened the back of the van and put on latex gloves, then got the dust-pot and extension poles ready for action. At the front of the house, high above the front door, was the dormer window. In the thatch just above it was a round hole about two inches in diameter. The wasps were flying in two distinct streams, one going into the hole, the other leaving it. As I attached the six foot poles together I tried to guess what the CID men were asking Gabriel. No doubt they wanted to establish whether he had returned to Rowan Tree Farm early in the morning on Sunday with murderous intent. Perhaps they had gleaned some evidence of his journey there, or found his DNA, or fibres of his clothes on the body. Whatever the reason for the interview, it took only about thirty minutes to complete. By this time I had finished dusting the wasp nest, and knocked on the cottage door to receive the payment. A few minutes later, as I was just putting the dust-pot and poles away, a rear passenger door of the Land Rover opened and Gabriel got out. He had a one of his strange half-smiles on his face as he limped over to me. The police car remained where it was, the engine still running. I imagined the two detectives discussing their findings, perhaps trying to decide whether to take Gabriel Miller back to Martlesham Heath police headquarters for more interrogation, maybe even to charge him.

But no: the Land Rover's engine revved slightly, the driver indicated that he was about to pull out, and the vehicle moved off. We watched it go, in silence, as if under a spell. Gabriel fumbled in his cargo trousers pocket for his tobacco.

'Are those wasps all dead?' he asked quietly.

'Yes, and I've got the money, too.'

I handed it over, and he stuffed it in a side pocket without checking the amount. As he rolled the cigarette, I decided not to ask him about his meeting with the police.

Twenty minutes later, as I drove us to the next job, much to my surprise Gabriel broke the silence.

'Well, Ivan, what do you make of that? Those

policemen knew exactly where we were, yet we'd told nobody where we'd be today.'

'Do you think they came looking for us, then?'

'I suppose so,' he said, rolling his cigarette, 'but we could have been anywhere in Suffolk or beyond. It doesn't make sense.'

Then, a thought struck me.

'It's your phone, Gabriel – they must have tracked you by tracing your phone signal.'

Gabriel slapped his knee, as if the penny had dropped.

'The silly fools – why on earth are they interested in me?'

'I've no idea,' I said. 'What did they ask you?'

He licked the edge of his cigarette paper and rolled the tobacco into a thin white tube. He lit his roll-up, and drew the smoke deep into his lungs.

'First they asked me if I had any means of transport, other than the van. So I told them I often used Naomi's Renault, especially at the weekends.'

He paused, smoking his cigarette.

'Was that all?' I asked; 'You were in their car for quite a while.'

'They asked me if I'd been angry with Anne-Marie Chalmers and her husband for letting the kids have an unruly party.'

'What did you say?'

'I told them the truth,' he said, 'That it was bloody Beatrice who got my goat, she was the one I blamed for letting her friends get drunk and drugged up. Also, I said that although I was angry about a bunch of kids being given the means to go haywire, I didn't feel so mad about it that I'd actually *harm* anybody.'

'And what did they say?'

'Nothing – that's the thing about those plain-clothes officers, they were so smug and insulting, trying to get me to lose my cool and say something incriminating. But when I asked *them* why they were wasting their time talking to me, when the real killer is still out there, they just said they were *'following several lines of enquiry.'*

He puffed on his cigarette, his brow wrinkled, and for once, that strange little smile was banished from his face. After a brief silence, he said:

'I even asked them outright if I was a suspect, and they just looked at each other, but wouldn't say either yes or no. Then they came out with the biggest insult of all – asked if I'd ever had any problems with my mental health. So I told them straight again, I said talk to your own firearms department, they've already got the answer to that.'

'What do you mean by that, Gabriel?' I asked. 'How do the firearms department know about your mental health?'

'Because, Ivan, like all certificate holders I'd consented to let them ask that question to my doctor in Saxmundham. And he would have said Mr. Miller has never had any mental health problems. These days, firearms certificates are simply not granted to anyone who has the slightest mental defect. They even bar you for minor bouts of depression or anxiety, or things like that. But I've never had the slightest problem. If those policemen had done their homework they'd have known that. So why pick on an ordinary citizen like me, with his mental health already investigated, when there were hundreds of people there at that stupid party, some of them high on drugs, too? Then there were the other parents coming and going, picking up their kids. Perhaps the real killer was one of them.'

I have to admit, his protestations of innocence, and his facial expression of righteous indignation were pretty convincing. This was his most believable performance yet. I almost felt sorry for him. I had to tell myself again, that I was sitting beside a ruthless killer... wasn't I?

By a quarter to five we were back in Fordley, parked outside Hawthorn Cottage.

'That's enough for today,' said Gabriel; 'My ankle hurts, I've got a headache and I don't feel quite right. On the positive side, we've polished off all the outstanding jobs without crashing the van. Well done, Ivan, I'll give you a hundred for the day instead of eighty.'

'Thank you,' I said.

'I'll get Naomi to run you over to Middleton, while I get myself some tea and paracetamol. See you tomorrow at eight-thirty sharp. Come over here in your own car, of course.'

He left me standing on their driveway while I waited for Naomi. It was a full ten minutes later before she came out, no doubt after hearing a summary of the police's interrogation of her husband. On the way back to Middleton she stared straight ahead at the road, offering not a word of conversation.

Back in my own home, I let the dog out into the garden, then phoned my mother to see if she was on the way home. She was able to reply, as her car had the latest hands-free technology.

'What's up, darling?' she asked. 'Where are you, Ivan?'

I told her I was home, and about to get a shower and go over to Esme's house.'

'That's a pity,' she said, 'I was looking forward to seeing you. I'm just setting out from Ipswich, I'll be back in forty minutes. Can't you wait till then, and we'll have a meal together? You can go to your girlfriend's place after that.'

I agreed to wait for her, and she rang off, which, I am afraid to say, was my cue for entering her office and using her password and security number to log on to Suffolk Constabulary's PDCS network. I went straight to her emails, and found in the 'sent' messages two that had just been despatched to the Chief Constable. The first one had the title *'Summary for C.C./Re: Today's Press Conference'* and had details explaining that there would be another televised Press Conference and an appeal for information pertaining to the Minsmere Murder, which would go out live at 6.30 p.m. Senior detectives had been deciding whether to present this as the latest murder by the East Coast Killer and admit they had the wrong person in custody, or continue to treat the death of Anne-Marie Chalmers as a one-off. As there was no forensic evidence to link it to the sequence of five murders, the senior case detective, named as Chief

Superintendant Robert Kepler, had ordered that this second news conference should persist with the one-off incident approach until they had definite proof of it being the sixth crime carried out by a single killer.

After reading this message, my first thought was once again, *how could they be so stupid?* Surely the method of killing Mrs. Chalmers was reason enough to deduce that this was the sixth killing by the same person? And yet the public would be told that the Minsmere killing was not connected to the other murders. Evidently, after amassing evidence against Gerald Hadiscoe, some senior detectives were still clinging to the idea that he was their man.

I went to the second email marked *'Summary for C.C./Re: Suspects Minsmere murder/ Latest evidence.'*

It stated:

'Investigations into this case are of course ongoing, but initial investigations do not point to the guilt of the husband Daniel Chalmers, nor the instigator of an altercation at the young persons' party on the evening of 23rd August, name of Gabriel Miller. It is of note that this gentleman and his wife Naomi Miller were questioned by DCI Smethurst on April 21st after the Fordley murder occurred near to their home. Apart from the obvious fact that a serial killer does not leave bodies on his own doorstep, DCI Smethurst had satellite trackers placed on the Millers' vehicles on 29th April, the correct legal guidelines having been adhered to. The tracking data proves conclusively that both the Millers' vehicles were stationary outside their house at the time of the Minsmere crime which occurred at approximately 7.05 a.m. on 24th August. While Gabriel Miller did drive to Rowan Tree Farm at 8.45 a.m. to pick up his daughter who had stayed overnight with the Chalmers' daughter overnight in the farmhouse, he is just one of 23 parents who turned up during the morning to retrieve their sons and daughters. Therefore, Gabriel Miller's proximity to two murders has been conclusively shown to be coincidence.

As indicated in yesterday's summary, there were no witnesses to the murder, the first on the crime scene being the daughter Beatrice Chalmers at 7.10 a.m. followed by Daniel Chalmers at 7.12 a.m. While it is possible the latter did follow his wife out of the house earlier and then return indoors, thus allowing his daughter to discover the body, this theory has been shelved for the time being until motive is established or further evidence is forthcoming. Daniel Chalmers' DNA, clothing fibres and bodily fluids including perspiration were found on the body, but this is to be expected and deemed normal in the case of a husband and wife relationship.'

After scanning the rest of the summary I found nothing else of any great significance to the Minsmere crime, nor was there any other information of note in the rest of my mother's correspondence. I took a photocopy of each email, and logged off, being careful to leave everything in the room just as my mother had left it.

I went into the kitchen, and sat down. I breathed a long, drawn-out sigh of astonishment. So, according to this summary, Daniel Chalmers was a possible suspect! While I had no doubt as to his innocence, I was also not surprised that the cold and calculating detectives were keeping him on their list of suspects. With so many murders perpetrated by family members, it was normal practice to scrutinise relatives during their enquiries.

Of greater surprise to me was the fact that electronic trackers had been placed on the Millers' vehicles in April at the behest of DCI Smethurst, and that Gabriel did not drive to Rowan Tree Farm before 8.45 a.m. in either his van, or in Naomi's car. This seemed on the surface of it to let him off the hook. And yet, my first thought was *there had to be a third car*! I had followed Gabriel Miller around all summer, had seen his horrible character at close quarters, while all the time my gut instinct told me he was the guilty one. But the team investigating the East Coast Killer at Suffolk Constabulary had looked closely at Gabriel Miller, suspected him to the extent that those tracking devices were secretly placed on his vehicles, but then used the data collected to virtually dismiss him from their enquiries.

Given their findings, logic seemed to dictate that I, too, should give up my attempt at proving Gabriel's guilt, and admit that I had made a huge mistake. And yet, try as I might, I could not give up the notion that I was on the right track, that eventually I would find something that proved, once and for all, that he was the killer.

Glancing at my watch, I saw that it was now 6 p.m., thirty minutes before the latest TV news conference. I went to the freezer, selected a family sized ready-made vegetable lasagne and read the instructions. Oven cook in forty-five minutes, microwave in fifteen. As my mother pulled up outside, I put the lasagne in the microwave oven and set the timer.

By 6.30 p.m. I had greeted my mother, made a salad and phoned Esme to say I would be over at eight. With the lasagne ready, my mother and I sat down in the lounge for a TV dinner. We watched together in silence for twenty minutes as the grisly news was announced. The concluding sentence of Chief Superintendant Kepler was *'We are not at present linking this murder with any crimes committed earlier in the year, but we are keeping an open mind at this stage because of the possibility of copycat murders.'*

'I suppose you knew this would be on,' I asked my mother innocently.

'Yes, of course,' she said; 'It was pretty much the same stuff they put out twenty-four hours ago, except that tonight they added on the appeal for information. They also gave out a few more details about the murder, now that they've got all their facts straight.'

'But they *haven't* got their facts straight,' I said. 'The murderer is still on the loose. Do you think the detectives could have arrested the wrong man when they took in that Hadiscoe fellow? That would mean the *real* East Coast Killer is the one responsible for the Minsmere murder.'

My mother gave a little start of surprise.

'That's exactly what half of the staff at headquarters are saying. And the other half think it's either a different murderer or a copycat killing.'

'It doesn't give me much confidence in the police,' I said. 'If the killer is still out there, he's been at it for eight months, and they're no nearer to arresting him now than they were in January.'

She shuddered.

'Yes,' she said, 'I don't feel safe, even at home. Good thing I've got you in the house – well, some of the time anyway.'

'I'm off out again in a minute,' I said, a little shamefacedly. 'Esme is expecting me.'

'*Please* stay here with me tonight, Ivan. Do you really have to go there again tonight? After all, you hardly know her.'

'She's the one, Mum, I've met the one I really want to be with.'

'That's what you said about Georgia, and she turned out to be a right little cow.'

'Esme is different, in so many ways.'

'And what happens when you get to Cambridge? You'll both be meeting lots of new friends, how will all that work out?'

'It'll work out fine,' I said. 'Now, tell me something: you've listened to the senior police talking about this latest murder. Do any of them still think that my boss Gabriel miller is responsible?'

'What makes you ask that?'

'An officer called DCI Smethurst interrupted our work and questioned him for thirty minutes. I'd say that means he's still a suspect.'

'If he'd been a *prime* suspect they'd have taken him in for questioning. I can't really give too much away, but I can tell you Gabriel Miller is absolutely *not* under scrutiny for the murder, it's just that every possible avenue has to be followed in these cases. If Gabriel Miller was ever a prime suspect I'd not let you work with him, you can be sure of that. I told you before, your boss is an odd one, but that doesn't mean he's any more likely to commit a murder than we are.'

Half an hour later, I'd got myself ready to see Esme. I made my excuses for leaving my mother alone, and drove off in the direction of Framlingham. I felt strangely uneasy, guilty that I'd broken into my mother's private stuff once again, and that I'd left her alone when she'd specifically asked me to stay. Her words were still in my mind, too, that Gabriel was no more likely to commit a murder than we were. Once again, doubt seized hold of me, and I felt myself half accepting that he was, after all, innocent.

Then, half way to Framlingham, like a bolt of lightning it struck me: *I have to go back to Hawthorn Farm to check out that building behind the farmhouse.* Something deep inside me told me that, hidden in that dilapidated outhouse was the evidence I needed. And even if I were wrong, I nevertheless had to look behind that door, or be forever wondering if my instincts, my gut feeling, were right after all.

CHAPTER EIGHTEEN:
PARTNERS IN CRIME

Wednesday August 27th 1 a.m.

It was one o'clock in the morning. I lay wide awake in Esme's arms, her bedroom lit by the last light of a single candle on her antique dressing table.

'I have to go,' I whispered.

Her eyes flicked open, and she said, very sleepily:

'You're having second thoughts about me, and you're going back to Georgia, aren't you?'

'Good gracious no!' I said, 'Whatever put that thought in your head?'

She sat up, propped herself on one arm, and looked me in the eye.

'All night you've been kind of distant, distracted. You've said some sweet things, but there's definitely something wrong.'

'Everything's all right,' I said, 'But there's something I have to do. Something really, really important.'

'Something really, really more important than *me*?'

'No,' I said. 'Absolutely nothing is more important than you.'

She smiled, sleepily.

'You'd better tell me what it is,' she said, 'that would get you out of bed at one o'clock in the morning.'

'It's that murder thing,' I said, we talked about it earlier, that horrible thing that happened after the party.'

'I knew it!' she said, seeming suddenly to be fully awake. 'I thought it was that – and I bet it has something to do with that creepy old boss of yours.'

'How did you know that?'

'I kept thinking about seeing him after the murder, and I had a really uneasy feeling. I think he might have had something to do with Mrs. Chalmers' death.'

'To tell you the truth, I think the same. But how did *you* come to that conclusion?'

'Call it intuition... but we can soon find out for sure if he's involved.'

'How?'

'Wait here,' she said, 'and I'll show you.'

She slipped out of bed, threw on a dressing gown, and left the room. Two minutes later she returned with something in her hand.

'What's that you've got?' I asked.

She held out a pack of cards so that the candlelight caught them.

'Are we going to play cards or something?'

She sat on the edge of the bed, very beautiful in the flickering light.

'It's a tarot pack,' she said. 'Have you ever come across them before?'

'Not really, I've only seen them in films and things. I take it you know how to read them?'

A slightly devilish look came into her eye.

'Oh yes,' she said. 'The cards are going to tell me about this Gabriel Miller you've been working for. Put on some clothes and we'll do a little bit of divining. But be warned, before we find out about your boss, first I'm going to ask the cards about *you*. Are you OK about that?"

'I think so,' I said, feeling slightly apprehensive.

I put on my boxer shorts and T-shirt. She gave me the pack, and signalled for me to sit on the floor near the dressing table.

'Shuffle these,' she said, 'Don't stop till I tell you.'

I did as I was told.

'Now stop,' she said, 'and give them to me.'

'Cards,' she said, *'Tell us all about Ivan Salter.'*

She set about arranging the cards, one by one, face down on the floor. She put five in a cross shape, and another on top of the centre one. Then she put four in a vertical column to the right of the cross. Next, one by one, she turned them over.

'Oh my God,' she said, looking at the cards. 'That explains everything... well, almost everything.'

'Well?' I asked, 'What do they say?'

'You're a liar,' she said.

'Pardon?'

'The cards say you've been dishonest. The one representing your current situation is this one, at the centre of the cross. You got the 'hanged man,' who's suspended upside down by a rope.'

'Is that bad?'

''No,' she said, 'It just means you're seeking some kind of truth or enlightenment, but you've had to surrender something of yourself – I'd say your sense of freedom – to try to get what you want. Your pursuit of your goal means you had to become a liar. But see here, the devil card is on top of the hanged man, keeping him in limbo.'

'Wow,' I said, 'I guess the devil represents–'

'Your boss, Gabriel Miller, I'm pretty sure of that. But look at card three, the top part of the cross which represents future possibility, you've got the knight of swords. That means danger from violence, possibly a knife or other sharp instrument.'

'Now you've got me worried. What's next?'

'Number four, the bottom of the cross, meaning motives or the basis of your actions – you've got the ten of pentangles, you greedy boy!'

'Why *greedy?*'

'Because your real motive is money, as represented by those gold circles around the pentangles. Am I close to the truth? Don't lie to me – please don't ever lie to me, or hide the truth – if we're going to be soul-mates, we've got to be one hundred percent honest, all the time.'

'Don't worry,' I said, looking at the cards, 'I won't ever try lying to you. I think you'd just look at the cards and find me out.'

A small, wicked smile flickered on her face, and she pointed to the next card.

'Position five is your challenge – and your card is the moon, meaning dreams and illusions. The card came out upside down, so it means you are following an illusion, or dream that won't come true.'

'That's worrying,' I said; 'What's next?'

She pointed to the card on the right of the cross.

'This number six position is an important one, it

represents your future, and you've got the lovers card.'

She turned to me and smiled, but then her smile faded.

'But you've got the lovers card upside down, which could mean you don't really love me, and love someone or something even more.'

'Impossible,' I said, and reached out to touch her. But she pulled away, and her eyes flashed in anger.

'No, don't touch me yet. The cards say you've something or someone more important than me on your mind. Let's see what it is, then we'll talk it over.'

She touched the next card, the bottom of the column of four, to the right of the cross.

'This one is the self card, which represents the real you. You've got the chariot, which means you're stubborn, wilful and possibly very selfish when you try to get what you want. This is your worst outcome so far, and I'm getting upset, so we'll move on.'

'The next card in the vertical line of four represents your environment, and you've got the justice card reversed, which means either you're breaking the law, and therefore a criminal, or that you're a person who's doing things you know aren't right.'

I must have looked guilty, as she added:

'Take this as a warning, and mend your ways, young, man.' She fixed me with a scornful look, and held her gaze for several seconds before touching the third card from bottom of the column.

'The penultimate card represents your hopes and fears, and you've got the seven of discs, which represents failure. Needless to say, you're terrified of failure, which brings me to the last and most important card, which represents how the emotional ordeal outlined here is going to end. Do you see the card you got at the top of the column?'

'Yes,' I said, 'I've got temperance. That can't be bad, can it? After all, I could have got the death card, couldn't I?'

'Actually the death card would have meant an end to your suffering and illusions, but let's not go there. Temperance in this position means you'll end up well-balanced and true to yourself, *if* you do the right thing, and get your life back on track.'

'But what exactly is the right thing? It's true, I've got myself in a bit of a mess, trying to get something, but I really don't know what to do next.'

'Take a card from here,' she said, 'and we'll see.'

She held up the pack of cards, the ones remaining after she'd made the cross and column.

'Should I take one from the middle?' I asked.

'From anywhere you like.'

I pulled a card from the pack and laid it on the floor. It was the high priestess.

Esme looked at it, and began to laugh. She looked a bit sinister in the candlelight, chuckling away, rather witch-like, truth be told.

'Don't look so frightened,' she said, 'You just drew the best card you could ever possibly draw.'

'But what does it mean? 'Tell me, for God's sake!'

'All right,' she said, 'I'll tell you.'

She touched the card with a long beautiful finger, the ring finger of her left hand, and the diamonds of the engagement ring caught the candlelight and sparkled for a split second.

'That card is me,' she said. 'That's your salvation. If you let me help you, everything will be all right. If you try to go it alone, well, either the devil will get you with a sharp blade, or you'll end up emotionally crippled and hanging in suspension forever.'

'In that case,' I whispered, 'is there any way you could possibly help me?'

'Yes,' she said.

'*How?*'

'Well, you can start off by telling me the truth. I want to know all your horrible, grubby secrets, all your despicable plans to take over the world or whatever awful thing it is you're planning to do. From what I've seen of you, you're not a bad person, but something must have got a hold of you to make you so weighed down. So let's start at the beginning, you tell me everything, and I'll do my best to make things right for you. However, if you lie to me, or confess to any attraction whatsoever for another woman, I *will* slaughter you. Do I make myself understood?'

'Perfectly,' I said.

It took me nearly half an hour to tell her the whole sorry story of how I'd taken up with a nutty animal slaughterer, in the hope of shopping him for fifty thousand pounds, how I'd hacked into the police website, how I'd endured Gabriel's horrible company and compromised my vegetarian values while I sought out that one piece of evidence I needed to shop him. I finished up by telling her about the Millers' farm, and the locked outbuilding behind the old farmhouse that might conceal something conclusive, and that I couldn't rest or relax till I found out what was behind that outhouse door.

She listened to me without once speaking, her eyes wide with surprise, as I told her about Gabriel's cheerful killing of deer, squirrels, moles, rats and rabbits, how a murder had taken place a few yards from his back garden, how he stole, lied cheated and deceived everyone who came in contact with him, how I believed he was capable of absolutely anything, including serial killing.

After I'd finished, she went over to her dressing table. The luminous digital clock indicated the time of 2.05 a.m. From beside the clock she picked up a vape. Then she returned to the bed, and beckoned me over to her. She took my right hand in her own right hand, and looked me in the eye.

'That was a really horrible story,' she said, 'but tell me something. When you first took up with Gabriel Miller, how long was it before you decided he was the killer?'

'The very first day,' I said.

'So why didn't you go straight to the police?'

'Because I had no evidence that would definitely prove he was guilty, just a gut instinct that he was pure evil.'

'And what was it about him that convinced you he was the East Coast Killer?'

'I saw that he had a small hatchet in his cargo trousers pocket, just the type of thing the newspapers said had been used on those poor women. He used the hatchet that first day I was with him, at the beginning of July, to clear vegetation from rat burrows in a garden so that he could put poison in them. But the thing that took all doubt from my mind was when he killed that cow. It made me feel really sick, and I felt like leaving, that very day.'

'So why didn't you? You could have found another job, if you needed money so badly.'

'I thought about it carefully, but as I'd already had this instinctive feeling that he was the killer, I hatched the plan of sticking with him and finding some evidence to get him convicted. Then I could collect the money.'

'So you're saying the money was your main motive?'

'I have to plead guilty to that one. Obviously I wanted to stop a serial killer, but it was the thought of the money that made me stick with him.'

'I see,' she said, switching on her vape. 'And what about the fact you had to take part in, or at least witness the killing of all those wild creatures, how did you reconcile that with your conscience? After all, you are a vegetarian.'

'I didn't reconcile it at all,' I said. 'And I still feel guilty as hell. But I took the money for the work, so I suppose I'll have to live with it.'

She looked at me with her big round eyes, the look of

disappointment in them painful for me to see. She put the vape in her mouth, and breathed in deeply. She held her breath for a few seconds, breathed out, then handed the vape to me.

'So you really think it's him?' she asked. 'You really think Gabriel Miller is the East Coast Killer, but the best detectives in the area have let him off the hook?'

'That's about the size of it,' I said.

I took a puff of vape, and discovered this one was stronger than usual. It made me cough, which seemed to amuse her.

'That'll wake you up,' she smiled. 'You'll need to be wide awake to drive us over to that farm. That's where you want to go, isn't it?'

'Well, yes, but what do you mean, *we?*'

'If you're going,' she said, 'then I'm coming too, your story's stirred up my curiosity. But first I'm going to ask the cards about Gabriel Miller.'

'To see if he really is the guilty one? Can the cards tell us that?'

'Maybe, let's see.'

She picked up all the cards, and gave them to me to shuffle. Then she took them back and told me to ask the question.

'Is Gabriel Miller the East Coast Killer?' I said aloud.

'Now take three cards, one by one, and lay them face down in a line on the floor.'

I did as I was told, and she turned over the first one.

'The hierophant card,' she said, 'is in the position of the enactor, which in this case is you. It means you are in search of knowledge and enlightenment, which we know already.

She turned over the second card, and smiled.

'The queen of wands card,' she said, 'is in the position of the enabler. This means a female of great strength is part of the answer, but I'm really not sure what part she plays. This card either relates to me, or possibly Gabriel Miller's wife. But it's the third card that shows us the answer – are you ready?'

'I'm ready all right,' I said, feeling my heart beat a little faster. Esme took the vape, and drew in a deep breath, before gently blowing out the sweet-scented fog.

She turned the card. It was the strength card, but was upside down.

'Oh my God,' she said, cupping a hand over her mouth. Her eyes widened even more than usual, and she looked straight at me. '*Strength* usually means balance, empathy, sympathy and good human qualities, but reversed like this represents an evil or amoral character. I haven't been frightened by what you said so far, but this card has put a chill right through me.'

'Yes, but is it him? Does the card say it's Gabriel?'

'It says it's the evil one, so I suppose the answer is yes.'

'That's it, then,' I said, 'I'm going to Fordley.'

I started to put the rest of my clothes on.

'I'm coming too,' she said.

'Are you sure? It's a horrible deserted old farm, creepy enough in the day time, but at night it'll be *really* spooky.

'Yes she said, 'especially if the mad axe-man comes at us in the dark.'

'God, don't say that.'

'I'm kidding,' she said, 'It's two thirty in the morning, everyone's asleep – even serial killers.'

'I bloody-well hope so,' I said, 'But just in case, we'd better arm ourselves with something. Also, we'll need tools to get in that outhouse.'

'Ooh, this is getting exciting,' she said. 'We'd better go take a look in my dad's garage workshop and see what we can find.'

Once dressed – and feeling rather excited – I followed Esme to the big double garage outside. The strip lights flashed on to reveal a shiny new Audi A3.

'Nice car,' I said.

'It's my mother's,' she said. 'Dad's driven them to the airport in his own car.'

At the back of the building was a workbench, above which were various shelves holding a variety of tools.

'This is exactly what I need to remove the lock,' I said, taking down a pair of bolt croppers. There was also a spare brass padlock and key, which I slipped in my pocket, figuring to lock up and seal any incriminating evidence inside when we'd finished investigating. Esme selected a big stainless steel torch, and a large screwdriver. I also asked her to fetch some rubber washing-up gloves from the kitchen, these being needed to prevent me contaminating any evidence with my own DNA and fingerprints. She came back with a brand new pair still in their clear plastic packet. I stuffed these into one of my pockets.

'You do realise,' I said, 'if we get stopped by the police at 3 a.m. we'll be arrested for having these tools. It's a crime known as *going equipped for theft.*'

'I wouldn't worry too much about that,' she said, 'Meeting the police tonight might be the least of our troubles.'

'The farm is half a mile from Gabriel's house,' I said; 'There's no way he'll know we're there, and in any case he can hardly walk at the moment.'

'But just in case,' she said, 'take this.'

She handed me a blue metal crowbar with a tapered end, ideal for forcing a door – or stopping a serial killer in the dark.'

'Thanks,' I said, 'I feel a bit more confident now.'

'Tell you what,' she said, 'If he does come after us, *I'll* dazzle him with the torch, and *you* clonk him on the head with the crowbar – that should stop him all right.'

'Very funny,' I said. 'Now, no more talk, let's just go and get this over with. But, before we go, I'm going to ask you one last time, are you *sure* you want to come with me?'

'Are you kidding?' she said, 'Imagine me lying in my bed worrying while you went there on your own. I couldn't bear it.'

She put down her torch, picked up a small hatchet and waved it around a bit.

'After all,' she said, 'What's the *worst* that can happen?'

CHAPTER NINETEEN:
THE STUFF OF NIGHTMARES

Wednesday 27th August 3.15 a.m.

Driving carefully through the moonlit country lanes, I held Esme's right hand in my own left one, her head resting on my shoulder. From time to time she put one of her watermelon flavoured vapes in my mouth, and I inhaled deeply, the occasional strong hit of nicotine enough to keep me from feeling sleepy.

Through the sleeping villages of Dennington, Badingham and Yoxford we rolled, then into the deep, dark woods between North Green and the outskirts of Fordley.

'We're almost there,' I whispered, and she took one long, last lingering breath of vapour, and made me do the same. I slowed down as we neared Hawthorn Farm, and switched off the car's lights. We drove very slowly onto the driveway, with the storage barn on our right, the farmhouse and its outhouse straight in front of us.

The two car doors clicked open. We got out, brandishing our various tools and the big torch, and closed the doors ever so quietly behind us.

'You were right about it being creepy,' she said. 'That old house looks like something from a Scooby-Doo movie.'

'I ain't afraid of no ghosts,' I said.

She punched me lightly in the ribs.

'That's not from the Scooby-Doo film, that's from

"Ghostbusters". But let's concentrate on the matter in hand. Now, where's this outhouse? I want to get this done as quickly as possible.'

'Straight ahead, here, give me the torch, I'll show you.'

I led her by the hand along the driveway, as overhanging branches, twigs and leaves reached down like fingers in the darkness trying to touch us, as we crept toward our destination. Overhead, partially screened by the trees, shone a big yellow moon, surrounded by wisps of circular cloud that interlocked to form a magnificent dapple-grey sky.

We took the narrow path, walking now in single file, past the decrepit old farmhouse, with brambles, nettles and ragweed brushing our flanks and hemming us in. I pointed ahead, as, looming out of the darkness, the old brick outhouse grew larger and larger as we approached.

Then, we had a shock, as we heard the distant hum of a car's engine approaching from the direction of Fordley village – the direction of the Miller's house. Esme and I froze, as the long, probing beams of the car's headlights filled the road beyond the barn. But the car passed harmlessly by the end of the driveway without slowing down.

'Thank God it's gone,' I whispered.

'Come on,' said Esme, 'Let's go open that door, before anyone else comes, I've beginning to feel a bit panicky.'

I heard her pause and take a deep breath of vape, then exhale, before her hand reached out for mine and we moved on. At the door of the old building, which was no more than six feet wide and eight feet deep, we were confronted by the padlock. I handed the torch to Esme and grasped the arms of the bolt croppers, forcing the jaws open. In a second I had the steel ring of the lock in the jaws. I pushed the two arms together, but at first the lock resisted and held firm. A little more pressure, and I felt the jaws biting, until a loud snapping noise announced the parting of the ring of steel. The broken lock fell to the ground.

I felt Esme's hand squeeze my shoulder in congratulation. I pushed open the outhouse door, and Esme shone the light to illuminate the interior. Howard Carter looking into the tomb of Tutankhamen could not have felt more hope and anticipation than we both felt at that time. For this moment I, in particular, had suffered and striven all summer, in the hope of the reward money, fame, and glory...

But, looking inside, at first my heart sank in disappointment. The only thing visible was a large green canvas cloth, draped over what seemed to be a four feet by two feet irregular box shape. The 'box' was placed touching the right hand side of the outhouse. Ahead of us was the wooden toilet seat with its gaping round hole where Naomi's departed ancestors had once squatted to relieve themselves in days gone by.

'Oops,' said Esme, 'There doesn't appear to be anything here in the crapper. Let's get out of here.'

'Wait,' I said, putting on my rubber washing-up gloves. With my hands now covered so as not to leave my own DNA or finger prints on potential evidence, I took a step forward and pulled at the canvas sheet. After a few tugs I'd removed it from the shape it covered – causing Esme and I to gasp in astonishment.

'Oh my God,' she said, 'So that's how he did it!'

There before us was a motorcycle, a very old scooter, to be precise. Its insignia proclaimed it a 'Honda 90' model. It was a light green colour, with chrome mirrors, handlebars and wheel-rims, and it had a white plastic wind-faring to protect the rider's legs. Hanging off the handlebars by its chin-strap was an old full-face crash helmet with a dark tinted visor. Draped over the seat was an old Barbour waxed jacket, slightly spattered with mud on its lower hem from the road. There was a white top-box behind the seat, bolted to the luggage-carrier. When I opened the box, I couldn't believe my eyes: there before me was a small hedger's bill-hook, a box of latex gloves and a large pair of boots. Even a quick examination of the heel of the left boot was enough to spot the tell-tale damage on the heel, as described in the forensic team's reports.

'Christ Almighty!' I said; 'It's all here, all the evidence, even the damaged heel I told you about.'

I used the torch to peer into the interior of the boots.

'There's another shoe inside it, a sort of sheepskin slipper,' I said. 'And look, there's a kind of curved blade with a hook at one end that could have been used in all the murders. It looks shiny on its sharp edges, as if it's been sharpened fairly recently.'

'What exactly is that thing?' she asked

'I think it's a hedger's bill-hook.'

'That's a gruesome thing to use as a murder weapon,'

she said. 'So the killer must have stashed all this stuff here, then used the motorcycle to get to and from the murders. It's a simple but brilliantly clever way to travel incognito with that visor over his face. No wonder the police couldn't find evidence of a car being used.'

'Yes, they even put trackers on the Millers' vehicles, and the fact these couldn't be linked to any of the crime scenes made the police believe Gabriel was innocent. Wow, what fools those police must be, to let him kill six women so close to where he lives.'

Just then, I felt Esme grip my arm.

'Shh,' she said, 'Stop talking – I think I heard something...'

She turned the weak beam of her phone's light back along the narrow path. I stepped back out of the building and shone the big torch past her. At first, nothing was visible. Then, we caught sight of a dark figure standing in the darkness, its features obscure due to its distance from us.

'Oh my God – there's somebody watching us,' she whispered.

'Who's there?' I said, rather stupidly.

No reply. The figure did not move.

'Phone 999,' I said to Esme.

She punched the numbers into her phone.

'No signal,' she said.

'Keep trying.'

I took the crowbar into my right hand and moved past Esme towards the shadowy figure. The black shape seemed to turn, and move back past the storage barn, then glide towards the road. I followed a few steps, before Esme called out:

'Don't go after him – I'm through to the police, they want to talk to you.'

'Hello,' I said, 'I've found the murder weapon and items used by the East Coast Killer, and I know for sure who he is...'

It took twenty minutes to convince the duty officer at Suffolk police's headquarters at Martlesham Heath that I wasn't a hoax caller, that they must send officers immediately to arrest Gabriel Miller, and that I had discovered items of evidence that proved both the means and method of the murders. Esme and I spent a further nervous twenty minutes waiting for a patrol car to arrive at Hawthorn Farm and secure the site and the evidence. Almost simultaneously, as we learned later, another car went to the Miller's house with instructions to block their vehicles in their driveway and wait for back-up before arresting Gabriel. This caution was the result of my reminding them that Gabriel had firearms and was often in possession of a small but deadly hatchet.

After waving and flagging down our patrol car with two officers on board at the farm, we were told, in no uncertain terms, that we had acted very foolishly by coming to the outhouse by ourselves. Furthermore, when we told them of the shadowy figure, an officer pointed out the danger we were in by staying in the vicinity of the discovered weapon and accessories.

'You put this young lady's life in danger, too,' said the first officer; 'What on earth were you thinking of?'

'Oh, but I insisted on coming,' said Esme, 'though to tell you the truth, until we saw that bill-hook thing I thought we were on a wild goose chase, and that building would be empty.'

'You might still be mistaken,' said the other officer. 'I can't see how you can be so sure you've found the murder weapon.'

Esme and I exchanged glances.

'Not just the murder weapon,' I said. 'That building contains the boots and jacket the killer wore, and the motorcycle he used to get to and from the murders.'

'If what you say is true, you've made a somewhat incredible discovery, said officer number two. 'But how in heaven's name did you happen to come by this information?'

'That's a long story,' I said. 'Let's just say I got to suspect my boss shortly after I began working for him in July, and I've been looking for evidence against him ever since. I suspected he might have hidden the murder weapon in his lock-up in the barn over there, then discovered a track leading to that outbuilding. We decided this morning to take a chance and look in it... and I guess we got lucky.'

'Quite the amateur detective, aren't you?' said the first officer. 'Well, we'll find out later if what you say is true.'

'You seem to have been very clever,' said the second officer, 'but why didn't you come straight to the police as soon as you had your suspicions?'

'Because,' I said, 'I knew he'd already been interviewed and released, so without firm evidence I'd have been laughed at, and told not to waste police time.'

The first officer's radio crackled into life.

'We've apprehended a male,' it said, 'from Hawthorn Cottage, Fordley, name of Gabriel Frederick Miller, and taken away a number of firearms and a quantity of ammunition.'

Esme squeezed my hand, and I breathed a sigh of relief at this news. The voice from the radio continued:

'Miller is now on his way to headquarters, but we need to speak to his wife, Naomi Jane Miller, for routine questioning. She wasn't at home when we arrested the suspect. Her car was not at the property, so she is believed to have driven away in it, a red Renault Clio registration number FB61 VHG. We are currently interviewing their daughter, Fleur Alice Miller, and awaiting a forensics team, who want to conduct their searches here. A second forensics team is on its way to you at the farm, so stay where you are and await their arrival. Detectives are on the way to interview the young man and lady who first alerted us. Are they still with you?

'Roger that,' said the first officer, 'We're still at the farm, and aren't going anywhere.'

He turned to me and Esme, as he said:

'I'm due to finish my shift at eight a.m., but something tells me you guys are in for a long and tiring day.'

That police officer was right. While an officer drove Esme back to Framlingham, I was taken to police headquarters at Martlesham Heath, and spent a gruelling three hours being questioned about my boss, and what had prompted me to suspect him, how I'd managed to find the murder weapon and accessories, and how I'd had the audacity to accompany a suspected serial killer for nine long weeks. After every answer I gave them they seemed dumbfounded, that a mere slip of a lad had likely led to the solving of the case that had perplexed them for so long.

At seven a.m. that morning I'd phoned the Eastern Daily Post to offer them my story and initiate my claim to the fifty thousand pounds reward. Another phone call to my mother left her shocked and confused as she prepared to leave for work. In all my dealings with the police, the Daily Post, and my mother, I'd had, of course, to be ultra-careful I didn't give away the fact I'd hacked into Suffolk Constabulary's communications system. I couldn't, for instance, let on that I knew about that defective left heel of the size twelve boots, nor that the Miller's vehicles had been fitted with satellite-linked trackers. But, all said and done, my illegal hacking – and my mother's giving away confidential police information, for that matter – hadn't been crucial in my finding the evidence.

It had, however, been useful for confirming the guilt of Gabriel Miller – or so I thought at the time.

Alas, my triumph was to prove short-lived.

Two days later, just as Esme and I were sitting in my garden at Middleton, eating our bowls of spaghetti with passata, we were rudely awakened from our loved-up reverie by the arrival of a certain silver-coloured Scudo van. As we sat in our deck-chairs, bowls in hand, forkfuls of pasta half-way to our mouths, who should emerge from that familiar vehicle but Gabriel Frederick Miller himself. Tilly gave a single bark of alarm, then came to my side, half-afraid of this stranger looming over us.

'Hello, Ivan,' he said, half-smiling, *'I've just been released, and if you've got a minute, I've come just come over in person to have a little word with you...'*

CHAPTER TWENTY:
UNEXPECTED VISITORS

Friday August 29th 1 p.m.

Full of fear and apprehension, and caught completely off guard, Esme and I were at first stunned into silence. Then, after scanning Gabriel up and down in a search for weapons, and seeing none, I managed to blurt out:

'Gabriel – we heard you'd been arrested... so how come you're *here?*'

'Don't look so shocked,' he said; 'The pair of you look like you've seen a ghost! Well, the reason I'm here is to give you your last month's money... and clear up a few odds and ends with you. First, here's your wages, with the bonus I promised for Tuesday.'

He handed me an envelope stuffed with cash, his customary way of paying me. By this time I was beginning to see that he wasn't there to murder us, and, apparently, he wasn't even aware that it was because of me that he'd been arrested.

'What happened to you?' I said tentatively, as an opening gambit to draw information from him.

'They arrested me, of course,' he said, his half-smile now fading; 'Took samples of DNA from me again, took my guns away, searched my house, searched my van, put the fear of God into Fleur, and whisked me away to Martlesham Heath. From their questioning, it was pretty clear that this time they really did think I was the East

Coast Killer, and they were really aggressive and insulting to me. At first I answered all their questions, but after a day I told them to go to hell, that they had better charge me or let me go. I went against their advice and declined to have a solicitor come to me, as I've done nothing wrong. All day Wednesday and Thursday this went on, and they kept asking me about a motorcycle I kept at Hawthorn Farm. I told them straight I didn't have a motorbike and that I'd never even learnt to ride one – I went straight from a bicycle to a car when I was seventeen. The only motorcycle we ever had in our household was an old Honda 90 that Naomi's grandfather gave to her when she was in her teens and courting me. But that was over twenty years ago, I haven't seen it since she got a car. Anyway, the police seemed very interested in that, and I told them to ask Naomi about it. I also told them I wanted to see my wife, and it was only then they gave me the news she'd been missing since Wednesday morning...'

A tear fell from the corner of his eye, but he wiped it away instantly. His lips quivered slightly, and he seemed unable to go on.

'What did the police tell you about Naomi?' I asked softly; 'Did they give you any explanations about why she might have gone missing?'

'That's the ridiculous thing,' he said, sniffing, 'They kept asking if Naomi liked to go off on her own, either in her car, or on the motorbike.'

'And what did you say?' I asked.

'I said the same thing I've just told you, that she

didn't have a motorcycle any more, that she always took her car. As for going off on her own, she does have the funny habit of getting up out of bed and going for a walk in the early hours sometimes when she can't sleep... you see, she's had insomnia for years and years now, ever since we lost our little boy. She's been on several kinds of tablets for her depression and anxiety, too, but that's nothing special – half the world takes something or other for their nerves or whatever.'

Esme and I exchanged glances.

'Mr. Miller, where does she go,' asked Esme, 'when she gets up and goes for walks?'

'Well, I don't know for certain as I'm not with her, but in the daytime she likes to spend hours and hours up at the barn packing up things she's sold on eBay, so every time she's out of the house I just assume she's gone there. The police did say she might have been spotted there on Wednesday morning, in the early hours.'

'Did they say *who* saw her there?' I asked.

'No, not at all, I suppose it was the same police they sent to arrest me and search my property. But why the hell have they got it in for me, Ivan? I've always obeyed the law, and never did anything to make them suspect I might be some sort of *serial killer*. I mean, that's just bloody ridiculous...'

'Yes, of course it is,' I said. 'But why do *you* think Naomi has gone missing, and where has she gone? Does she have any relatives in the area?'

Now the tears began to flow down Gabriel's cheeks, and this time he didn't brush them away.

'I can't think why she went off like that,' he said. 'She doesn't have any close relatives any more, only her great-uncle Walter who said on the phone he hasn't seen her for weeks and weeks. The police went there too, and were told the same thing. She does have a cousin, Miriam, who lives in Woodbridge. She last saw Naomi two weeks ago, and the police say they've also visited her address, and drawn a blank.'

'Hasn't Naomi contacted you,' I asked, 'using her mobile?'

'No,' he said, 'and I can't get through to her when I ring her number. So, either her phone is out of charge or it's switched off, which tells me something is very, very wrong. I had to buy a new phone, by the way, as the police have still got mine.'

'What about her car?' I ask; 'Haven't the police been able to find it?'

'She has her car with her, but it's as if she and it have disappeared off the face of the earth. Unless... unless... *the killer's got her!*'

Here he burst into tears, unable to continue. He sobbed and sobbed, falling onto his knees, the very picture of a broken man.

I had a brief impulse to go to him and put an arm around him, but after a second's thought I found this idea quite repulsive. Esme and I exchanged another long look, and we both knew what the other was thinking: *how could Gabriel Frederick Miller, this wreck of a man, be the East Coast Killer?*

From what Gabriel had said, the only logical

conclusion was that Naomi Miller was the guilty one. *Naomi Miller!* Could she *really* be the murderer of those six women? If so, why would she do these things? And where was she now?

The other question in my mind was why, even now, had Gabriel Miller not worked out or accepted that his wife was the most likely the serial killer? Surely the police must have told him that Naomi was a wanted person. But the man seemed to be stuck in a state of deep denial, believing Naomi herself was a possible victim of the East Coast Killer.

'Gabriel,' I said, 'Can you think of any other place she might go to avoid the police?'

'That's the thing,' said Gabriel, 'There's no other obvious place. I'm completely stumped. I can only think that something terrible's happened to her and now she's unable to get in touch with me.'

We were interrupted by the arrival of a familiar vehicle which pulled up behind Gabriel's van. It was a silver Land Rover Discovery, and one of the two men who got out and showed Gabriel his warrant card was none other than our old friend DCI Derek Smethurst.

'Good afternoon,' said the detective, 'I've come to speak to you, Mr. Miller.'

'I would have thought you'd seen enough of me lately,' said Gabriel. 'And I won't even bother asking how you knew I was here.'

'Oh, we have our methods of finding people,' said Smethurst. 'Now, Mr. Miller, there's no easy way for me to tell you this, but I'm afraid I've got some rather bad news.'

'Have you... found my Naomi?' asked Gabriel, wiping his eyes with the back of his hand.

'If you'd like to come with me,' said Smethurst, 'I can talk to you in private.'

He led Gabriel over towards his car, but this time they didn't get in. Instead, they stood talking on the roadside for about fifteen minutes. Then the two officers got in their Land Rover and drove swiftly away.

Gabriel walked back to where we were sitting. Strangely, though he'd looked shattered and broken before, his face had now taken on its customary frozen half-smile, which, given the circumstances, I found rather sinister.

'They're found Naomi's car,' he said, with one hand gently rubbing his temple. 'It turned up in a car park next to Dunwich beach. A fisherman saw a woman swimming out to sea this morning – fully clothed, so he said – and called the coastguard. When the local police arrived they recognized her car. The coastguard and police have been there all morning, some of them riding up and down the beach on quad bikes, and a helicopter is searching the sea, but they haven't found her... yet.'

'That's dreadful news,' I said. 'I hope they find her safe and well soon.'

'There's more,' said Gabriel, still rubbing his temple. 'They told me Naomi is wanted as a suspect in the East Coast Murders case, and in the unlikely situation she turns up at home, I have to contact them immediately. But what the hell are they on about, saying Naomi is a *suspect?* My Naomi would never harm anybody, there must be some mistake. I'm telling you for a fact, it just doesn't add up. And, good Lord, Ivan, what am I supposed to tell Fleur? She's been questioned several times by the police, and what with me being taken into custody, and her mother missing, the poor girl's already in a terrible state.'

'Would you like us to go and speak to her?' asked Esme. 'I know we hardly know her, but she might need someone her own age to talk to.'

'That's very kind,' said Gabriel, 'but she's already with someone her own age. You see, when I got back this morning I discovered Beatrice was in my house staying with her. Apparently, she turned up two days ago.'

Esme and I exchanged yet another look of utter surprise.

'My first instinct was to throw that little bitch out,' said Gabriel, 'but on reflection I suppose it's probably a good thing they have each other as... you know, *friends.*'

There was a long period of awkward silence, with Gabriel, head bowed, continuing to massage his temple.

'Ah, well,' he said, finally, 'I suppose I'll go over to Dunwich and see if I can help find her. Maybe she's swum up the coast a bit, and come ashore somewhere further along the beach. She's always been a very strong swimmer, so it's possible she's gone a very long way. Or maybe the police have found her safe and well somewhere on the beach already. Anyway, I'm off now to see what I can do.'

Gabriel's hand dropped to his side, then he slowly

turned and walked, with shoulders drooping, back to his van. He got in and drove off, without even bothering to put on his seatbelt.

Esme got out of her deckchair and came to kneel beside me, then placed her arms around me.

'After all that,' she said, 'I think I need a hug.'

'Me too,' I said; 'Looks like I was wrong about Gabriel Miller after all. Bang goes my reward money, too.'

'But it was still your information that led to Naomi Miller being shown to be the killer. In a minute you should call that newspaper contact of yours and give him an update.'

'Good idea,' I said. 'I'll tell Bill Tweedie at the Daily Post that the evidence we unearthed relates to Naomi Miller, not her husband.'

We were silent for a while, held in each other's arms, still digesting the afternoon's startling news

'Poor Fleur,' said Esme, breaking the silence; 'How on earth will she deal with the worst possible news about her mother?'

'And God knows what all this will mean for her relationship with Beatrice,' I said. 'But do you think that Naomi Miller really is the east Coast Killer? Only a short time ago we were absolutely sure that Gabriel was the guilty one, now we're faced with a completely new reality.'

'Yes,' she said, 'I've been thinking about that. The things Gabriel Miller just said about the police questioning him make it pretty certain it's Naomi who's the real serial killer. After all, if it's not her, who else could it be?'

'I wonder,' I said, 'if *Fleur* knows how to ride a motorcycle?'

'Surely not!' said Esme; 'I really can't imagine her being, you know, some sort of killer. Besides, the three card tarot spread we did seemed to point to someone older. That 'strength' card in the last position usually relates to a mature person, not someone who's just left school.'

'I think you're right. The way I see it, Fleur is just the unfortunate and slightly grouchy child of horrible parents. But before I phone the Eastern Daily Post, I have to be certain. So, there's only one thing for it – I have to check the police computer again to see what forensic evidence they got from that outbuilding at Hawthorn Farm.'

'Oh no!' said Esme, recoiling from me, and placing me at arm's length. 'You absolutely can't do that. If you get caught doing that, you'd be in such a heap of trouble, it doesn't bear thinking about. I'd hoped you were finished with that hacking business, once and for all.'

'But I *have to*, Esme,' I said, 'It's the only way to find out for sure what forensic evidence the police uncovered from that bill-hook, clothing and motorbike. I've got to be sure that the stuff in the outhouse is linked only to Naomi Miller.'

'Who else would it be linked to, Ivan? You've already given the police the vital evidence they needed to catch a serial killer, so why risk getting yourself in trouble now that you're almost home and dry?'

I know I should have taken her advice. But, fool that I am, I decided I had to do things my way. So, at 5.15 p.m. when I knew my mother would be on her way home, I left Esme in the garden and went to my mother's room. I had just hacked into Suffolk Constabulary's supposedly secure network, when I felt a soft hand on my shoulder.

'Oh Ivan,' whispered Esme, 'I don't like it. I'm worried for you.'

I kissed her hand, then resumed my work by getting straight into the summary my mother had completed only thirty minutes earlier, a document destined for the Chief Constable's inbox. Despite her reservations, Esme remained with me, and soon we were both staring at the forbidden data before us.

In my mother's 'Sent email' I soon located a message sent to Richard Garnham with an attachment that bore the now familiar title of: *Summary for CC/ Latest Developments/ East Coast Murders'.*

Part of the document read:

'Results of the forensic tests on the bladed instrument recovered at Hawthorn Farm show traces of 3rd, 5th and 6th victims' blood is present on the blade and handle. Traces of blood of these two, plus victim 4 also found, despite attempts to clean, on the right sleeve of the Barbour jacket. The boots show the defective heel print detected at murders 2, 3 and 6. All the items recovered from the shed at Hawthorn Farm bore the DNA of Naomi Miller. The motorcycle was in good running order, and had been used recently. The crash helmet also showed traces of hair and other

DNA from Naomi Miller. The sheepskin slippers inserted in the size 12 boots also showed her DNA.

NOTE 1. the working hypothesis is that these slippers were worn inside the boots to disguise her true shoe size.

NOTE 2. It appears Naomi Miller employed great cunning and skill in locating and stalking her victims and avoiding detection.

Note 3. She apparently guessed her car might be fitted with a tracker and on 27th August inserted a GPS blocking device to stop its transmission, the latter bought online some time earlier.

NOTE 5. No DNA matching Gabriel Miller was found on any object at Hawthorn Farm, nor does he appear to have any knowledge of his wife's criminal activities. The data from the trackers placed on his van and car in April this year show that neither vehicle was in the vicinity of subsequent murders at Yoxford or Minsmere at the times the crimes took place. Thus, it is likely Naomi Miller transported herself to these, and earlier murders on the Honda motorcycle.

NOTE 5. Every available officer is now working to locate Naomi Miller ASAP. Our helicopter is also searching the coast and countryside for the suspect.

NOTE 6. All senior case officers now recommend we go public with naming Naomi Miller as a wanted person, and issue photographs and descriptions, plus information of the last sightings of her to all media outlets. This will inevitably lead to considerable criticism of our strategy and

accomplishments to date, not least the detention and charging of Gerald Hadiscoe. The latter, while he will face lesser charges for wasting police time and claiming to be the perpetrator of the first five murders, will of course, now be released.
NOTE 7. All senior case officers will attend the 9 a.m. meeting tomorrow morning in the main briefing room to discuss these latest developments and agree upon our next courses of action.

My concentration on these momentous words was broken by Esme squeezing my shoulder.

'Time to sign off,' she said, 'We've seen enough.'

'*AND SO HAVE I!*' my mother called out from the doorway. 'Oh, Ivan – what on earth are you doing?'

Neither Esme nor I had heard her car arriving, nor noticed the dog leave us and go into the kitchen in anticipation of my mother coming through the door. It had been a relatively windy day, and the sound of the breeze outside had been enough to obscure the noise of the car pulling up outside.

And that was the moment when my relationship with my mother was utterly changed. She realised then, that her unreserved trust in me had been betrayed. As for me, it was as if a halo of shame had descended and was now illuminating me as a despicable, untrustworthy and treacherous person in her eyes. I cannot even begin to explain how shamefaced and lousy I felt.

My mother spent half an hour giving me a good

dressing-down. She had treated me like an adult, she said, given me a car, never questioned where I went at nights, taken me into her confidence and discussed work matters, she had *trusted* me. She had thought I was loyal and sensible, believed me one thing when in fact I was another. I'd also put her in a serious position as regards her job, having breached the strict security of Suffolk Constabulary so that she was obliged either to report me immediately to her bosses, or risk being prosecuted herself for not admitting her secure pathway to the police's IT system had been used in a criminal way. She hung her head, cried real tears, and pushed me away when I said I was sorry and tried to put an arm around her.

'You told me on Wednesday evening,' she said, 'when I got home that you'd had a hunch your boss Miller had hidden his murder weapon and clothing at that farm in Fordley, and that is why you went there, then called in the police. But if you used police evidence and data to find that secret location you'd better tell me now, and we'll just have to own up to it and take the consequences because the detectives on the case may sooner or later cotton on to the fact you've tapped into their confidential information.'

'No!' I said firmly, 'There was nothing in the police's IT system that ever gave me so much as a clue about Gabriel Miller hiding stuff in that outhouse, nor did I see anything earlier about him being the guilty one. I caught him – or thought I had caught him – using my own methods, after having a gut feeling he was the killer. I saw that he was cruel and ruthless, and I saw with my own eyes he possessed a possible murder weapon. I looked at your personal stuff to confirm what I already knew, and see what evidence the police needed to clinch his guilt and claim the reward money.'

'But he *isn't* guilty,' said my mother, 'It's someone else my colleagues are searching for now, so all your prying and sneaking through my personal PDCS account was all for nothing.'

'I disagree,' I said; 'I was doing what I thought was right, and what I found out led to Naomi Miller being identified as the murderer. And if I hadn't suspected Gabriel, that evidence would never have come to light. I still think I can still claim the reward money from the paper...'

'*Reward money?*' she said with disgust. 'Is that what all this is about, then? You've broken into my account because you were so keen to get *money*, and to hell with everything and everyone else?'

'At first it was the money, I said, 'and maybe being famous for catching the worst criminal in the country, but lately it's been more than that. I just had to see the East Coast Killer stopped before he – I mean she – killed again. The police didn't seem to be on the right track, and I knew I was on to something. I'm sorry I used your IT system, but I was desperate to get the job done, and I figured the police might have some information that would help me. The funny thing is, I didn't need their help at all, really, as all I found were details about things I'd already discovered. You have to understand, I was really afraid, especially for *you*, mum. We're right in the middle of the killer's murder zone, and the victims so far were all around your age. The police were focused on that Gerald Hadiscoe fellow, and I felt I just had to try to do *something*.'

At this my mother's tear-strewn and crest-fallen face became a little more tender. Her lips were quivering and, at last, she held out her arms to me.

'I could get in so much trouble,' she said.

'No, mum, *I* could. *You* had nothing to do with it. I'm so sorry, so very sorry. It will never happen again.'

She gave me a kiss on my cheek and pushed me gently away.

'Make some tea,' she said, 'while I think what to do.'

'Do nothing, Mum, please,' I said; 'I haven't acted on anything I learned off the computer. Even today, I heard about Naomi Miller being the principal suspect from my own sources.'

'How can that be?' asked my mother; 'That information hasn't been made public yet.'

'We've had Gabriel miller over here this afternoon ranting and raving about how he's been treated, and then two detectives turned up and told him how his wife had been spotted at Dunwich, and had probably tried to commit suicide by swimming out to sea.'

'That's awful news,' said my mother. 'I suppose he was pretty broken up by all of this?'

'That would be an understatement. I never thought I'd end up feeling sorry for *him*,' I said. 'Lord, what a couple, the couple from hell.'

'We need to feel sorry for poor Fleur,' said Esme. She'd come back into the kitchen, and was filling the kettle for tea. 'I don't know her at all, but she must be having a pretty hard time, trying to cope with all this terrible news.'

'Yes,' I said, 'I don't think she's had a very good life, either. Imagine being brought up by parents like that.'

There were a few moments of heavy silence, then my mother turned to me and said:

'We're straying off the subject – I'm still trying to decide what to do about you, Ivan. I just can't get over the fact that you'd betray my trust in you like that.'

She hung her head, clasped her hands together, and seemed on the verge of tears once more.

'Look, I know you two have had a bit of a falling out,' said Esme, gently putting the electric kettle back on its stand and switching it on, 'but can I just say this? I haven't known Ivan very long, but he's the most considerate and well-brought-up person I've ever met. He's always saying nice things about his mother. I know he shouldn't have meddled with your emails and stuff, but I'm sure his intentions were good – kind of *noble*, in a way – and even though it's none of my business really, I'd just like to say you two mustn't let this thing mess up things between you. I hardly ever speak with my own parents, they just sort of ignore me, but you two seem really close, and you should never let anything come between you.'

My mother reached out and took Esme's hand in her own.

'Thank you,' she said, 'But nothing you can say will ever change the fact that my son has been doing a terrible thing. I'm supposed to report any breach of security immediately, and even if I do, I could still lose my job. But I'm in two minds, as Ivan would be facing serious criminal charges if I do tell my department.'

'Then don't tell them,' said Esme softly; 'Give Ivan another chance, ask him to promise he'll never do this again. If ever this thing is found out, you can say you didn't know he did it, which puts you in the clear. I can't see how you can turn in your own son, it would haunt you to see him in so much trouble, and, as you say, you'd probably lose your job, too. If you let the matter lie, everything stays the same, and you both stay out of trouble. And remember, Mrs. Salter, Ivan didn't use the information from your IT account for anything bad or to gain an advantage. Ivan was always one step ahead of the police's thinking, and without him they wouldn't have known who the real killer was.'

My mother looked at Esme, looked at me, and another tear rolled down her cheek.

'Oh Ivan, what have you done?' she said. You've made a criminal out of me. But what Esme says is true, I really can't turn in my own son. So I guess I'll just have to hope we never get caught, and live with the fact that I thought you were honest and reliable, when really you were capable of doing this terrible thing behind my back.'

I hugged my mother again, but I could feel that she was holding something back, that something had changed between us. And when I looked at my mother's tear-filled eyes I felt a pain in my heart, and realised I'd hurt her so badly that our relationship would never be quite the same again.

On the drive back to Esme's house we were silent, sullen, brooding. From time to time she handed me a cherry flavoured vape, one of her stronger ones, and I was glad of it. I inhaled deeply, my head swam, and for a couple of seconds after each hit I had to concentrate hard on my driving.

When we were almost back in Framlingham, Esme squeezed my shoulder and said:

'My parents are back tomorrow at midday. You can stay with me tonight and go back home after breakfast.'

My immediate thought was to get back to my mother that night. I had a feeling that, after our traumatic meeting earlier, she wouldn't want to be on her own. Watching some TV or a film with her would have been a good way to help restore some goodwill between us. I had a vague feeling too, that with Naomi Miller still not accounted for, there was even now a threat to women of my mother's age and background in the area.

But instead I heard myself telling Esme that I would spend the night with her. As usual, I ended up feeling full of guilt, thinking in odd moments of my mother sitting by her television all alone, going off to her lonely bed with only a dog to keep her company. But, there again, I would soon be off to Cambridge, in which case she would be left forever alone, unless one of the men on her dates turned out to be her Mr. Perfect, or whoever it was she sought.

Later, with Esme snuggled next to me fast asleep, for some reason I awakened in the early hours with a feeling of deep dread in the pit of my stomach. I thought of my mother alone, and wished I had not left her. But then I reassured myself that she was locked up securely in the cottage with the dog, and all must be well... wasn't it?

Though I dozed off again, I awoke at seven a.m. and though I had intended travelling later and being back home by noon, I decided to phone my mother. I rang her mobile, three times, but it went over to the answering service each time. I tried the landline, but there was no reply to that call either. My vague sense of dread grew stronger, and I woke Esme to tell her I was leaving. Her beautiful blue eyes regarded me sleepily as I told her I was setting off right away.

'Come and see me this evening,' she whispered, half-smiling, with tresses of chestnut hair hanging over her face. 'And in case I didn't say it enough last night, I love you, Ivan Salter...'

'I love you too, Esme Harmon,' I said, and kissed her rosy-red lips one last time.

In the car on the way back home I broke the law and dialled my mother's number on my mobile phone.

Again, there was no reply.

All the way to Middleton I tried to override my gut instinct by telling myself over and over again that my mother was perfectly all right. She was probably just sleeping deeply, the effects of her nightly medication keeping her drowsy and insensible to the phone's ringing.

But when I pulled into our driveway behind her car at five minutes to eight I saw that the door was wide open and a surge of white-hot fear pulsed through me. She *never* left the door open like that; and when I walked in, through the kitchen and into the hallway, I somehow knew already what horrific sight would meet my eyes even before I opened her bedroom door.

CHAPTER TWENTY-ONE:
PURE EVIL

Saturday 30th August

At first I could not believe what my eyes were telling me. I remember my legs buckling as I fell onto my knees, calling my mother's name though I knew she could no longer hear me.

I could see through my tears that my mother was lying perfectly still, fully clothed, on her bed with a small gash in her temple. Blood had trickled down the side of her head and soaked into her bedspread. Her arms were by her sides, her legs were straight and in a natural position, and her eyes were closed as if she'd been struck while taking a sleep on her bed. On the floor, on the other side of the bed was the body of our dog Tilly. She had also been killed with a blow to the head.

I knelt down beside my mother, bent over, and hugged her for a long, long time, ignoring the blood on her head which had seeped into her pillow. Despite the shock of seeing her like that, strangely, my first thought was not to call the police or an ambulance. I knew it was already too late for that. Instead I found myself talking to her. I told her I was sorry, what a bad son I was, how much I loved her...

A slight noise behind me in the doorway caused me to turn round.

'*Hello Ivan,*' smiled Naomi Miller, her brand new hedger's bill-hook held high in the air. 'I've been waiting for you. All night actually, but it doesn't matter how long it took. You see, I have all the time in the world.'

She was poised with the blade held high over me as I sprang sideways from my kneeling position and hit a chest of draws. While I was in mid-air she'd swung her weapon and grazed the side of my head, probably the first time that she'd ever missed her mark – but then, I was a moving target, unlike her previous victims. And, unlike those unfortunate souls, I was now very aware of her intention of making an end of me.

Though I'd hit my head so hard on that chest of drawers that I saw bright flashes of light before my eyes, I knew I had to get up, and be ready to move fast if I was to survive. I found myself standing, dazed, literally cornered, there in my mother's room. Naomi stepped purposefully towards me and took aim for a second time.

'Don't make this harder than it needs to be,' she said, still smiling, 'Now, just stand still, and I'll try to make it as quick and painless as possible.'

If she actually thought I had any intention of standing still while she hit me she was very much mistaken. My hand felt sideways for a weapon, grasped a lamp off the chest of drawers and hurled it at her. Unfortunately it was attached by its cable to the wall, and as it reached the end of its wire it was yanked harmlessly to the ground. Naomi didn't even flinch, but her smile morphed into a delighted laugh.

'You're being very *silly*,' she said. 'As you can see, there's absolutely no way out for you.'

I could see her narrowed eyes calculating how best to

deliver the deadly blow she meant to give me.

Instinctively, as I stood tensed, my gaze fixed on that arm holding up the bill-hook. I should have kept quiet, but instead I heard myself say:

'Why did you have to kill my mother? What did she ever do to you?'

'Oh, she was just another one of those smiling, painted bitches, flashing their eyes and sticking out their tits, trying to lure my Gabriel astray... but I'll tell you something, every time I hit one of those whores I suddenly felt normal again. Yes, that's right, don't look so bloody shocked, hitting them on the head made me feel so *good*. There was a time I wanted to die every day, but after I had that fight with Katy Tranmer and saw her lying dead I suddenly felt *normal* again. She'd been seeing my Gabriel on the sly, you see, but I found out. After then I realised it was either those other bitches or me that had to die... but I made it *them,* and I'm glad I did.'

She laughed again, and her eyes grew a little wider with delight at the thought of what she'd done.

'And what about me?' I asked; 'Why do you want to do me harm? I'm a friend of your husband–'

'Ha!' She snorted, 'You're no *friend* of his, I know it was you who called the police and reported him as the one they wanted. It was *you* who ruined everything – and now you're going to pay for it, you nasty little hypocrite. I hated you the first time I saw you, I could see in your high and mighty eyes that even though my Gabriel treated you so fairly, you only looked down on him and me as if we were some sort of low-life...'

I could see by her eyes it was pretty pointless talking to her. She was in some kind of a frenzy, fixated on only one thing, and that was delivering a single blow to my head in one of her trademark strikes.

And I was fixated on only one thing too, and that was dodging the blow of that blade. Strangely, my principal emotion was not fear, most probably because I was still in shock from seeing my mother dead. Instead, I was full of rage and hatred for this twisted piece of humanity who sought to add me to her list of victims. So, like a mongoose watching a cobra poised to strike, I stood tensed ready to evade her swing. She made a couple of feints, laughing as I flinched, evidently taking great delight in her murderous work. I shall never forget the look on her face as she manoeuvred her feet an inch or two towards me.

Suddenly she swung, her arm becoming a blur as the bill-hook descended on me in a fraction of a second.

I still don't know how I did it, but in that split-second between life and death I darted sideways and the blade smacked harmlessly into the top corner of the chest of drawers. I pounced on it, wrenching it from her grasp. She came at me with a scream, her fingers grasping at my throat but I used all my strength to push her backwards a couple of steps. I had the bill-hook now, but she, fearless in her frenzy, came at me again like an angry lioness thwarted at losing out on a kill. I could have struck her down, but even in that desperate fight I didn't want to kill her, so I pushed her away again as hard as I could, causing her to stagger backwards and crack the back of her head on the door frame. The sound of her head striking the wooden post reminded me of the noise of one of those hard wooden balls at a fairground hitting a coconut on its shy. Naomi Miller's eyes rolled in her head and she slid down with her back against the door jamb.

I took a step forward and stood over her with the bill-hook raised in my right hand, threatening her, my intention being to frighten her into remaining on the floor. She looked up at me with a dazed demeanour. Then, her face, slowly changed from a look of pain to one of mockery. She was looking from my face, to the blade, then back at me.

'Go on, then,' she said, smiling and nodding her head, 'Go on, do it!'

Seeing me hesitate, she attempted to provoke me, saying:

'Look at your mother, Ivan, I just killed her with that sharp little blade, I killed her and I enjoyed it. Now be a man and do the same to me.'

She made a movement as if she was about to get up. I took a step forward, glanced sideways at my mother on the bed, and felt my right arm raise the bill-hook a little higher ready to give her the coup-de-grace she so desired...

'*No, Ivan!*' shouted Esme from the doorway; 'Don't do it.'

She rushed in and stood between me and Naomi. I lowered the bill-hook, but as I did so, Naomi tried to rise. Quick as a flash, Esme's leg shot out and delivered a kick straight to Naomi's chin, knocking her head against the door frame for a second time and immediately rendering her unconscious.

Esme took the bill-hook out of my hand. She looked into my eyes for a second, and, realising I was still in shock, led me into the kitchen. After she'd phoned the police she went back to look at Naomi, who had started to come round.

'We need string or tape to bind her,' she said.

'There's duct tape in the kitchen cabinet drawer,' I said vaguely.

With Naomi bound and under control, and the police on their way, I went to look at my mother, touched her hand, smoothed her hair and kissed her cheek. Then I looked down at Naomi Miller, whose mocking eyes, now conscious again, watched me with deep satisfaction. I paused next to her, thought of kicking her, hard, but instead did nothing.

Esme watched me with pity in her eyes, took me in her arms in the kitchen, held me while I sobbed for a long, long time.

Presently, I recovered just a little, and sat down in a chair to await the police, while Esme, in true British style, and somewhat absurdly, I thought, decided to make tea.

'I wasn't going to do it,' I said; 'Hit her with the hatchet, I mean...'

'I would've,' said Esme.

'Hey,' I said, remembering how Esme had appeared so

suddenly, 'How on earth did you get here? I left you half-asleep in your bed in Framlingham.'

'Took my mother's car and drove over. She'll have a fit when she gets back at midday and reads the note I left her. She never lets me take her car, you see.'

'But I didn't even know you could drive.'

'There's a lot you don't know about me,' she said.

'Like the karate kicks?' I said.

'That was aikido,' she said with a shrug. 'I've been going to classes since I was seven.'

'But you still haven't said *why* you came over. I know I said I felt something was wrong at home, but I hardly expected you to take me seriously.'

'I saw that you were really spooked when you left, so I quickly did a four card tarot spread.'

'And what did they say?'

'They said that the hierophant – that's *you* – was in danger of death. That woke me up, all right, and I decided to borrow my mum's car and follow you over.'

'But you didn't call the police?'

'And tell them *what*? That I had a sinking feeling that something was wrong, and that my fears were based on a tarot reading? At that stage I wasn't sure the danger was real – and I certainly didn't think Naomi Miller would turn up here. Oh Ivan, I'm so very, very sorry...'

Her voice trailed off. The kettle was boiling. She poured water into the teapot and sat down next to me and we put our arms round each other. From outside came the distant wailing of the first police car.

And from the bedroom came the noise of a window

opening and a person scrambling over the sill.

As the police discovered later, Naomi Miller had chewed through the tape on her wrists and around her legs, jumped out the ground floor window and landed in the flower bed below. She then made her escape on foot. By the time enough police had arrived to form a decent-sized search party, almost three-quarters of an hour had passed, and, needless to say, Naomi Miller was now nowhere to be found.

Nor was the horrible hedger's bill-hook she had used to kill my mother.

Chapter Twenty-two:
The Tarot Cards Again

Saturday 30th August 8 p.m.

Back in Framlingham at 8 p.m. in the evening, still in shock, I met Esme's rather snooty parents. They sat me in an armchair in their huge lounge and drank gin and tonics (without offering me so much as a glass of water) while they carefully examined me. Her mother was about forty-five, with short chestnut-coloured hair, a tiny red-painted mouth and sad blue eyes. She had that well-groomed, slightly uptight look of affluent English women.

Esme's father was a tall, lean fellow of about fifty with hawk-like grey-blue eyes, and a great beak of a nose that was bright pink from drinking too much alcohol. He had a post-box of a mouth with no lips, and his teeth were yellow. I hated his dry, humourless way of talking down to Esme – and me – and though his daughter had already briefed him on the phone of my distress, he insisted on grilling me for half an hour about the events of the day. He wanted to know the reasons I'd suspected Gabriel Miller, and how I'd found the evidence, and finally, how I was feeling after my brush with mortality. I answered him briefly and honestly, watching the old fellow's eyebrows rise higher and higher as I told him about how my plan to secure the reward money may well have led to my mother's death, and that I would never forgive myself. I knew I was giving away too much information, but once I started, I couldn't stop talking.

'Don't be so harsh on yourself,' he said, 'Nobody could have predicted that woman would get into your house like that, and if you'd been at home last night she may well have killed you too.'

I was too tired to argue the point, but his words at least made me feel a little better. When he asked me how long I'd known Esme I told him that though I'd seen her around in school, I'd only been her boyfriend for a week.'

'And what are your future intentions regarding my daughter?' he asked, with a wry smile on his face. 'You do know she's off to Cambridge University in a few days' time?'

'Yes,' I said; 'Of course she told me. And I told her that I was studying at Anglia Ruskin just down the road. So my intentions are to continue seeing her, and try my hardest to make her happy.'

As this exchange was taking place, Esme was standing in the doorway behind him, squirming with embarrassment. Esme's mother, fortunately, decided to intervene at this moment, saying:

'Of course, Ivan, you can't go home alone tonight, so you can stay the night in our guests' room. Esme will show you where everything is, and get you some food if you want it. But before Victor and I turn in, we'd just like to offer you our heartfelt sympathy – wouldn't we, dear?'

'Yes, of course,' he said. 'Now, Esme, take this young man into the kitchen and get him whatever he wants.'

Esme led me away, quietly closing the lounge door

behind us.

'Sorry about that,' she said. 'See what I have to put up with?'

'I'm not surprised they're so curious,' I said, slumping into a kitchen chair; 'It must be pretty weird for them coming home to find out their daughter has a new boyfriend, and then be told his mother has just been murdered.'

'Forget about them,' she said, 'I'm only concerned about you. Can I get you something, some coffee, or maybe some pasta?'

'I couldn't eat a thing,' I said, 'but some tea and a few puffs on one of those extra strong vapes would be good. And I guess I'm going to miss your arms being around me tonight, even though you're just in another room.'

'About that,' she said, 'I'll come to you as soon as they're in bed, which is usually pretty early. The spare room is just across the hallway from me. I can't bear to sleep without you any more.'

I pulled her towards me and sat her on my lap.

'Yes, I feel the same way,' I said. 'Lord, what's happening with us, Esme? We've only known each other a few days.'

'It must be love,' she said, gazing on me with her big, sorrowful blue eyes.

I gazed back at her, hugged her to me, buried my face in her long tresses of chestnut hair. A sudden thought came to me.

'I wonder if they've caught Naomi Miller yet?'

'Probably,' she said; 'before we left Middleton the

police said they'd called in dozens and dozens of officers into the area, and even a search helicopter with infra-red cameras to help find her. Surely she can't get far, with all those resources after her.'

'That's what we said on Monday, though, and they didn't catch her then. She must have some secret hide-out in the area, and found some way of getting around without being noticed. A stolen car, maybe.'

'Yes,' said Esme, 'She's obviously pretty cunning and resourceful when it comes to avoiding the police. I wouldn't put it past her to kill again – and we would both be targets, if she knew where we were. God, I hope they catch her quickly.'

'Maybe we could try the tarot cards again,' I said. 'They've been pretty accurate at predicting stuff so far.'

Esme found her leather bag, rummaged amongst the collection of vapes and other stuff and took out the pack of tarot cards.

'I brought them with me today, she explained, 'in case they were needed. I'll try a simple four card spread. Here, you shuffle them, then put the pack on the table.'

I did as I was told.

'Where is Naomi Miller?' whispered Esme. *'Cards and spirits, reveal to me where she's hiding...'*

Then, one by one, she placed three cards in a line, face down, with a fourth card crossing the middle one. She turned the left hand one, to reveal the tower. The picture showed a tall tower hit by lightning and burning fiercely.

'That's her!' said Esme, 'The tower is a symbol of

death and destruction, and represents that evil cow Naomi Miller.'

She turned the right hand card, to reveal the moon. The picture showed two shadowy dogs howling up at the stars and a full moon.

'That one reveals that she is most active at night, that she will use her womanly powers to achieve her aims, and that she can sometimes be almost invisible.'

Next, she lifted the card crossing the centre one, and, while keeping it hidden, turned the middle card to reveal the chariot. The picture showed a woman in armour with a spear on a chariot pulled by two white horses.

Here, Esme paused, staring intently at the card.

'Well?' I said, after a couple of minutes.

'She has a car,' said Esme, and she's on the move. The armour suggests she's somehow hidden, or protected by something such as a disguise, which ties in with the moon card. Now let's see the last one, which may show her weakness, or something that might lead to her capture.'

She turned over the last card, and placed it across the chariot one. It depicted the emperor, a picture of a crowned man on a throne.

'Ah,' she said, 'now it's beginning to make sense. The emperor here shows she's moved to a new place, and has the help of a wealthy or powerful man. That would explain how she's able to disappear and hide so well.'

'But who would ever want to help her... except maybe Gabriel, I suppose.'

'The police will be watching his house day and night,' said Esme, 'So I don't think it's him. Does she have any other relatives in the area? Someone who has money, perhaps?'

'None that I can think of. Wait! There is a rich old pig-farmer, called Walter Tranmer, who's her great-uncle. Gabriel said he was the richest farmer in Suffolk, though I thought he was only joking when he said it.'

'It's him!' said Esme; 'It must be him... that farmer – whoever he is – is protecting her, I'll bet you.'

'Gabriel said he'd phoned Tranmer, and the old fellow said he hadn't seen her.'

'That old man was lying,' said Esme; 'It's the only explanation.'

'But why would he be protecting a suspected killer, even if she is a relative?'

'I don't know,' she said; 'Maybe she's spun him a yarn and he doesn't know she's a killer... yet.'

'We'd better tell the police immediately,' I said.

I took out my phone, and selected the direct line number I had been given to the East Coast Murder team. It was already nearly ten p.m. so I didn't really expect to receive an answer. Evidently, however, the team were working overtime that night.

A rather gruff voice asked who was calling. It turned out that I was speaking to none other than DCI Derek Smethurst. I explained that I'd had a hunch and worked out that Naomi might be hiding out with her great-uncle at Kelsale Green in Red House Farm.

'And how did you come to that conclusion?' said an

incredulous Smethurst. 'We've already sent officers to that gentleman to ask if he's seen her, and he said he hadn't. It was actually her husband who suggested we spoke with Mr. Tranmer, by the way.'

'Did you search the house?' I asked.

'Well, of course not, we had no reason to issue a warrant, we were merely making enquiries. And I'm afraid we can't go in and search the place without some concrete evidence.'

'I'm pretty sure she's in there with him,' I said; 'I don't have any 'concrete' evidence, as you put it, but just as I worked out where the murder weapon, motorbike and boots were hidden, I've come to the conclusion she's there. Also, I think she's got some means of transport there, possibly a stolen car – or maybe Mr. Tranmer has been lending her a vehicle.'

There was silence for several seconds. Then Smethurst gave his verdict.

'If it were anyone else but you I wouldn't act on this sort of information; but I'm going to get a search team with a warrant there first thing tomorrow morning.'

Then there was another short silence, before Smethurst said, very quietly:

'Pardon me for asking this, but are you by any chance some sort of *psychic?*'

Had I not been so full of grief and sorrow I would have laughed at these words. Instead, I told him:

'I'm no psychic, officer, but I do have a gut feeling she's there, and you'll appreciate I've met Walter Tranmer before, and I think there's something very peculiar about him. And you'll be aware his wife disappeared two years ago, in strange circumstances.'

'My word, sir, you are well-informed. I was part of the investigation into Mrs. Tranmer's death, and I can tell you now, that we found absolutely no evidence that old man had anything to do with her disappearance.'

'Listen, I've just remembered that Naomi Miller said she'd killed Katy Tranmer while she was attacking me. She said something about it being vengeance because Katy had an affair with her husband. From the way she said it, I don't think Walter Tranmer was in on the murder, or knows she did it. I think he's just shielding her because she's a relative. Most probably, she told him she was in trouble, and innocent of any crime.'

'Good Lord, you should have told us all this before.'

'I'm sorry, but I've been in a kind of daze since my mother died, and it's rather affected my thinking. Also, I think I've been blocking all thoughts about Naomi Miller attacking me and what she said as she swung that billhook thing at my head...'

'I'm not surprised it's affected you in that way. Remember, I gave you the number of a counsellor to ring if you need some help.'

'Thanks,' I said, 'but I've already got someone here to help me.'

'That's good. I'd just like to say that we're very grateful for your contributions. Now, returning to the matter in hand, I've heard enough. I'll personally lead a team to search Red House Farm first thing tomorrow morning. We'll let you know how we get on. Till then, take care young man, and may I say again, how very sorry we all are for your loss.'

I'd had the phone on 'speakerphone' mode so that Esme could hear the policeman's side of the conversation.

'Hey, Ivan,' she said, after Smethurst had rung off, 'Why don't we go to that farm and watch the police bring her in? I'm sure she's going to be there.'

'I was thinking about that already. I'd really like to be there when the police finally get her. But I'd better go alone, I think, I can't ask you to go anywhere near that killer.'

'If you're going there, I'm coming with you.'

'Absolutely out of the question – what if she sees us and comes at us with a hatchet again?'

'There'll be a few burly police officers she'll have to get past first. But if she does, then having someone with you with a second dan in aikido won't do you any harm. Anyway, I've already decided, we're going together, to finally see this thing through to the end.'

'Well, that's supposing she's there at Red House Farm with old Tranmer in the first place.'

'Oh, she's there all right,' said Esme, her strangely animated eyes looking quite fierce in the flickering candle-light. 'We'll go and watch her taken, and something tells me that evil creature isn't going to go quietly into captivity...'

CHAPTER TWENTY-THREE
THE RAT HUNT

Sunday August 31st 5.45 a.m.

If I hadn't been so full of sadness and grief, it might have been the most exciting day of my life. But only those who've lost a member of their family suddenly and in circumstances like I have can truly understand how I felt the next morning as I opened my eyes after sleep and the realisation hit me: *she's dead, she's dead, and nothing in the world can ever bring her back.*

To be killed, murdered by a serial killer, is an incredibly unlikely and unlucky thing to happen to anyone. You never believe it possible for a lightning-bolt of fate to strike someone close to you, until it actually happens. And after it does, you are tortured by the thought that if only you had acted differently, had somehow warned them, or kept close by them, that this terrible thing would never have happened.

And yet, with all this going on in the back of your mind, you have somehow to carry on, to get out of bed, to eat, to breathe, to go through the motions of everyday humdrum life... that my mother could never know or experience again.

But revenge is a powerful motive to someone in my position. I felt I had to see Naomi Miller safely locked away in prison, or a secure psychiatric hospital, or better still, swinging from a gallows as some of the baying lynch mob on social media would have it.

So, at 5.30 a.m. when my phone alarm beeped, I woke up Esme, got myself out of bed, dressed and readied myself for my first full day of grief.

I can't help thinking that final pursuit of Naomi Miller was like a kind of rat-hunt, a very appropriate way for her to finally lose her freedom.

By 6.15 a.m. we were in position parked half-way along Tranmer's driveway. Ahead of us, we could see the officers surrounding the big farm house. We'd actually arrived a few minutes before the officers, and were heartened to see that the farm house's curtains were still closed, and there was, as yet, no sign of the guard dogs. When the ten or so marked and unmarked police cars and vans drove past us, one of them stopped. It was a familiar-looking silver Land Rover Discovery. DCI Smethurst got out and walked back to my car.

'What on earth are you doing here?' he said. 'You shouldn't be here, you know that.'

'I just want to see her arrested,' I said.

'*If* she's in there,' said Smethurst. 'All right, you two wait here on the driveway, don't get any closer.'

'Tranmer has two German Shepherds,' I said, 'and they're pretty aggressive.'

'I know that,' said Smethurst; 'One of our officers got bitten yesterday when he knocked on the door. But thanks for the warning. Now, for goodness sake, sit tight while we go in.'

Twenty officers got out of the cars and vans. Ten of these moved off to surround the big house, leaving five men and five women officers outside the front door. Two uniformed women officers had police dogs on leads – German Shepherds, as it turned out. Two other men were carrying dark objects in a double-handed grip.

'Are those guns they're carrying?' asked Esme, pointing. 'Do you think they're going to shoot her?'

'I hope so,' I said.

Smethurst rapped on the big front door, which opened immediately, to reveal Tranmer and his two dogs, which ran past him and sprang on the two police dogs. While half of the officers boldly went into the house, the others were distracted by the dogs fighting. While trying to separate the dogs, officers were getting bitten. Then, two shots rang out, followed by a man's loud bellowing. The shouting turned out to be Walter Tranmer's protest at seeing his two companion guard-dogs slaughtered before his eyes. Clearly, the police were in a determined mood.

Now it was Tranmer's turn to be intimidated by German Shepherds, as the police dogs barked at him in response to his aggression. He was shouting, and swinging his long walking stick at the nearest officers. A big policeman grabbed him, and, despite his old age, the old farmer was unceremoniously placed head first down on the gravel, and had his arms pulled behind his back, ready for the handcuffs. After he was secured, one officer remained with him while the others disappeared into the house, leaving the door wide open. The officers who had been covering the flanks now came to the front door, and followed the others inside.

There followed what seemed an eternity. Ten, then

twenty minutes passed. There were no sign of the officers.

Then, at the right-hand side of the building, on the first floor, a small window was flung open and a black-clad figure leapt down onto the ground.

'That's her!' said Esme, 'Naomi Miller just jumped out of the first floor window!'

We watched in horrified fascination as she picked herself up, and ran limping across the lawn. She bolted through a gate and onto a small meadow, heading for the cover of some nearby farm buildings, which happened to be the huge pig fattening sheds.

I leapt out the car and shouted back towards the house:

'Hey! Hey! She's running towards the piggeries!'

The officer by the front door was concentrating on restraining his prisoner, and showed no sign that he'd heard me.

'Run up to the house and warn the officers she's jumped out and gone toward the first piggery,' I shouted to Esme. 'I'll follow her at a safe distance and see where she goes.'

Esme hesitated, obviously not wanting me to go after Naomi alone; but then, seeing how far off the fugitive now was, she left me to sprint after her, and ran towards the farm house for help.

I darted off in pursuit, across the lawn, into the meadow and over a hedge. Before me, Naomi Miller half ran, half hobbled, like a wounded animal. However, unlike a wild beast, Naomi Miller was holding something in her hand, an object whose metal head glinted in the early morning sunlight.

I learned later that Esme ran to the police officer by the door and screamed at him to follow Naomi Miller. But instead he got on his radio and called his colleagues out of the house. Out they all tumbled, before finally, taking up the chase.

Imagine the scene that followed, twenty police, two of them with dogs on leads, two of them brandishing pistols, sprinting off toward the big factory farm buildings where thousands of pigs were quartered.

Meanwhile, I had already followed Naomi Miller into the shed marked number 1. Inside the building it was not as I'd imagined. The big sliding door, left open before me by the fugitive, led to an open concreted area surrounded by metal gates. This enclosure was designed for holding the fully-grown pigs after they were driven out of their small pens and assembled ready for transportation on livestock lorries. The rest of the building consisted of row after row of square breeze-block enclosures, with paths running between them like streets. Each individual pen had a gate, firmly closed of course, bordering the paths. Thus, from the holding pen end you could select a row and access any of the 'kennels', as the workers called them.

Each of these pens was about ten feet broad, fifteen deep and six feet high, and though there was a corrugated steel roof to the building high overhead, for added warmth each small enclosure had a plywood roof at about head height. The lower roofs area was accessed by mounting steel ladders, and, as I discovered, the flexible plywood bounced as you walked over it. Every pen had tubes conveying meal into a trough on one sidewall, and a pipe carrying water into a smaller trough on the other. As mentioned earlier, earlier, the piggeries used the Danish-invented 'Psycho-Dynamic' method of fattening, whereby food is periodically withheld from small piglets, and fed into the troughs at the signal of a buzzer. Later on in their lives, when growing, the pigs automatically consume huge quantities of meal every time they hear the buzzer, allowing the fiendish farmer to induce them to eat to excess and thus fatten more quickly.

From the holding pen area, I adjusted my eyes to the dim light, and ran to scan each 'street' that ran between the rows. At first I couldn't see her, but then I heard a commotion as pigs squealed and milled around madly in a pen somewhere along the second row of pens. The first of the police came in behind me.

'She's in there!' I yelled, pointing to the place, 'hiding among the piglets.'

'Stay where you are!' shouted a policeman, but whether he was calling to her or me I couldn't tell. Four or five police clambered over the metal gate and ran along that second row. Before they reached the pen of pigs where she was hiding, Naomi Miller mouthed an obscenity and sprang out of her dark corner, into the street about thirty yards in front of them. She hobbled along the concrete till she reached one of the steel ladders that led up onto the kennel roofs.

A dozen officers ascended other ladders onto the pen roofs and quickly surrounded her. I climbed a ladder at my end of the building, and watched to see what would happen next.

Far from being intimidated, Naomi Miller only laughed at the brave policemen closing in on her with telescopic truncheons extended. She was swinging her bill-hook from side to side in defiance. In her frenzy, she didn't seem to realise that two of the officers had pistols ominously brandished in that business-like double-handed grip ready for action.

'Don't shoot her if you can help it,' shouted Smethurst. 'Try to knock that weapon out of her hand, and then we'll have her.'

Some things are easier said than done. She was over the roofs of the third street when officers finally had her surrounded, and moved in on her with truncheons. She fought them off like a female Viking berserker, severely wounding three brave but foolish officers who got too close to her, who'd mistakenly believed they could hit her before she hit them. Finally, on Smethurst's orders, an armed officer shot her in the chest and knocked her off her feet. Severely wounded, she still tried to strike out from her position on the ground at the officers who were now closing in to assist her. She was alternately laughing, cursing and spitting like a cat as the life ebbed from her.

Kicking out at her would-be first-aiders, she rolled, still conscious, over the front edge of the roof, bounced off the front gate and landed in the empty meal trough of a pen of full-grown hogs. As we found out later, these were some of the un-castrated special order wild boar crosses I had been warned about back in July. And, as bad luck would have it, Naomi Miller landed just as the buzzer of the Psycho-Dynamic system signalled the influx of a feed of soya meal. It was the first offering of the day, and the hogs were ravenous. The twelve big boars barged and pushed each other aside to get to the extra large helping of blood-tinged protein in the trough. A high-pitched scream rent the air, but it was cut mercifully short after a few seconds, replaced by the roar and growls of the savage beasts as they tore and chewed at Naomi Miller's squirming body.

The two armed police officers were the first to arrive at the mouth of the pen after descending the steel staircase back down to the level of the front gate. By this time the body was unrecognisable, and the hogs were in no mood to let humans into their midst to rescue the pitiful remains.

I watched as a brief discussion ensued, followed by the two armed police kneeling by the gate and levelling their pistols at the nearest pigs. For men trained to kill, who discuss and dream daily about getting the chance to use their guns in a live fire situation, it must have seemed that Christmas had come early. Shot after shot rang out, as the hogs realised, too late, how dangerous it was to attack those wicked humans who had, after all, placed them in that dark and dingy place of humiliation, discomfort and, in effect, psychological torture.

I watched in horror and fascination as both of the

pistol-toting officers blasted away, emptied their guns, replaced the magazines, re-cocked their pieces and continued to shoot until the last hog had ceased to twitch.

A pall of blue gunsmoke rose slowly over the gate of the pen, drifted into the air, and gradually dispersed in the foul-smelling air. A pool of blood was seeping under the metal gate and trickling into a gully that led to the grid of a drain.

'Sausages, anyone?' remarked one the armed response officers, with grim black humour, to his watching colleagues.

The police broke the news of my mother's death in a news conference that evening. They also said that a forty-two year old woman, a suspect in the East Coast Murders case, had been shot by armed police officers. She was, they explained, unfortunately killed while resisting arrest and wielding a bladed weapon. Within minutes, social media channels, online news outlets and TV and radio broadcasts were buzzing with news of the latest murder and the sensational demise of the real East Coast Killer. Esme and I retreated to Framlingham to avoid the inevitable flood of news reporters to Middleton. Fordley, too, we heard, was inundated with journalists and photographers milling around the now notorious Hawthorn Cottage. In the midst of all that storm, somewhere, was poor Fleur Miller, who, as we heard later, was ultimately rescued by Beatrice Chalmers and her father, who invited her to stay at Rowan Tree Farm, Minsmere.

As for Esme and I, we had no choice but to live under the roof of her parents, for the time being. After a week, we went to sort out things at what was now my house in Middleton.

The next few days and weeks were a time of incredible stress and busyness for us both, but particularly for me. Esme began her course on time, staying in a student hall of residence (where, luckily, overnight visitors are allowed for up to three nights per week). I enrolled on my English and Drama course, but had to miss several days early in the first term as I was obliged to go to and from Suffolk to tie up numerous legal matters, and later attend my mother's funeral in Middleton's Holy Trinity Church.

With Esme's love and support I managed to get through it all, but only just. My nerves were shattered, my guilt and remorse almost overpowering. I suffered from terrible flashbacks, and was sometimes awakened by nightmares. I found it very therapeutic, however, to continue writing my diary, and later to write about the events of that summer with the idea of completing a book. I had already been contacted out of the blue by Lizzie Donovan, a senior editor from Round World Books. She'd explained that her company was keen to publish an account of how my detective work had helped catch the East Coast Killer. I agreed to send her three chapters of a potential book. Writing those first few pages put me on the road to recovery, and I determined that I had to tell the whole truth this time, and confess my whole story regardless of the consequences. As the book would sooner or later result in me being investigated for hacking into Suffolk Constabulary's PDCS network, at Esme's suggestion I wrote them a letter outlining what I'd done. After being interviewed by them all over again, I received a written caution from Suffolk Constabulary for my crime, but it was ultimately deemed 'not in the public interest' that I was prosecuted. I have also traced the elderly couple from whom I stole the first edition of Charles Dickens' Bleak House, and sent them a cheque for one thousand, six hundred and eighty pounds. I think my mother would have been proud of me for putting right at least two of the wrongful things I've done in the last few months.

Esme and I ultimately found a tiny flat to live in, conveniently half way between our two colleges. This was just before the Christmas holidays. Much to her parents' dismay, we told them we were spending Christmas day together in our cosy little love-nest.

Parents are rather fond of telling their children how love between young people is destined to end in heartache and failure. Esme and I, however, have a rather more optimistic view of our future together, and we fully intend to make the most of our love, and to hell with what others may think of who we are, or what we do because, as far as we are concerned 'Amor Vincit Omnia'.

Chapter Twenty-four:
Another Murder

December 5th 4.30 p.m.

On our very first evening in our little flat, I asked Esme to read the tarot cards one more time. The question was a relatively trivial one, concerning whether I should accept the advance proposed by my would-be publisher, Round World Books, or hold out for more and risk losing the proffered amount of no less than thirty thousand pounds.

We closed the curtains, poured two glasses of red wine, and lit a candle. I shuffled the pack as I asked the question aloud:

'Should I take the thirty thousand pounds, or ask for more?'

Esme put the cards in a line of three, with a second card across the centre one. The result came out clear enough: the centre card was the ten of pentacles, a card indicating financial gain, crossed on top by the emperor, a card of power and control.

Esme looked at me, laughed, put her arms around me.

'You are the one in the driving seat,' she said. 'The cards say the publisher will certainly pay you more.'

We hugged and kissed for a while, and ten minutes later, my phone began to ring. It was none other than Lizzie Donovan, my contact at Round World Books. I put her on speakerphone, and we listened to her words, as she explained how her company wished to *'move things forward'*, as she put it.

'We really liked the first three chapters you sent us, and my colleagues and I think it would be *amazing* to have you on board, so we'd like to increase our offer to fifty thousand pounds now as an advance, plus royalties at our normal rates. The initial print run will be one hundred thousand copies, so we'd like the rest of your first draft as soon as possible. Don't worry too much about editing matters, our people will guide you through and see to all that. But Ivan, we need your agreement pretty much straight away, as this is a time-sensitive project, and it's important to get it to press as soon as possible.'

As she paused, I put the phone on mute, and looked at Esme, who seemed to be weighing up Mary Donovan's words.

'I'm inclined to take the offer,' I said: 'But what do you think?

She reached out and turned over a single tarot card, the hierophant. At this development, she nodded sagely, pointing a finger at the card.

'That card means "good judgement" and suggests you will be very well-mentored and have success in your writing,' she said. 'I think you should accept.'

I un-muted the phone and graciously agreed to the proposal. My hands were trembling with excitement.

'That's *amazing*,' said Lizzie Donovan; 'The draft contract will arrive tomorrow in your inbox. Congratulations, Ivan, we're really happy to welcome you on board.'

As I put the phone down, Esme jumped into my arms and we hugged for a good five minutes.

Later, sipping our wine, I asked:

'How the hell do you do that tarot thing? You seem to get it right every time.'

'I guess I'm a *witch*,' she shrugged, reaching for her favourite watermelon flavoured vape.

'Was that a *witch* or a *bitch?*' I teased, 'Well, I always have thought there was something a little strange about you.'

She punched me lightly in the ribs.

'I'm definitely a witch,' she said; 'Not only can I read tarot cards, I can cast spells too, you see. Did you hear about my ex-boyfriend James?'

'You mean the guy that used to hobble around the sixth form common room in a plaster-cast? Fell off his motorbike, so I heard.'

'Mmm, but that was my fault, I'm afraid. I didn't want him to get hurt, but after I cursed him with the tarot cards he rode his bike into a horse and fell off.'

'Good gracious, that's horrible. Was the horse all right?'

'Yes, but its rider fell in a ditch and got all shirty. But when he realised James had a broken leg, he was all right about it.'

'That was very nice of him.'

'Then, a month after James came out of hospital, he offered to go back with me.'

'So, what did you say?'

'I said I didn't want him any more because he was damaged goods.'

'Because of a broken leg?' That's a bit harsh, isn't it?'

'Not really, he'd been going out with my friend Rosalind for almost two weeks by then. I told him to go back to her. But she'd already ditched him because he kept talking about me.'

'Sounds like good material for an Australian soap-opera.'

She punched me a medium-strength dig in the ribs.

'Poor old James,' I said, 'So nobody wanted him any more?'

'Don't know, don't care. So, remember, I have incredibly high standards when it comes to men, so be careful.'

'I'll never let you down.'

'Don't say that, it's a promise that's impossible to keep.'

'Oh, I'll keep it all right.'

'Are you absolutely sure?'

'Oh yes, otherwise you'll curse me and I'll crash my car into a herd of cows on their way to be milked, or something horrible like that.'

'There aren't any cows around here – we're in the middle of Cambridge. But remember, if you let me down, I definitely will curse you... horribly.'

'Even after a relatively short relationship?'

'Especially after a short relationship.'

'Damn, you've got me all scared now. Still, I was planning to be really kind of perfect for you anyway, so I guess as long as I don't let you down in any small way I'll be perfectly safe.'

'Yes, perfectly safe, as long as you obey my every whim and small wish.'

'I don't suppose I could have the ring back, then?'

I got another punch in the ribs, quite a hard one this time.

'Not a chance,' she said, 'I'd definitely curse you then.'

'Bugger, well all right, then I guess we'd better see if we can make the most of our relationship.'

We hugged one another for a few minutes, then she pulled away suddenly and looked me squarely in the eye.

'So, Ivan Salter, I know things have been really hard for you, but are you happy with *me*? I mean *really* happy?'

'Definitely. It's a case of so far, so good, I think.'

She continued to hold me at arm's length.

'That's not very romantic,' she said, frowning.

I pulled her close to me, and whispered into her ear:

'All right then, then let's do something really silly. I want to marry you right away, no more thinking about it, we'll just do it. We've got the money from the reward, and Round World Books has offered me that huge advance for the book I've started to write, so things are looking rosy for us. And remember, that money's not mine, it's *ours*. You were in at all the dangerous stuff, and without those spooky tarot cards we wouldn't have caught Naomi Miller. It seems that when we work together, miraculous things seem to happen. So, we'll take a chance on our love lasting for ever and ever, hunker down in our snug little love-nest here, and quietly do our courses. Then we're all set for the future, and nobody can say we're not doing the sensible thing. Well, Esme Harmon, what do you say?'

'I say *stop talking*, and kiss me, if you know what's good for you. And the answer to your question is yes, yes, a million times *yes*.'

Several hours later the doorbell rang and I had, very reluctantly, to leave Esme's arms and go see who had climbed the stairs to pay us a visit. I glanced at my watch, and saw that it was just after 8 p.m. I was a little curious to find out who might be calling on us at that time of the evening, but first I had to go to the bedroom to put on a dressing gown, as I had been wearing only my boxer shorts and a T- shirt. Esme, also curious about our late night visitor, threw her Indian cotton dress back on and followed me to our door.

A little tipsy from the glasses of red wine we'd drunk, we were feeling pretty euphoric, oblivious of what awaited us on the other side of the door. We both agreed later, that we'd expected to see a fellow student or group of students who were attending either of our courses, come to pay us a visit, maybe to bring a bottle of something pleasant from the pub or college bar to share with us.

But, a huge shock awaited us: as I unhooked the chain, and turned the handle of the mortise lock, the door was suddenly pushed into my face by the person leaning heavily against its outer side. I was shoved a couple of steps back, as the door was forced open, and a body fell forward and landed heavily on the floor. Esme and I both gasped and took a couple of steps back, staring at the man lying on his front with his upper body in our hallway and his legs on the landing.

Writhing in agony was a man in khaki cargo pants and a green pullover with leather shoulder pads and patches over the elbows. Sticking In his back was what looked like a short, thick-stemmed arrow with white feathered fletching. We found out later this was a crossbow bolt.

Still alive, the man tried to regain his feet by getting into a kneeling position and looking up at us for help. It was then that we recognised who the unfortunate fellow was.

My God!' said Esme, *'It's Gabriel Miller!'*

'Help me,' said the stricken man, as he fell back down onto his front.

'Lie still,' I said, 'You've been shot with an arrow.'

He looked up with a frightened look on his face.

'Help me,' he said, more faintly

Esme was already on her phone, summoning an ambulance and the police.

Gabriel Miller began to make choking noises. Blood was coming out of his mouth. Rightly or wrongly, I put him on his side in the recovery position.

'Help me,' he said again.

'Who did this to you?' I asked.

He looked up at me, his eyes beginning to glaze over

'Who did this to you?' I repeated.

He looked up at me with frightened eyes and at first I thought he hadn't heard me.

Then he said, quite faintly:

'They... drugged me. Put something... in my... food.'

'Who's *they?*' I asked; 'Who did this to you?'

His eyes flickered for a few seconds, then opened a little, as he said:

'There were... four of them. They said... they wanted... *to make an example of me*... and... you'd be... next...'

His eyes flickered again, then slowly closed. He breathed out for the last time and his body went limp.

The police were on the way, an ambulance too, but they wouldn't be taking away the body until an army of detectives and forensics experts had swarmed like vultures over and around the corpse for hours and hours.

Meanwhile, Esme and I were marooned in our little flat, interrogated within an inch of our lives. And when it was all over, and we were finally alone together in the early hours of the morning, I turned to her and said:

'I never expected trouble to follow us all the way here to Cambridge. But let's make a vow right now... to leave it to the police and not get involved in solving this latest horrible crime. I'm not sure my nerves could stand another period of worrying and fretting about murderers and what they might do next.'

'But how can we *not* get involved,' she said, 'when the killers said *you'd* be next? No, we've got to get this thing sorted once and for all, be proactive in getting these maniacs in prison before they strike again.'

I let out a long sigh.

'I guess you're right,' I said. 'I don't suppose the danger will go away if we just ignore it. And if Cambridgeshire police are as poor at catching killers as Suffolk Constabulary, the only way to keep ourselves safe is to get to the bottom of why Gabriel Miller was killed as soon as possible, and identify the crazy people who did it.'

Esme got up, walked slowly to the bedroom and came back with the tarot cards, a lighter and a candle in the top of an empty wine bottle.

'We'll start off by asking the cards what's going on,' she said; 'Then we'll decide what to do.'

'All right,' I said, 'but do you really think they'll help us solve this crime?'

'They worked before,' she shrugged; 'And every time I've ever consulted the cards they've always come up with the answers. When I first started reading tarot cards I didn't expect them to work the way they do. But there's something really uncanny and mystical at work, something very spiritual. It's as if the spirits want to help us, and this is the only way they can get through to us.'

She set the wine bottle on the coffee table next to our sofa, lit the candle, then sat down next to me. While I switched off the electric light, Esme shuffled the pack of cards, and whispered the question:

'Cards, tell us – who killed Gabriel Miller.'

She took the pack of cards and began to lay them on

the table face down to form the familiar shape of the Celtic cross. Then, as each chosen card was turned over in the flickering light, our eyes grew wider and wider at the astonishing narrative now revealed before us...

END OF BOOK ONE...

Dear Reader,
If you have enjoyed this book, why not leave a review on Amazon books? Your feedback is important to me, and your review helps other readers make an informed choice when browsing books,
Many, many thanks,
Ed Garron.

Other books by Ed Garron:

THE HUNTING OF JOE REDWOLF
WEST OF KANSAS CITY
THAT WILD WESTERN SPIRIT
WARPATHS AND PEACEMAKERS
WILD AS THE WIND!
BROTHER OF THE WOLF!
YARNS OF THE OPEN RANGE
THE SOLITARY TEXAN

Children's books:

THE RUNAWAY PONY RIDERS
THE FLYING FALCONETTIS

Printed in Great Britain
by Amazon